WARM RECEPTION

The course curved away from the intended direction: The helm was responding as if the *Klact* were approaching a large mass. The mass sensor said nothing.

Suddenly the star was there, huge, blinding, overwhelming the forward screen, looming directly in their path. A dozen sensors on *Klact*'s bridge blinked in alarm. The mass sensor was heading off scale. The ship's skin temperature was much too high and climbing. Motion sensors were confounded by the writhing, seething, flaring surface below. Radiation and particle sensors were flooded.

The *Klact* was falling into the sun.

By Leslie Gadallah
Published by Ballantine Books:

CAT'S PAWN

CAT'S GAMIT

THE LOREMASTERS

CAT'S GAMBIT

Leslie Gadallah

A Del Rey Book
BALLANTINE BOOKS • NEW YORK

A Del Rey Book
Published by Ballantine Books

Library of Congress Catalog Card Number: 89-91895

ISBN 0-345-36478-3

Manufactured in the United States of America

First Edition: March 1990

Cover Art by Barclay Shaw

KD2434-II

The moons rose, one after the other, like a tight constellation of cold stars. They alleviated the blackness of the night hardly at all.

A mean little wind drifted out of the west, blood-chilling and smelling of more rain. At the bottom of the rocky gorge, the invisible river dashed along its stony bed, the frothy roar of white water rising faintly to the narrow ledge where Ayyah sat shivering with her fur fluffed out and her tail wrapped around her legs.

To a superstitious person, the rare configuration of moons might have signaled either a propitious or a sinister occasion. Ayyah's culture emphasized the pragmatic and the provable. She had no belief in occult forces moving in the universe solely to thwart the ambitions of rational beings. The birthing had been hard because it was hard, because she was in midlife, because the place was wrong, the setting was wrong, the whole world was wrong. Oriani did not belong here. Their presence offended the natural order of—she stopped and gave herself a mental shake to pull herself away from those archaic patterns of thought.

She was exhausted, and her heart ached almost beyond endurance, and she could not have the comfort of blaming a malign supernature for her pain.

Sanity demanded she return to the Orian community where medical attention, food, and warmth were available. But in her grief, the company of others was what she wanted least. Hers was a solitary race. The language of her people contained no word for lonely. Distressed, she naturally sought isolation. Until her physical and mental hurt abated, polite words would be too hard to say, civilized behavior scarcely possible. Her instincts urged her to find a dark, sheltered place in which to hide.

She compromised. She sat unmoving on the ledge, regarding the alien stars.

Even that meager comfort was not possible for long. In the end, the icy wind rising and driving flicks of rain minutely removed from snow forced her to do the reasonable thing. Clouds boiled up over the western sky, and soon it would be too dark for even an Orian's keen night vision to show her the way along the unfamiliar track down. Oriani were new to this world. The females had not yet worn smooth the path to the birthing caves.

Once committed to going, Ayyah moved quickly among the boulders and the stiff, foreign brush, guided as much by scent and sound as by deteriorating visual clues. She came to the small cluster of stone houses by the riverside before the rain began in earnest.

The buildings of the community were constructed to a common, irregularly hexagonal design with flat, sloped roofs, well separated from one another by areas of untamed native vegetation, almost invisible in the shadows of the night. They were oriented so that no building's door opened toward its nearest neighbor and were connected by rambling walkways surfaced with packed river sand that showed vaguely pale in the rapidly diminishing starlight. With the wind ruffling her fur, Ayyah walked quickly along the paths. In front of the house that was hers, she hesitated.

Going in was hard to do. Light spilled from the high windows. Her mate, Lawr, was waiting within. She forced herself to open the door and enter. He had a right to know, to hear it from her.

The warmth inside was welcome. She shook herself. Lawr turned from his work as she came in, anticipating her announcement. Spread out on the plain table before him near the center of the single room were the myriad intricate parts of the controller of the power plant he and another engineer were trying to adapt to local fuels. Off to one side was another, smaller table holding a computer terminal, with a crude bench before it.

There were few other furnishings. The house had a rough, primitive air to it and contained a minimum of amenities.

Lawr's big feline ears pricked forward to catch her words. But he said nothing, allowing Ayyah to speak as little or as much as she chose. He did not approach her. By Orian standards, that would have been impolite.

She closed the door behind her, shutting out the wet, cold inhospitable night.

"All dead," she said weakly. "All dead."

She swayed there by the door, the saying of it bringing the pain close again.

Lawr's ears flattened slightly, but it was no more than he must have expected. One might always hope. Daily hope grew dimmer.

He came to her then, tail held low, head bowed, and gaze directed away to show he was nonaggressive, concern overriding good manners. She understood him well enough. They had been mated all their adult lives.

He guided her around a coarsely woven screen to the box filled with dried grasses that served as a bed. "I will bring the healer," he said.

Ayyah lay curled into a ball on the bed, too tired to protest though she knew the healer would have no relief to offer. The grasses were harsh and musty, not the least bit like the soft, aromatic hays of her homeworld. "We cannot live here, Lawr," she said. "There has not been one live birth since we came. We have to go home."

That she spoke so plainly embarrassed him. Births and birthings are not easy topics among Oriani.

"That's foolish talk. You know we cannot. Rest now, until the healer comes."

Ayyah's eyes closed and she drifted toward sleep. They opened again suddenly, and she said with determination, "I will find a way." But Lawr had already gone in search of the healer, and there was no one to hear.

The storm was in full fury, audible through the walls of the house. Rain smashed down on the roof; wind roared through tossing branches.

Facing the bare stones of the wall, Ayyah waited, expecting nothing. Roused from her sleep, the healer would nod once in her solemn way and get her things. Silent, she would follow Lawr into the night, concerned but helpless. She would have no help to offer.

The notion that had come to Ayyah on the rocky ledge, and which she had hastily suppressed, returned, and she could see the truth in it. Oriani did not belong here. This world truly was too cold and too wet, even here in the equatorial region, to suit them. The healer spent much of her time dealing with fungal infections, in clearing lungs better adapted to desert conditions. And, of course, coming to the aid of the bearers of dead babies.

There was little enough a physician could do for any of them with less than the minimum of equipment and almost no pharmacy.

The healer did try. The population of the settlement had eroded down to less than a thousand, and still they taxed her abilities. The ragged little community might well be all that remained of the once-respected Orian race. She did what little she could to preserve it. Ayyah did what she could to help. The healer was overworked, and Ayyah was a teacher without students, and therefore without an occupation.

She drifted into a half sleep filled with memories of a better time, at home, upon her own world. She remembered a desert, with her first child beside her, in the quiet hour of light before dawn. They were stalking the elusive ska. She remembered the spicy scent of the beast, overlaying the dry, warm smell of the desert, the alert, anxious movements of her son, the distant cough of a predator seeking its breakfast in the fading shadows.

Oriani taught their children the arts of the hunt in those days for the sake of the training and the discipline, though they no longer caught the animals they stalked. Ayyah no less than her child would have been appalled by the thought of killing the delicate little animal nosing with nervous haste among the rocky crevices for what forage it could find in the dry land.

The child of her youth, the youngster's name was Shirr. He had been bright and quick and strong, and Ayyah had discovered a deep, upwelling pride in his accomplishments that her society forbade her to express.

Shirr was almost certainly dead now. In that desperately frantic time when the Kaz were attacking Orion, the starships had been packed with whomever was near, without regard for family ties. Those remaining the Kaz had slain, without exception.

A few survivors were here, on this inhospitable world without a name.

She could appreciate the bitter irony of it. Kaz, like many races, were revolted by the Oriani way of population control and expressed their revulsion over the death of babies by slaughtering young and old alike. Now the refugees from that slaughter could propagate not at all. Oriani mothers, once vilified for their role in choosing only the strong of a litter to survive, now had no choices to make among the lifeless products of their aching wombs.

An element akin to Stoicism colored the whole of Orian philosophy, and it told Ayyah that nothing could be gained by regretting things she could not change. It did not tell her how to put the burning memories away.

Lawr returned with the healer, intruding upon her solitary thoughts. Only with difficulty could Ayyah keep her ears from folding back in annoyance.

The healer's quick examination told Ayyah nothing she did not know. She was healthy, strong, and resilient. No permanent damage had been done. She would recover quickly.

"Why can't we do something about this?" Lawr asked, as five hundred anguished males had overcome the difficulty of the subject and asked before. "There must be a reason. Why can't we find the cause and cure it?"

The healer looked away for a moment before replying. "When we have laboratory facilities, perhaps answers can be found. Until then we guess, and we have guessed wrong."

She paused, the debilitating sense of hopelessness she could not articulate plain on her face. Under other circumstances, she might be embarrassed by this display. But who could ask for the niceties of manners under these conditions?

Ayyah did not need words. She had assisted when, with clinical detachment, the healer had performed autopsies on her own litter and found her little babies perfect in every way, except they were dead.

"There is a greater danger," the healer continued, as much to herself as to her audience. "If we find the cause of the stillbirths this very day and overcome it tomorrow, the gene pool may be insufficiently diverse to permit our survival. In times past, when the tools of science were available, geneticists clearly saw the need for genetic diversity.

"Time is the enemy," she said.

Lawr nodded, forcing acceptance of hard reality. Ayyah understood his despair. Time must be spent building houses and planting crops and securing a supply of energy and establishing communications and trading relations with other societies, trying to make life livable in a hostile environment as the few resources they brought with them dwindled. There was no choice.

The healer kept the germ banks as carefully as she was able under primitive conditions, but had no way of testing the specimens to see if they were viable. Passing time, an aging population, accidents, disease—every day made survival less likely.

Long years yet must pass before luxuries like laboratories were possible.

They might have discussed it further, standing with bowed heads before her bed, but Ayyah, nearing the limits of her tolerance, sent them away with words that were barely civil.

Alone, she pursued sleep, the only escape from sorrow that she had.

Sounds of activity in the village roused her before first light. The season of the harvest was upon them, and the community was busy. The expatriate Oriani had discovered one resource on their new world with value for off-planet trade, the fruit of a small tree that grew in scattered clumps in their valley and was highly prized as a condiment and tonic among the Tuers and related races. Seeded, dried, and packed, it was their item of commerce in the interplanetary market, exchanged for the products of technology. When the fruit was ripe, all hands were pressed into service, for the season was short and their need was great.

A few of the seeds from the fruit were reserved for horticultural experiments that the Oriani hoped would lead to orchards suitable for automated farming; the rest were dutifully returned to the forest. The dried fruit was transported down the wild river and hoisted up the bank near the landing pad to await the arrival of the Tuers.

It was smelly, sticky work. Long, arduous hours spent shoulder to shoulder with other workers were required, and individualistic Oriani, by nature preferring privacy and solitude, grew tense and irritable over those few weeks. By the time the Tuer ship was due, and they faced the further effort of unloading and loading without the benefit of proper port facilities, tempers would be held only with the greatest of difficulty.

Ayyah's duty was there. Everyone's effort was wanted. The Tuer vessel would stop for nothing less than a shipload. A pioneering community trying to pull itself up by its own bootstraps needed everything—food and fibers and bearings, refined metals, machine tools, fuel, pharmaceuticals and medical supplies, electronics, and above all books, information, knowledge, all the lost techniques needed by any civilization, borne on microrecords. And, therefore, readers to make the records useful.

Still feeling hurt on many levels, Ayyah did not join in the work. But by noon she was too restless to remain in bed. She sat awhile in the doorway of her house, basking in the insufficient sun. That, also, was not satisfying.

The most respected Orian philosophers taught that guilt was a useless mental activity. Better one should act to alleviate the cause. Growing increasingly uncomfortable with idleness, Ayyah roused from her lassitude and walked the path along the riverbank to the clearing.

Two kilometers downstream from the Orian village, a natural meadow spread across about sixty hectares of flat ground before giving way on three sides to the ever-encroaching forest and on the fourth to the sharp plunge down to the river. Near the center of that open ground lay the remains of two great starships. Sometimes the morning sun would strike a glint from their broken metallic hulls that could be seen in the community. Fifty meters riverward of the wrecks an area of ground had been cleared and packed to form a shuttle landing pad. Some crude, newly constructed cranes and pulleys were mounted on the rim of the gorge. Beneath them, a waterwheel provided power.

Many members of the community were busy around the shuttle pad as the boxes of dried fruit were prepared for the arrival of the Tuers. She passed them without further pangs of conscience. Though few of the workers would have agreed with her, she had something else to do that she felt was more important. She entered the larger of the two downed ships by way of a wooden door that had been skillfully fitted into the warped frame to keep the weather out.

It was more than obvious that the great ships would never fly again, but they were carefully preserved. They were, and contained, the community's archives: The crumpled metal cylinders and their contents were all the Oriani had of their history. Some of the refugees complained that they needed metal more than monuments and urged the dismantling of the ships for their material. The majority disagreed.

The light inside was dim; the weak sun filtered in through dusty ports. Most of the ship's internal systems were still functional, but Ayyah did not turn the overhead lights on. She could see well enough, and scarce fuel was to be judiciously used.

Some of the bulkheads had been torn down and some of the furnishings removed to serve the early needs of the exiles, leaving the curved interior more open and uncluttered than it had originally been, but most of the ship remained intact. It was as if the packed refugees had just left, and would return at any moment.

Ayyah sat down before the terminal that had once been the navigator's station but now offered access to the library. The ship's computer housed those few documents the community had brought with them from their homeworld.

She began to search the reduced records for anything to do with the Kaz. She became wholly absorbed in her work and forgot about the healer's prescription for rest.

What she had was an impoverished, discontinuous collection. Fleeing Orion, people had snatched what they could. In the short hours available then, they could spare no time to be selective. Still, a surprisingly large volume of material was there. Without the comparative and summarizing capacity of a larger computer, sorting through the data was confusing and time-consuming.

Oriani had studied the Kaz for many generations, seeking to understand their ancient enemies. But few had studied the Kazi empire so deeply and thoroughly as had Ayyah's own father, Talan. Talan's whole life's work had revolved around his efforts to stop, or at least delay, the expansion of the empire. Some of his work had found its way here, much of it in Ayyah's own arms, though at the time of the flight from Orion, she had not anticipated her current need.

Talan's description of the organization of the empire was referred to by many scholars and had been called the most accurate ever compiled outside of Kazi space. Ayyah returned again and again to that document in her studies, gaining more respect for the troubled man who was her father than she had found in his lifetime. As a youngster, she had to fight her resentment of his preoccupation. She could not have known she would inherit it.

A coin-size record containing some of his work was in the reader. The words on the screen waited patiently for her attention:

The well-known Rayorian student Owye once likened the organization of the empire of the Kaz to the organization of an incredibly large but simple organism. Curiously, this comparison appeals to the Kaz, and is often used by them to describe the empire to non-Kaz, as follows:

The empire's smallest organizational units, like the cells of a body, are cells of activity centered on a broodmaster. Each cell carries on almost independently of the cells around it.

Therefore an attack upon one cell, or even its total destruction, has minimal effect on neighboring cells. This makes the empire impossible to defeat, for to have a serious effect, an enemy must destroy a significant fraction of the independent cells. Considering the extent of the empire and the number of cells involved, this is beyond the ability of even the most determined of enemies.

A cell may consist of individuals from one to a dozen broods, rarely more. A district supervisor oversees 144 cells. An area commander presides over 1,728 districts. (The awkward figures arise from the Kazi duodecimal base of numbering.) Of course, these individuals are also members of some broodmaster's cell, adding a degree of stabilizing recursion to the organization.

This could be considered the natural social pattern of Kazi life. It is overlain and strengthened by political and cultural ties to the emperor, and by ties of birth and mystery to a Broodmother.

The connection to the Broodmother deserves further consideration. Though a difficult topic for our people, it must be approached by anyone seriously seeking to understand the nature of the Kaz, for it underlies much of their effort and a high proportion of the loyalty to the group. Group loyalty is the empire's great strength. The Rayorians offer a description of the extremely strong and personal relationship between a Kazi and the Broodmother that gave it birth, but have given us no satisfactory explanation of its nature. It seems almost impossible that it should exist, since a Kazi rarely sees its parent, being removed from the presence of the mother while in the egg.

As with many aspects of the empire, most of what we know of the Broodmother comes from the dedicated students on Rayor. Later I will return to write more about this most significant individual—perhaps we should call her an institution—in the Kazi hierarchy and offer for consideration some new evidence for and against possible psi-level mind-to-mind connections between the Broodmother and her broods.

The individual Kaz forming a cell of activity are not necessarily together in physical space . . .

Ayyah looked up from the reader, surprised to discover that the ship around her had grown dark and, outside, it was night.

The curved walls reaching up into darkness enclosed her with familiar things, protected her, kept her separate from the unpleasant world without. She was warm here, and filled with memories. The physical beast would have been content to remain indefinitely.

If Talan ever did explain the significance of the Kazi Broodmother, it was not among the records available in the dead starship.

Indeed, she found herself with many fragments of knowledge, things half known, facts hinted at but not revealed. Too much was missing. Feeling restless and discontented, she abandoned her studies and left the comfort of the ship for the blustering chill outside and worked out her frustration with a long, brisk walk along the river's windy edge. She needed more information, but it was not to be had on KD2434-II. She must look farther afield.

When the Tuer shuttle landed, she returned to the clearing and lent her back to the loading, laboring with the others in the circle of artificial light, finding some relief and some inspiration in the heavy work.

When the shuttle lifted, she went with it.

Alpha Centauri IV

"Commander?"

Commander Raoul Desjardins, Terran Space Fleet, officer in command of the patrol vessel *Eagle Eye*, had been crossing the instrument-crammed operations area toward the ward room and some coffee when Ikiawa stopped him.

"Problem?" he asked.

Ikiawa was frowning down at his sensor panel. While Desjardins watched, he switched from motion sensor to infrared and back again.

"Sensors register a vessel, sir, right over the polar hole. Heading straight down, under power. Getting under the planetary monitors, I guess."

The polar hole was one of the more polite terms for the area above the magnetic pole where Centauri IV's curvature and magnetic field combined to make ground-based sensors ineffective. It was one reason the *Eagle Eye* and Desjardins and Ikiawa and a junior officer and a dozen men were in ninety-minute polar orbit for six weeks at a time.

Desjardins hesitated long enough to glance out the port at Centauri's surface rolling beneath them. Centauri wasn't exactly barren, but neither was it exactly well endowed with life. Mankind's puny efforts on this, the first and only of its system-external colonies, were invisible from this height. Something deeply philosophical lay hidden in that fact, he was sure, and he was playing with the notion to avoid coming to a decision.

What they were expected to do, of course, was report their finding to the ground station. The Kaz would scramble fighters to bring the vessel down. No one would suppose it was on legitimate business. Legitimate ships went through the port, where safety margins were much higher and facilities for doing business and finding personal comfort were available.

The *Eagle Eye* itself was unarmed. The Kaz didn't trust a ship full of Terrans with guns overhead. Not even a patrol boat, which had minimal maneuvering capability, no hyperspace facility, and spit for range.

"Any confirmation from below?" Desjardins asked.

"No, sir. Not a word." Ikiawa watched the panel. "She's touched atmosphere, sir."

Desjardins took a deep breath. He was about to take one hell of a chance on Ikiawa, whom he didn't know very well. This was the young rating's first tour with *Eagle Eye*. The lad seemed to have no great love for the Kaz, but that was a superficial assessment at best.

In the next few seconds, Desjardins would either recruit a new member for the resistance or find himself listed for reprocessing the minute he got one foot on the ground. For an instant he gave consideration to sacrificing the unknown vessel to his personal safety.

That wouldn't sit comfortably on his conscience. He wasn't often able to do anything for the crazy mavericks who ran their souped-up ships through Kazi control. The Kaz called them anarchists and hoodlums, but a good many people privately cheered them on as latter-day corsairs and a small indication that at least one person now and then could squeeze out from under Kazi tyranny.

Besides, a ship with supplies for the resistance was due, and for all Desjardins could tell from where he was, this could be the one.

"Ignore it," he told Ikiawa.

"Sir?"

"It's a ghost. Ignore it."

"With all due respect, sir, that's no . . ." Ikiawa's protest faded as he caught sight of Desjardins's face. "It'll be in the computer record," he said.

"Yes?"

"If the Kaz examine the record . . ."

"It's my neck."

"But, sir . . ."

"Mr. Ikiawa, am I expected to believe you've grown so fond of me in the short time you've been aboard that you'd be willing to risk your entire future in the Fleet just to argue with me about what should or should not be considered a ghost, and that you're doing all this just to save me from a fate worse than death at the hands—claws—of the Kaz?"

"No, sir, I didn't mean anything like that." Ikiawa was a gutsy youngster and not easily flustered. "But it could be a test. The bugs do put them up from time to time."

"Really?" Desjardins said with no small degree of sarcasm. "I didn't know that."

Ikiawa subsided into frowning silence.

"Log it as a ghost and forget it," Desjardins insisted.

While the commander watched, Ikiawa entered the incident into the computer as a false reading due to atmospheric refraction, overrode the sensor lock, and set the instruments back into their scanning pattern. Satisfied, Desjardins started away.

"Commander?"

"More trouble?"

"Ah, no sir. It's just, I thought, well, if it'd be all right, next time we're dirtside, I'd like to buy you a drink, sir."

Desjardins smiled. He had a rare but wide and infectious smile that was well known among his crew. "I'd like that, Ikiawa. I'm flattered, actually." He sobered again. "But for now, I'd appreciate it if you kept this incident between us, eh?" He started away once more, then stopped. "There's one other thing. You'd better be careful who's around when you call our Kazi masters 'bugs.' They don't like it, and besides it's not accurate. They're not bugs."

"They bloody well look like bugs."

Desjardins's smile returned. "They do that."

The unregistered vessel *Harrier* came to a neat and spectacular landing on the abandoned pad near the head offices of the now-defunct Colonial Mining Company, and MacDonald wondered, as he waited for his ground transportation, how he could arrange to send a bottle of bootleg scotch to the commander of the patrol boat.

In the navigator's chair next to him, Oscar Achebe exaggerated the gesture of wiping sweat from his brow and turned to MacDonald with genuinely frightened black eyes. "Next time I'm looking for a partner," Oscar said, "I'm going to look for one with a better sense of timing. That was just a bit too scary for my delicate nervous system."

MacDonald nodded. His timing had been bad. Maybe he was

getting too old for this game. His reflexes weren't what they used to be, and his own nerves didn't take the strain so easily anymore.

He was grateful for his trim little ship. She could whip down through the sky in a way damned few vessels could follow. She had gotten him out of a lot of scrapes in her time.

He had found her lying abandoned in a Caparan refitter's yard about the time he realized that the usual excesses of the pirate life didn't really appeal to him. The luxuries he enjoyed were those of comfortable living. He drank moderately and rarely used other drugs. He gambled not at all, and found women by mutual agreement rather than by hire purchase. Given a fair rate of success harassing Kazi shipping, he wound up with money in the bank.

The ship was old, and her surface was pocked and scarred when he found her, and her engines were running a bit ragged, but she was sound. A fast two- to four-man scout of a type built when humanity had no idea what they would encounter Out There, she had weapons mounts, atmospheric capabilities, space for more provisions than would normally be required, and one man could handle her in a pinch. A sweet thing although a little cramped, there would be no more like her now that the Kaz had taken over.

The price wasn't bad. The Caparan didn't appreciate what he had beneath the scratches and the dirt. With thoroughly serviced engines and a control systems upgrade, the little ship could keep up with anything in space.

The starship represented his dream of forty-nine years. He had been only a quarter million or so credits short of the Caparan's price. He was making that up as he went along. If the deal he was working on now went through, he would be just about clear of the debt.

He had her refinished with a flashy coat of black and gold, and renamed her *Harrier*. He was proud of her.

Outside, the wind howled across the treeless plain like a wounded banshee, driving hard pellets of snow sizzling onto the *Harrier*'s still-hot skin, and for the umpteenth time, MacDonald swore he would find a more hospitable place to do business.

In a few minutes, he could make out the ground car's head-lights through the blowing snow. Good old Sam was always on time. MacDonald wondered, as he and Oscar made ready to leave the ship, if positions were reversed, if he was Sam and Sam was paying him the little Sam got to defy the Kazi curfew and come out in this god-awful weather, if he would do it with such cool, good-natured equanimity.

If Sam wanted to make his fortune, all he had to do was bring a few Kaz with him one time. The reward for turning in the maverick ship and its crew would keep him in high style for the rest of his days. *Harrier* was not without a reputation in the sector.

When anyone suggested something like that to him, Sam rubbed his deeply seamed and weather-tanned face and said, "I reckon the bugs'll have to get along without my help as best they can." But life in the Centauri Colony under Kazi dominion was hard, and no one could blame a man too much if he was tempted.

When MacDonald had thrown his kit into the rear cargo area, accepted the parka Sam offered, and settled himself into the passenger seat beside Oscar, the old man in the driver's seat said, without taking his eyes off the windshield, "They shot down the *Sherwood Forest* last week. No survivors." He rammed the car into gear angrily, and it lumbered across the frozen plain.

"Oh, Christ." Oscar groaned.

MacDonald's eyes closed in pain. He didn't trust himself to say anything. He had been fond of Marion Jones. More than fond. In the tight, scattered fraternity of spacegoing pirates, MacDonald and Marion had been something of an item for a while. To be honest, he loved her, deeply, though he found it hard to admit, even to himself. And admired her, and had wanted desperately to cherish her and keep her safe.

She never would let him do that. Tough and full of mischief, the lady did take some awful chances, and she vigorously opposed any effort to restrain her risky, merry nonchalance.

Snow swirled around the car and the wind howled, and MacDonald fancied he could hear scraps of Marion's laughter. She laughed a lot, and took all sorts of strays and oddballs under her wing in spite of all the warnings she got that sooner or later one of them was going to be a Kazi spy.

Sorrow took MacDonald and held him in a cold embrace. He was unwilling and unable to speak his grief. Fortunately Sam was a taciturn man who didn't require continual chatter; he was content with his own thoughts as the balloon-tired ground car waddled off south toward the railhead. Oscar felt no more like talking than MacDonald did. Marion Jones, deceased, often referred to as Lady Marion, received a tribute of silence.

They made good time on an arrow-straight road running between bleak fields that once had contained experimental plantings of wild peas and the subarctic species of Cruciferae agriculturalists had been trying to adapt to Centauri's climate. Now the fields grew scattered, short, dark, twiggy plants the locals called bug berries. In the winter of this hemisphere, the thin, dead branches stuck up through the snow and made a strange landscape.

At the railhead, MacDonald got out, and Oscar handed him his gear.

"You okay?" Oscar asked.

"Yeah."

"Are you sure?"

"I'll be all right. You're not coming to the city?"

Oscar shook his head. "I'll stay and help unload. Maybe keep an eye out that some overzealous freedom fighter doesn't help himself to more than the group's got coming."

It was a good idea, but it seemed unfair. "Won't you get bored?"

"No, I don't think so," Oscar said. He was probably right. He had an intellectual approach to life and found interest in the most unlikely places. Furthermore, his big, well-kept body and smooth dark features attracted women as if magnetic. "A few days of the simple life will do me good. I'll wait for you in the camp." The rebel camp with its small, largely isolated population would be starved for off-world news and accommodating toward a friendly outsider. Oscar being friendly was a phenomenon worthy of respect.

MacDonald left him with a wave, pulled the parka's hood up against the driving wind, and found the artfully cut, nearly invisible hole in the fence around the rail yard. The high-speed freight train would never know it had a passenger for Centauri City.

He hunkered down in a crevice of the old, deserted terminal building to wait. He was doing good, functioning, carrying on in spite of the pain. So why were those stupid tears freezing on his face?

He wiped at them impatiently. They kept coming back.

Llevec

Delladar Oll let her mount amble along the rocky trail at its own pace. To her right, the mountain sloped irregularly up toward its snowy top. To her left, the tangle of small trees and brush was occasionally interrupted to allow a glimpse of the river valley far below. Springberry was in bloom, and its golden flowers and heady perfume decorated the way.

Another year she would have urged the beast she straddled to its limits, anticipating the delight of the homecoming and the hot fevers of the breeding season. This year the journey held little joy. Callous nature still stirred her blood, but the fever did not touch her soul. Home had lost much of its savor since the occupation.

It was a thin beast she rode anyway, tired and saddlesore, rented for more than its value in the foothills village of Waellsad where lines of modern transportation petered out before the high, jagged mountains of Delladar Oll's homeland. It had a prominent backbone and a cranky disposition.

She batted trail dust from her clothes, and her mouth bent with disgust at the plain brown tunic she wore, devoid of clan marks, like some tribeless peasant's shirt. The only sign of her status left to her was the long black mane that began between high hawkish eyes and flowed full length to her shoulders. Most people kept the mane clipped short for convenience, but mountain warriors grew it long to protect the long, vulnerable Lleveci neck. Even that had caused her trouble in the port city, where it brought her to the attention of the oppressors and the maggot-ridden, gutless, lowland defectors who bowed before black Kazi ugliness.

She did not know whom she hated most, the Kaz or the Lleveci who did their bidding.

She said as much to the one who was screening incoming passengers at the spaceport.

"I must do as I am bid," he had said, "or I will soon find myself in the reprocessing bin with your blade."

With her blade. Thrice damned rubber-necked old maggot. Only a lowlander could have said that so casually. Only one who had no idea of what the knife meant to her, who had no concept of how much a part of her it was. It had been almost more than she could bear to surrender it to that licker of Kazi feet. She would have much rather run it into his cowardly heart and taken her chances with the consequences. She would have suffered through the breeding season alone rather than give up that knife. Only the call from the clan's chief elder was strong enough to force her to part with it. Her duty demanded she answer the call, and it was not fitting to escape a duty by dying.

She felt as if a limb had been amputated. She felt naked and insecure.

Not that she was entirely weaponless. Broken down into pieces too small for the lowland bastard to recognize and scattered among the offworld gifts she was bringing to her family were the parts of a perfectly functional blaster. She was skilled in their assembly. Her attachment to the crystal blade did not mean she was ignorant of modern arms.

Her mount's gait changed as it crossed the top of the stony ridge and began the descent into the high valley. As it picked up speed, she felt it fill its lungs. It stretched its scaly neck and bugled its call over the mountain. Faintly another answered.

The clan was gathered in the village below as it had gathered for a thousand generations, never dreaming until now that a time would come when aliens would tell them that the ancient ways were no longer valid, that the clans were to be disbanded and dispersed and everyone was to find his proper place serving the empire.

It would be a damned cold day in hell when Delladar Oll stood beside that doddering lowland traitor entering the names of incoming passengers into a computer log for the benefit of the Kaz. They could take her blade away because her leader required her presence in the village, only because of that, but they would never take her soul.

She had fled her homeworld when the Kaz began to tighten the screws, and hired her not-inconsiderable skills out along the fringes of the empire, where Lleveci mountain warriors were in high demand as bodyguards and private soldiers. She lived well, if somewhat dangerously, and dreamed sometimes about finding a way to wipe the Kaz off the face of Llevec forever.

As it was with many expatriate warriors, much of what she earned found its way back to the tribes. Though the Kaz had not yet ventured into the mountains in force, they had done their best to cut off contact with more peaceable Lleveci. The hard mountain life had become harder for lack of commerce with the lowlands.

Across a boisterous stream, the village of Ollsad lay in the mountain's shadow, looking much as it had looked for millennia past. The huddle of small wooden houses with their conical roofs and brightly painted walls made a cheery spot against the dark backdrop of the forest, and the tidy streets between the buildings undulated up the hillside, seemingly untouched by the Kazi invasion. The mountains protected them from fancy vehicles and heavy weapons alike—for now.

Her mount plunged into the water, spraying her with icy drops. The beast had become lively, anticipating company. A group of children playing near the water stopped their game and shouted the news of a rider back to the village.

A group of breeding males lay basking in the sun on the streambank, their languor marking them as plainly as their flushed faces. During the season, they had energy only for the rut. Youngsters scampered among the houses, released for these few days from supervision of their elders, enjoying their holiday. The Aunts and Uncles, the people past breeding age, had their hands full looking after the breeders.

Delladar Oll knew without looking that her own face had begun to show color, losing its normal sandy hue around her eyes and on the planes of her cheeks and in the loose skin of the neck as surface veins and arteries opened, painting her red and blue. It was the great disadvantage to being Lleveci that one's passions were written on one's face for all to see.

She stopped at the streambank for a moment, enjoying the sight and taking pleasure in the ribald invitations to join the men at the river's edge.

With difficulty, she turned her mount and urged it up the hill toward the center of the village. She handed it over to the care of the Uncle who had come to meet her. She must see what the elder wanted of her before the fever took her sense away.

But first she climbed the hill to the crimson and deep forest-green house belonging to her parents, where she could clean away the dust of the journey and find some proper dress.

She stopped before the entrance and saluted the doorway with a nod, as was proper. There were no locks in the village. She pushed the heavy wooden door open and went inside.

The house seemed smaller than she remembered it. Solidly built against the winter storms, well kept, it was filled with reminders of happier times. The pelt of the first animal she had ever brought home for the table still occupied the place of honor on the wall directly opposite the door in the entry hall.

Her parents were happy to see her in the restrained way of mountain people, a brief stiff embrace with averted eyes lest one read in another unseemly sentimentality. They were properly appreciative of her gifts.

But there was a strangeness, too, that her years offworld had made, which would take time she did not have to overcome, and it saddened her. They had aged, too, overmuch, it seemed, for the time she had been away; they were thin and tense.

Delladar Oll had no way of knowing if she had any biological connection with these she called her parents, any more than she could know if any of the youngsters running around the village were her offspring. She had deposited four embryos with the Aunts and Uncles when she was last home, to be activated randomly among those of other females, according to the needs of the village.

When an embryo was activated, it was placed with a family, a stable association of male and female—an Aunt and an Uncle, since breeding pairs were anything but stable, partnerships forming and dissolving like crystals of ice in the winter sun—to serve as parents. This Aunt whom she called mother and this Uncle she called father had raised Delladar Oll and taught her and made her what she was. When, as a young apprentice, she had sat by a winter fire carving scenes of her family history into the red-black stone that was to become the haft of her warrior's knife, it was the deeds and triumphs of these people she depicted. Neither she nor they knew if any blood bond existed. Neither she nor they cared. They were her family within the larger family of the clan, and she was fond of them.

Her time with them was short. Her duty and her body were both demanding. Soon a messenger came. She went with him into the center of the village to meet the chief elder.

* * *

"Greetings, Mother," Delladar Oll addressed the chief. It was an honorary title. Once a Lleveci's few years of sexual activity were past, the concept of femaleness gradually lost both social significance and biological definition. Younger Aunts and Uncles retained residues of sexual distinction, but the older one got, the more neuter one became. The chief elder was the oldest member of the village; the title was a courtesy, used regardless of original gender.

The elder looked her over. "Welcome, Delladar Oll. I am happy to see you have decided to rejoin us. The Uncle said you entered the village clanless."

"Not of choice, Mother," Delladar Oll said. She was much more comfortable in the sky-blue tunic she now wore, with its clan signs and marks of rank and symbols of successful hunts and battles, tied with an embroidered sash bearing her family emblems. She felt more herself. Still, there was that empty place at her side where her knife should have been.

"The Kaz do not allow one with clan signs to clear the port," she explained. "They would have us all dress and act like humble vassals of the emperor." She ducked her head to hide the blanching of embarrassment. "They took my blade from me."

The elder shook her full mane as a sign of sympathy. It was still a magnificent growth, even though the years had turned it white. She motioned for Delladar Oll to sit by the fire pit where coals glowed red. The day was warm enough. There were better ways to heat houses in modern times. The fire served a ceremonial purpose, a tradition retained from a time when the keeper of the flame was responsible for a stone age community's most valuable asset.

The elder took a second bench a short distance away. "I appreciate the sacrifice, Delladar Oll. I know you did not give it up easily. No warrior would, and you are among our best." Delladar Oll ducked her head again. Praise was not common among the mountain people.

"You are among our best," the chief elder repeated, "and you have spent much time offworld. You know your way around among aliens. Therefore, I have need of you."

"How may I serve, Mother?"

The chief did not answer directly. "The Kaz hold most of our world in their grip now. Only a few pockets of resistance remain—the desert tribes, ourselves, I think also some of the island nations. Small thorns in the massive Kazi side that in time they will seek to pluck out. Soon the Kaz will be invading these mountains, and we must be prepared to defend them."

"We cannot win, Mother."

"But we will fight. We are warriors, and we will fight to preserve the ancient ways as long as we are able. Who knows what the future brings? It has been said the empire will eventually collapse of its own weight. Pray the gods, some of us will live to see the day. In any case, the Kaz will pay dearly to put their foul feet in these sweet meadows."

"As you will, Mother."

"It would be satisfying to use traditional weapons in this battle to preserve tradition, but modern armaments are more practical against computer-assisted missiles. We will need heavy equipment to hold the passes. We need defenses against aerial attack.

"A supplier has been found. He is a wily fellow, and a hard bargainer. I need you to negotiate in our behalf. Are you willing to serve as merchant in this cause?"

"If it pleases you and serves the clan, I am willing, Mother. Such poor skills as I have in the marketplace are yours to command."

"It will be so, then."

"Purchase is one thing, delivery another. The Kaz hold the spaceport."

"Leave that to me. The arrangements will be made known to you when the time is right."

Delladar Oll nodded, seeing the wisdom of the Mother's caution. "May I know who this dealer of arms may be, and where found?"

"He is a Terran, known as MacDonald. You will find him in the Terran colony on Alpha Centauri IV, where the Kazi presence is less formidable than it is on Earth proper. He is expecting one of us to approach him. You will not have difficulty in that regard."

The elder regarded Delladar Oll carefully, taking note of the color in the warrior's face. "However, we can surely discuss these details another time. We must serve nature as well as tradition. I will not keep you much longer from those impatient men by the river. Wait here a moment."

Delladar Oll waited, trying not to fidget, while the elder disappeared into the interior of the house. Her mind was more on the men than on the task she had been given, but she was pinned to the fireside by the elder's command. She could not move until she was given leave to go, no matter how much her blood raged. It was hard to be still. Not only the men were impatient.

The elder returned shortly with a bundle wrapped in a shimmering silken cloth the color of the night sky, with tiny white stars woven into the fabric. She laid the bundle in the startled Delladar Oll's lap. "I would have you accept this," she said. "As the gift of the older generation to the younger, with our combined prayers to the gods for those carefree young scampering about outside, that they may never be Kazi slaves."

Delladar Oll carefully turned back the folds of cloth and, when it was done, found herself so overcome with emotion she could scarcely speak. She dared not look at the elder. With closed eyes, she whispered, "Mother, I cannot."

Lying in her lap was a near-perfect blade, glowing with the patina only age can bring. Delladar Oll tried to imagine the old warrior as a young apprentice making the journey to the mines to select the perfect crystal that was to become her most precious possession, spending the long, tense, arduous hours fashioning the weapon from the brittle quartz when the slightest error meant one must begin again, sitting by the winter fire carving scenes of her family's history into the magnesite haft. Delladar Oll had only known the elder old, but once she had been young, and had done all this.

The chief sat on the bench beside Delladar Oll. "Once," she said, "no one doubted the strength of this arm, the boldness of this heart. Now the arm grows weak, the heart, erratic. I doubt I will see another season. How better to honor the weapon that has served me well these many years than to see it at the side of a valiant warrior? Take it, Daughter. Use it well. If sometime it should be stained with Kazi blood, I will be well pleased."

Silently Delladar Oll wrapped the knife back into its silken cloth, moved beyond the ability of words to express.

"Go now," the old woman said. "Go to your pleasures by the river. These old bones must rest."

Ayyah

The Tuer captain wrapped an elongated, rubbery proboscis around long, intertwined flexible arms and snorted into the knot of flesh.

"This vessel, she not for passenger, you know?" He spoke the Orian language at the simplest level, like one whose tongue had grown stiff in a mouthful of foam.

Meeting the captain had tested Ayyah's diplomatic skill. The Tuer had been disinclined to bother with a persistent lunatic and protected his privacy with a string of stubborn crewmen. He obviously thought of Oriani as impoverished laborers without the resources to become tourists. Convincing the last of the guardians at the cabin door otherwise had taken a noticeable bite from Ayyah's slim resources before the journey even began.

"You know?" the captain asked again, as if repetition would make his meaning plain.

"Yes, I know," Ayyah answered. "I also know you can make room for one."

"Where this room?"

"Enough could be found in this cabin. I require little space. Passage can be paid in fruit, gold, or labor. You choose."

The captain snorted again. "Take captain's bed? How much gold you got, Orian?"

"Sufficient. I neither need nor want your bed."

"So?"

"Move some of the crates of fruit from the other room and give me the space. This is all I require."

The captain's intertwined appendages unraveled, and it began paying serious attention to the furry mad thing. "What you say here? You talk bad. Who is telling you bad things? No passage.

24

No. Bad talkers I got lots already in not-so-good crew. Go away, Orian.''

"No one told me. More crates go into this vessel than appear on the manifest or in the hold. It is reasonable to assume some have been stored elsewhere. I am not so knowledgeable about starships as you are, of course, but it is my understanding they do not commonly have quantities of waste space.''

"You too much talk bad. Go away.''

"Diverting some of the cargo for your personal use is, of course, your business. It is Tuer law which states that all members of a crew share a vessel's profits according to a strict formula. Oriani have no reason to intervene.''

"You threaten?''

"No. I seek passage, nothing more.''

"Too danger. Kaz hear, shoot first, question unwilling captain later if living.''

"It would be advantageous not to tell them.''

"Ha. I tell no one, for sure.''

"Including your crew?''

The captain cocked his head and waited for the explanation. He was beginning to see potential in this nonsense.

"The fewer who know, the more secure the secret. Their knowledge could be costly.''

The spasms traveling along the Tuer's proboscis were the equivalent of laughter. "Costly? Ha. Crew costing half. Smart, Orian. You pay gold?''

"Gold is hard to get. Would you take fruit?''

"Fruit already got. Gold want.''

"As you wish.''

"To Tuer homeworld only. Is understand? No stop. No extra going.''

"I understand.''

"You stay cabin whole time.''

"Agreed.''

"Crew is finding, you pay twice.''

"No. If the crew finds me, it will be your error, not mine. I will not pay for your errors.''

"My vessel. You do not say will do, will not do.''

"But there are conditions to our bargain. Quarreling is not in anyone's best interest. You agree to the conditions?''

"You mad, Orian. Stay here. Safe here. Kaz eat you very soon you leave this place. That your error you pay for.''

Waiting in the bay for the shuttle to take her back to the surface, Ayyah knew the Tuer captain was wrong. Others also would bear some of the cost, beginning with Lawr.

She had told herself she was prepared for his distress. As much as she regretted it, it was necessary. She knew no gentle way to present the news. A swift, clean strike was best, she decided.

Before the sun rose to start the next day's work, she cruelly roused Lawr from his sleep and revealed to him her intentions. In that coldest hour before dawn, when she explained the bargain made with the Tuer captain and her need for a quantity of gold, Lawr, already stressed by the tensions of harvest time, came alarmingly close to losing his temper. If that happened, he would never recover his self-esteem. The one greatest sin in the Orian culture was to allow savage passions to overrule the rational mind. Lawr was a good man, industrious, careful, and gentle, and also very, very formal and restrained.

Ayyah knew him so well. Her sensitive and well-trained eye caught the brief flick of ears, the slight tightening of the mouth, the tail held rigidly immobile to keep it from betraying the turmoil within.

Lawr turned on his heel and stalked out of the house into the predawn forest and did not come back until he had been so sufficiently cooled by the morning mists that he was flirting with a bout of lung congestion, and had better control himself.

Ayyah waited tensely for his return.

He was shivering when he came in. She found a small oil heater to warm him and a towel to dry his dampened fur.

His first words to her were sharper than they should have been. Ayyah left her worry about the effects of damp air and began to appreciate the effort Lawr's self-control was demanding from him. Her resolve wavered in those moments.

"This is too long for the birthing madness to stay with you. Consult the healer," Lawr demanded.

Had he chosen any other words, he might have defeated her. But remembering the pain of bearing dead babies reinforced her sense of a dead future closing in on the community. "There is no madness here," Ayyah said, and meant it.

"Ayyah," Lawr said, and it was almost a groan. His hands were clenched. He was stiff with the effort of fighting for reason.

"Even as you begin, you begin with deceit, with threats, with trickery, to take advantage of an innocent Tuer."

"My father would call it diplomatic negotiation. I would not call the captain innocent. His intention is to cheat his shipmates of part of their profit. I deceived no one, cheated no one. Nor have I any intention to do these things."

"Your father is said to have been a great man. His greatest talent seems to have been speaking the truth in a way that made it appear other than it was. You follow him well."

"You have become insulting. This is not worthy of you."

"Ayyah, I am trying to make you think."

"I have thought."

"Your father spent his whole life trying to stop the Kaz when Orion was strong, and even then he felt he needed the entire strength of all the Rim Worlds working in concert to accomplish his goal. And he failed, Ayyah. With all those resources, he failed. How do you suppose that now you might succeed, when we are a few infant-weak individuals struggling desperately for our own survival?"

"First, I must learn."

"Learn what?"

"Come, I will show you."

Ayyah was prepared. Lawr allowed himself to be led across the room to the screen of his computer terminal. He had not given up the argument.

"Here," he said. "Do you understand? This we have in place of the Communications/Computer Net that once tied worlds together. Communications technology was Orion's chief export in the days before the Kaz."

"This will serve," she said, not able to admit she understood his illustration of all the lost Orian strengths, diplomatic, economic, and political, as well as technological.

"Does the technology survive anywhere?"

Ayyah resisted the Orian love of argument. Possibly Lawr's question was innocent rhetoric; possibly he was deliberately trying to deflect her. In either case, a distracting debate on the survival rate of technological applications would not serve her now. She called a map of the near side of the galaxy onto the screen. Just to the side of the galaxy's center, across the core, was a yellow, ameboid blotch representing the Kazi empire. A long, jagged pseudopod extended deep into the Orion arm. A much shorter, blunter extension pushed into the Sagittarius arm.

The Perseus arm was not marred by the faintest hint of yellow.

"They know the answer," Ayyah said.

Lawr shut his eyes. Ayyah could almost taste his dismay. He was certain she was insane. She could hardly blame him.

"You do understand the distances involved?" he asked. "Do you imagine you could cross vast tracts of space, establish a relationship with unknown peoples, discover the mighty secret, if such a secret exists, and return with it in one lifetime? You say there is no madness here?"

"I say it is the greater madness to wait placidly here to die."

"I say it is the greater madness to chase blindly after death until you catch it."

Ayyah did not reply. She regretted the pain she was causing but refused to let it sway her.

"You would do this how?" Lawr insisted. "Our small society has no resources to spare for quixotic journeys across half the galaxy."

"In whatever way possible," Ayyah said, "with whatever means present themselves. The time is past for gentle niceties of manners. We must fight for our survival."

"Fight?" Lawr repeated, appalled.

"Or end here."

Lawr was silent a moment, the implications of her statement biting deep. "You would abandon all pretense of civilization in this cause?" he asked.

Ayyah caught herself bristling. If Lawr had wanted to be deliberately offensive, he could have done no worse.

She did not, or would not, believe that offense was his intent. More probably he sought to shock her into rethinking her position. Nonetheless, she had to turn away from him to keep her automatic response within acceptable bounds.

"Our civilization is gone," she said finally, when she thought she could speak with a reasonable semblance of calm. "We have already abandoned it, except for the façade. We build on the banks of the river and foul its water. We cut living trees for fuel and building material. We plant crops alien to this world with no notion of the damage we do. We labor like rude beasts in the forest and snarl at one another like savages. We have laid waste a tract of land to make a place for the Tuer shuttle, all in the name of expedience, and still we die. Still we die. One by one, we go down to righteous death. When we are all dead, who will carry our precious civilization then?"

"This is not the answer."

"Waiting here, suffering silently in this poor place until the Kaz find it, wondering if age will take the last before the Kaz arrive, that is a better answer?"

Lawr grabbed Ayyah's hand, an almost obscene violation of her person by Orian standards, and pushed on the knuckles to make her claws extend. They were long and sharp, a set of tiny scimitars. Normally an Orian would keep his claws clipped short and blunt, a symbol of separation from his barbarous, bloody heritage, a symbol of his affirmation of the ancient Creed of the Pacifist of Owr Neg that no hand or product of hands and no mind or product of mind should ever be raised against another living thing except in immediate defense of one's own life. Ayyah had started to let her claws grow out when she had first realized she was pregnant. No one asked her why, assuming, as Oriani would, that it was her personal concern and no one else's, assuming, she supposed, that it was one of those quirks of motherhood. Perhaps it was. Ayyah herself had no better explanation.

Lawr shook the clawed fingers. "A descent into savagery is a better answer?" he demanded.

Ayyah's ears had flattened, and her hackles were starting to rise. Her own anger was almost out of control. Lawr let her go, tail limp with embarrassment at having gone so far in his desperate attempt to make her see reason.

"All other considerations aside, the journey is not possible," he said more quietly. "You cannot even begin to cross vast tracts of Kazi-held space. You will need fuel and supplies even if you manage to obtain transport by methods I don't wish to contemplate."

A long silence ensued, during which neither Orian looked at the other. When at last Ayyah spoke again, her words were calm and polite, as if a few moments previously raging passions had not threatened to rip away all seemliness and dignity. Decorum, her father had once told her, was the collection of behavioral lies that made civilization possible.

"It may be not necessary." She touched the screen and the scale changed, displaying a section of the Orion arm of the galaxy with their place of exile just out of the yellow fringe. The yellow blotch occupied most of the screen. But it was not uniformly colored. There were holes in it. Ayyah pointed to the star in the center of one, inward from their present location.

"Forty Eridani," she said. Another, deep in Kazi space: "Mira." A third, closer: "Riga."

"Isolated worlds, to be cleaned up at Kazi leisure."

"Islands, where one might rest and possibly find what is needed. My father writes of another, Rayor, long known to be a place of great learning. Talan spoke highly of the wisdom to be found there."

"Also in Kazi space?"

"Yes."

"And you want to go there?"

"Yes."

"It is not shown on your map."

"The location is unknown."

Lawr's teeth came together with an audible click. Ayyah waited. After a moment he said, "It is not possible. No vessel would carry an Orian into the heart of the empire, assuming you knew where you wanted to go."

"I have heard of a human whose fast ship dares Kazi space. I will seek out this one."

"What, a Tuer merchant's tale, half fable, half rumor? Humans are unreliable. You cannot trust your life to one."

"My father did."

"Your father did not succeed in what he sought to do. Talan is not the best authority you could cite."

"Those of lesser courage who followed did not succeed either. We no longer have a home."

"I cannot agree to this."

"You cannot prevent it. I shall make the attempt."

Lawr capitulated, realizing argument would not prevail. He reasoned, as Ayyah knew he would, that if his mate was truly mad, no purpose would be served by preventing her from acting out her fantasy. If she was not mad, one thing was certain: Through her father, one-time ambassador to Earth and elsewhere, Ayyah had experienced more contact with outworlders than any other Orian in the community. It was minutely possible that she had an insight others lacked. In any case, as she had pointed out, if she was determined, he could not stop her by any means short of physical restraint. Though Ayyah had little good to say about the present state of Orian society, she did not believe it had degenerated to that degree of savagery just yet.

If he had been strictly honest with himself, Lawr might have seen that his resistance was based not a little on another factor.

Ayyah had watched it grow between them over the long years of their life together, a thing without a name. The Oriani did not admit interpersonal ties such as Ayyah had seen among members of other races. Perhaps these things did not occur between Oriani. But something bound them together.

They could not speak of it. There were no words in their language. The inhibitions ran generations deep.

Ayyah knew that in the end he would find gold for her, reluctantly lent by the electronics workers, not because he agreed with her, but because he cared for her.

It was a strangeness, this caring.

"Do as you wish," he said finally. Ayyah did not see the relaxing of tensions in him that his surrender should have brought.

Centauri City

"A baby!"

MacDonald sat bolt upright on the bed. His ardor had shriveled away to nothing in an instant. He switched on the bedside light and looked down at Shirley's bland face.

"Wouldn't you like to have a baby, MacDonald?" Shirley wheedled. She watched him coyly from modestly lowered eyes.

"Holy loving Saint Agatha on a blanket. No. No, I most emphatically would not like to have a baby."

"I would. I'd like to have yours."

"No way, Shirley."

"I don't know why you feel like that. It wouldn't have to bother you much."

"My dear girl, I'm much too old to embark on any twenty-year projects. Besides, I don't need the responsibility or the pain. Besides, why in heaven's name would you want a kid that's going to grow up to be like me?"

Shirley shrugged on the bed, abandoning all pretense of girlish embarrassment. "Well, you don't know, maybe it'd look like me."

MacDonald didn't see where that was much to cheer about. Shirley had a soft, bovine prettiness of a common sort, which was rapidly heading into overstuffed middle age. She had a soft, bovine mind to go with it.

"You've got a breeding permit?" he asked.

"No, but I could get one."

Probably you could, MacDonald thought. You're just the kind of compliant, unimaginative type the Kaz would like more of.

He padded naked over to the window and looked out. The bottom of the polyglas was just aboveground, giving him an odd

32

knee-level perspective on the street. On Centauri, buildings tended to be deep rather than tall because of the endless wind.

The bowing trees bent to the northeast under the street lights. They were engineered Sitka spruce, the only thing bigger than a bread box that would grow in Centauri's ugly climate and inhospitable soil, many of them more than a century old and still not much more than man high. Most had a permanent northeast lean.

Proxima Centauri rode above the horizon, a hazy red disc and a damned poor excuse for a third sun, though it made a good enough moon if one didn't mind red moonlight.

MacDonald didn't care much for red moonlight. He felt he was beginning to lean a bit to the northeast himself. He was tired of waiting. He was nervous about leaving his ship on the ground. If the Lleveci didn't show up soon, he was going to chuck the whole deal and get away from Centauri and its miserable weather and the neck-prickling presence of the Kaz.

Oscar must have exhausted the scanty interests of the rebel camp.

A meteor crossed the upper sky, a brief line of light that reminded him of the fate of the *Sherwood Forest*. He had managed to put the hollow around his heart out of his mind for a little while, but the void was back now, achingly empty.

Marion Jones had roused in him the closest thing to love he had felt in a long, long time. Maybe ever. They had been good together. He felt he should have prepared some appropriate memorial. He should be marking the event with something more significant than bouncing silly Shirley.

Maybe he should go out and trash a bar. That would suit his mood and be more fitting. He had sometimes made jokes with Marion about having picked her up in a bar, but that wasn't really the way it had happened.

He never knew how the free-for-all had gotten started that evening on Riga. The usual debris of dispossessed and futile noncitizens of the new order were sitting around the establishment known as the Outworlder, each quietly imbibing his favorite central nervous system stimulant. They were people of fragile temper for whom, as the Roothian often said, the blood lay close to the skin. A quarrel broke out and spread like oil on hot iron. Suddenly it was chaos, with shouting and the breaking of glass and everyone hitting everyone else. MacDonald would have liked to back quietly out of the place, which turned out to be a difficult thing to do with everyone on his feet—or other, very different nether appendages—milling around, taking umbrage, and it soon became a matter of hit or be hit.

For reasons known only to horned folk, MacDonald became the special project of a red-eyed Brodenli. He suffered one good blow to the gut before he wound up and smacked his assailant right between the eyes.

It was like hitting a brick. The bony skull plate that supported a Brodenli's horns extended down between the orbital ridges. Pain flashed up MacDonald's arm to his earlobe and sent him staggering backward. He found himself against a wall, with a horn on either side of his neck and the owner preparing to deliver the stake through the heart with a chair leg broken off into a long point.

Then there was an audible *thok*, and the Brodenli collapsed into MacDonald's arms. The lady had applied the metal base of a lamp firmly to the vulnerable base of the skull. Marion looked down at her handiwork, then up at MacDonald, and asked, as if it were the most normal question in the galaxy, "What's a nice man like you doing in a place like this?"

MacDonald rubbed the bone in his hand that had been broken that long-ago day.

"Aren't you coming back to bed?" Shirley asked.

He shook his head. "Want some coffee?"

Shirley thought about sulking for a bit, but remembered it was not too successful a technique where MacDonald was concerned.

"Yeah, I guess," she said.

MacDonald went to work with the miniature cooker and three cubic feet of cupboard space the landlord lovingly referred to as a kitchen. Shirley half sat against the headboard of the bed with the sheet tucked under her chin.

"I get lonely, you know," she said. "You're not here much."

"Mm," MacDonald answered noncommittally. He turned with a coffee cup in either hand and was startled enough to almost drop them.

A Lleveci was standing beside the door.

A little hot liquid sloshed over one hand, and MacDonald swore.

"I'm bloody sure that door was locked," he snarled. "Don't you knock?"

The Lleveci regarded him levelly and said nothing.

Shirley squeaked and pulled the sheet closer.

Many Terrans upon first seeing Lleveci compared them to turkeys. It's the long wattled neck that does it, MacDonald thought. But once one got the full effect of the sharp, highly placed eyes, some other comparison came to mind. Eagles, maybe, or even vultures. Definitely not turkeys.

This one would be darn close to two meters tall with the neck extended, was narrow as an oak plank, as hard looking, and about the same color, with a full mane, the mark of a warrior clan. Not to be taken lightly.

"Who is he? Tell him to get out of here," Shirley squealed.

"Her," MacDonald corrected. Seeing all the colorful regalia, he was suddenly acutely conscious of being mother naked. He put the cups down on the bedside table and reached for his robe.

"Here Delladar Oll," the Lleveci said in heavily accented English, slapping her chest with a long-fingered hand. "Do business, MacDonald?"

MacDonald rubbed his own hand over his face and thought about it. He didn't want to look overly anxious. Nor did he want Delladar Oll to think he was not interested. Nor did he want to spend one more minute in the Centauri Colony than he absolutely had to. It was not the safest place in the universe for a known pirate.

"Well, I, uh, wasn't expecting you in the middle of the night."

"Night best. Kaz not move in night."

"And as you can see, I have company."

Delladar Oll turned to Shirley for one slow blink of fierce eyes and decided to disregard her.

"This dangerous. For me, also for you. Longer time, more danger. Dismiss companion. We talk now, quickly."

Imperious dame, aren't you? MacDonald thought. He turned to Shirley nonetheless. "Maybe you wouldn't mind? I'll call you later."

"Well, gee, thanks." Shirley's eyes were wide and round, not the least bit sure of what was happening. However, she did seem sure of one thing. "I'm not going anywhere till curfew ends. I don't care what you say—I'm not. I'm not ending up in some reprocessing bin just so you can do your weird business."

"Half the people in the colony don't pay any attention to the curfew. Chances are, you won't even see a patrol."

"I don't care. I'll scream the house down if you try to make me."

"Relax. Nobody's going to make you do anything." MacDonald turned to Delladar Oll. The Lleveci squatted down beside the door with her stiff back flat against the wall.

"I wait," she said. Nothing about the announcement suggested she was pleased.

MacDonald consulted the chronometer on the wall opposite the window. The instrument approximated the ephemeral data of a world subject to the influence of three suns—the rotation of the planet, the date according to the Terran system of dating, various sun risings and settings, the location of a few significant constellations in Centauri's inconstant sky, and a guess at the state of the confused tides on the Inland Sea. It was more accurate than MacDonald could be in five minutes with a pencil, but less accurate than he could be in half that time at a navigation console.

Memories of the Fleet Academy surfaced. Navigation 513, Approximate Solutions to the Classic Four-Body Problem. He was good at navigation. From his sophomore year until he graduated, he made his pocket money tutoring wealthier but less capable students.

Those were happy days, for the most part blissfully free of political considerations. Young MacDonald studied hard and graduated near the top of his class with a reputation for an innovative and sometimes mischievous approach to problem solving.

A lot of people glared enviously when he took the prime assignment aboard *Starchaser*. Other people's envy didn't hurt too much. Under the demanding eye of Captain Singh, who did not believe ensigns should ever imagine their education was completed, he made more rapid progress than anyone expected. Ten years later he found himself second in command of the *Rising Dragon* and within six weeks of taking command of the *Great Bear*. That same six weeks would see his thirty-fourth birthday.

He was damned pleased with himself in those days. He even dared to hope his father might be finally won over. The old man was bitterly disaffected with the son who, by willingly, even enthusiastically, joining the Kazi-controlled Fleet, became in the old man's mind an accomplice to Kazi oppression. Seeing him with a captain's bars on his shoulders, Pop might, MacDonald hoped, understand at last that his boy was realizing a childhood dream.

Could you take your old man in hand and shake him and tell him "My dreams are important, too"? The stern old lunatic would never have believed it. He had held his own dreams about ending Kazi rule, and MacDonald's dream never did materialize.

The Kaz announced a major change in their policies toward the Space Fleet. Henceforward, all Terran deep-space vessels would have Kazi captains.

A hell of a good way to control offworld traffic.

MacDonald left the service without even saying good-bye, which, of course, put him on a good many lists. All sorts of people were on lists back then. He fell in, as the ancient saying went, with bad companions.

The Fleet had made him a good pilot. A good pilot could always make a living. He learned his way around the community of outlaws that populated the chinks of Kazi-controlled space, acted out his resentment by screwing the Kaz in whatever little ways he could, and fully expected to end his days reprocessed. Pop's restless spirit probably approved.

The chronometer predicted primary dawn in a little less than an hour. He wondered if he ought to offer the Lleveci some breakfast, and if so, what. He settled instead for getting some proper clothes on.

Alpha I just cleared the horizon when the clouds rolled in and the rain began, beating against the window as if determined to drown the colony once and for all. The Centaurians, long resigned to foul weather, went briskly about their business as soon as the curfew was lifted.

Shirley got dressed, somewhat shyly in the Lleveci's presence, refused breakfast and even coffee, and called a ground cab at MacDonald's expense to take her off to work at whatever it was she worked at. When MacDonald said he would call her, she told him not to bother.

Throughout this activity, Delladar Oll had not moved. When the door closed behind Shirley, she stood up. "Now?"

MacDonald nodded. "You understand, I don't have the stuff here. All I can show you is a sample. What you have to do is prove to me you have access to the necessary credit."

The Lleveci produced from a pocket of her tunic a Securitaped flimsy indicating a substantial line of credit on an Eridani bank.

"Okay," MacDonald said, impressed. "My show-and-tell is

going to take a few minutes. Why don't you relax a bit until I'm ready?"

Delladar Oll remained ramrod stiff beside the door. MacDonald shrugged and went about gathering the parts of the laser cannon from their hiding places and laying them out on the floor beneath the window. One reason he kept this apartment at considerable expense even when he was offworld most of the time was the modifications he had made to its structure to accommodate such situations. He doubted he had been clever enough to defeat a serious search, but several casual inspections had been made without his secrets coming out.

He worked in silence. He couldn't even hear the Lleveci breathing. But some small sound or motion brought his eyes to the window about the time he was done. He was surprised to see a sodden kitten out there in the rain peering anxiously through the glass, its little pink mouth open wide with cries he couldn't hear. Go away, cat, he thought at it. Don't like cats. Never did. Much preferred dogs, if you want to know.

There were no dogs anymore. Dogs hated Kaz on sight, and after a few startled times of being chased down the street by a barking, snarling hound, the Kaz consigned all dogs to reprocessing.

The same thing was supposed to have happened to cats. As much as dogs didn't like Kaz, Kaz didn't like cats. But cats were wilier, more suspicious beasts, and there were still a few about.

The kitten realized it had caught his attention and renewed its cries, pushing its wet little body against the glass.

"Shove off," MacDonald said aloud. "If you're still there when the patrol comes by, you'll be molecules faster than you can say 'Holy meow, Pussycat.' "

"Talk to me?" Delladar Oll asked.

MacDonald shook his head. "Talking to myself. If you'd like, come take a look at this . . ." He rammed the firing mechanism in place and stood aside for Delladar Oll to make her inspection. "This is just the business end. It's powered by a standard high-efficiency photon pump."

"Included?"

"If you're willing to pay."

Delladar Oll prowled around the gun and removed and replaced bits, adequately demonstrating her familiarity with the mechanism. "How to have weapons of Kaz?"

"That's none of your business."

"I see work."

"Hey, come on. Even if I had a power pack handy, I can't fire the damned thing around here. Aside from blowing away a few innocent bystanders, we'd have every Kazi within ninety AU standing on the doorstep in fifteen minutes."

The thought made him glance first at the chronometer and then at the window. The Kazi street patrol was due any moment. The kitten was stretched up on its hind legs, pawing frantically at the pane. Its gaunt ribs showed beneath its plastered-down fur. Its little feet were torn and bleeding. There was a streak of blood on the glass.

"Where?" Delladar Oll asked.

"Where what?" Stupid kitten. Why didn't it go away? "Oh, for chrissake." MacDonald opened the window and pulled the kitten inside in a gust of wind and rain. It clung to his arm like an animated burr.

"Where test weapon?"

"Deep space?" MacDonald suggested. The kitten was hanging on for dear life. He could feel its tiny body shivering. He carefully disengaged its claws from his skin and set it down on the floor. It leaned against his foot and tried to purr. "Look, cat," MacDonald said, "don't think you're going to stay. This is strictly temporary."

To Delladar Oll he added, "The patrol is due. I've got to get this out of sight."

Delladar Oll was looking past him, her cheeks showing a little color. "Not routine patrol."

Two of the heavy-duty ground vehicles known locally as Kaz carriers had turned into the street and were approaching at speed. When he listened for it, MacDonald thought he could make out the motor of a skysled through the noise of the rain.

Delladar Oll had unsheathed the long knife she carried at her side and held a formidable-looking blaster in the other hand; she looked ready to make a gallant stand at the door.

MacDonald shook his head vigorously. "Let's get out of here."

The Lleveci asked about the gun with a gesture. She was reluctant to give up the weapon.

"Leave it. It'll give them something to do for a minute. Skin is more valuable than machinery any day of the week. Take the corridor to the left, the door at the end, stairs leading down."

Delladar Oll moved with admirable speed. MacDonald started

out behind her. The kitten mewed plaintively. MacDonald hesitated a fraction of a second, swooped the wee beast up, tucked it into his shirt, and ran. "Not a sound, you understand," he whispered to it.

The stairway went down several levels and ended in a wandering, badly lighted tunnel. Bundles of pipes and conduits hung overhead. Cryptic maintenance-man symbols were stenciled on the wall here and there with arrows pointing this way and that. Other tunnels joined it to form a maze that underlay the entire colony. When he first came to Centauri, MacDonald had taken the trouble to explore the maze sufficiently to have an escape route established.

Delladar Oll bumped him into a narrow branch and motioned for quiet. He put his hand over the lump in his shirt that was the kitten, stifling a tiny squeak. In a moment he heard the *scritch* of Kazi feet on the tunnel floor.

He peered around the edge of the junction and made out the two black, many-legged forms just rounding the curve ahead, coming toward them, blocking the way to the surface, weapons very evident in the manipulative forelimbs. He took a reading on the branch he was in. It ran arrow straight for bloody ever. Back was the apartment, which would be crawling by now. There was no place to go.

It seemed particularly dumb for it to end like this, in a service tunnel in crummy Centauri, of all places. No grand gesture, not the slightest hint of a blaze of glory, the only witnesses fated to die with him. He thought he had become completely fatalistic over the last fifteen years, but a little dash and ceremony would have been nice.

He looked at Delladar Oll and shrugged an apology. There didn't seem to be much else he could do. He felt bad about the kitten who was an innocent bystander in all this.

The Lleveci jabbed him with a sharp elbow and glared him into silence. She shoved the blaster into his hand hard enough for it to bump him in the gut and pulled him tight against the wall closest to the Kaz. Her sign language was universal in form and simple enough in the seconds available to be incapable of misunderstanding. He was reluctant to give up the kitten. It was silly. Now or moments from now, dead was dead, and he didn't even like the beast. Delladar Oll reached under his shirt and took it, a too-intimate contact from an alien that left him taken aback even under these circumstances.

The sound of Kazi feet was close. No chatter passed between them—the Kaz had no auditory language—but MacDonald caught a whiff of them, and their smell was the smell of damp, sunless places.

Delladar Oll dropped to one knee, put the cat on the floor, and gave it a push toward the main corridor. It went a few hesitant steps, then stopped and looked back, puzzled. Then it suddenly fuzzed itself out and arched and spat and whirled and dashed back by them along the narrow straightaway like a hairy bullet.

The first Kazi who rounded the corner in pursuit met Delladar Oll's blade held rigidly in close with her elbow braced against her side about a meter off the floor. The Kazi impaled itself on the point and died instantly, with hardly a spasm.

MacDonald, firing over her head as instructed, smoked the second one but was allowed no time to admire his marksmanship. Retrieving her bloodstained knife, Delladar Oll urged him along the narrow branch. "Where goes?"

"I don't know."

She made no comment, but he could sense her disapproval of his improvidence. She had good reason. However they did it, the Kaz knew when one of their number died. They always knew. All the Kaz on Centauri, and God only knew how far beyond, would sense that two had died here, and hordes of them would descend upon these tunnels in no time.

They jogged on for what seemed well over a kilometer until MacDonald, who thought he was in reasonably good shape, was feeling every one of his forty-nine years. Anticipation of Kazi fire from the rear kept him moving without complaint, until their narrow banch met another wide, main tunnel.

One arm was abbreviated, ending with a ladder on the round face. Delladar Oll started up without hesitation.

The kitten huddled against the wall in the nearest thing it could find to a corner. MacDonald swept it up before following the Lleveci to find himself in a bottom-floor hallway with a lift shaft nearby, leading to the surface.

"Now where?" Delladar Oll asked.

"Do you know how to get to the northern railhead?"

"Find way."

"I'll meet you there. If I don't show up, look for a big man called Oscar Achebe. But be careful who you ask."

She looked at him as if she were doubtful about the wisdom of all this. All she said was "Get rid of animal. Dangerous."

"He just saved our skins," MacDonald answered. "We owe him a chance."

That explanation may have touched some Lleveci sense of the proprieties. In any case, Delladar Oll did not argue further. She started away, hesitated, and turned back to him. "Hide in tunnel. Kaz live in tunnels. Not smart." And she stepped into the lift shaft and was gone.

By the time MacDonald arrived on the surface and stepped out into rain turning to sleet, she was nowhere in sight. Shrugging, he hailed a cab, charging the extravagance against the cost of doing business.

The driver, a prune-faced old woman with an illicit cigarette butt hanging out of the corner of her mouth, was curious about the kitten. MacDonald offered to give it to her.

"No thanks, Bud," she said. "I got enough troubles in my life without bugging the bugs deliberate. I was you, I'd get rid of it."

MacDonald took it with him on the train. He decided its name was Cat.

Sam didn't want Cat either. His sentiments were about the same as the taxi driver's.

Oscar, wise in the ways of his partner and friend, and wanting to jeopardize neither relationship over an animal that was cute enough to melt a hardened heart but was out of place on a starship, said nothing.

Riga

Aboard the Rigan freighter *Gan Gorfed*, Ayyah fastidiously avoided the carnivorous Rigans at their meals. She was sickened by the sight of them stuffing bits of dead animals into their great toothy maws, chins running red and claws bloody, by the smell of meat long dead and only sometimes somewhat cooked, by the sound of crunching bone and the grunts of pleasure. Revolted, ignoring the fact her ancestors might have happily joined the repast, she retreated to her bunk space.

Offended sensibilities offered one compensation—a few moments of privacy. The crew quarters aboard *Gan Gorfed* consisted of a bare room filled with stacked bunks barely a Rigan-width apart. While the Rigans ate, she had it all to herself, and that eased the tensions somewhat. She could stretch her arms and nibble without apology at a dry seedcake purchased in Tuer Port for an outrageous price that raised anew her doubts about her right to spend the colony's few precious resources. She could spread out hardcopies of her father's notes and try to plan her strategy. Bunk space barely big enough for a Rigan was room enough for an Orian to camp in.

Well, not quite. In her mind's eye, Ayyah could see her father squatting down to child's level and telling her solemnly, "An exaggeration is half a lie."

The transfer at Tuer Port had been less difficult than she had imagined. Tramp freighters were endlessly in need of labor, and Rigan freighters were not the first choice of most deckhands. She had simply walked across the staging area to the *Gan Gorfed*'s shuttle and told the first Rigan officer she saw that she was available for an inbound trip. The captain of the *Gan Gorfed* seemed happy enough to get her and satisfied with the work of his temporary crewman. She was quick to learn, strong for her

43

size, and spent some of her first brief leisure period making adjustments to the life-support systems so that the atmosphere lost some of the stink of recycled air that commonly marked Rigan vessels as less-than-pleasant habitats.

If the captain's slow Rigan curiosity had been touched by the fact of a proscribed Orian on Tuer willing to work as engine-room gofer on his ship, he had scratched his scaly brow a bit, but by the time he was sufficiently moved by it to consider investigating, *Gan Gorfed* was already under way, and Ayyah was aboard.

So he did not ask, perhaps because the whole situation had been rendered academic by then, and he was not too fond of Kazi directives in any case; perhaps because communications between a vessel's captain and its engine-room flunkies were spotty at best; or perhaps because they would have to address one another in halting pidgin Sindharr, a language of unknown origin that was developing into a *lingua franca* among space-going people and was foreign to both of them. Ayyah was reasonably adept at it. The captain, she heard, was not.

Ayyah worked to overcome these limitations, for by the time they reached Riga, she wanted the captain favorably disposed when she approached him for help getting onto the planet undetected.

Her bunk, like everyone else's, consisted of a piece of heavy fabric slung between rails the width of her forearm supported by thick aluminum pipes extending from floor to ceiling. The preferred Orian attitude of rest, curled into a semicircle with the tail wrapped over the flank, was almost impossible. She made herself as comfortable as she could and reviewed her father's teachings.

Riga was an anomaly in the empire.

No one seemed to know the real reason Riga remained free of Kazi governance when worlds all around were absorbed, digested, and regurgitated either wiped clean of sentient life and ready to be repopulated by Kaz, or else with populations subjugated and enslaved as hewers of wood and drawers of water, providing essential materials and services to fuel the ever-expanding empire.

Some said it was because when the first Kaz landed on Riga half a century earlier, the indiscriminately carnivorous native population regarded them more as potential lunch than potential conquerors. Others said Riga was so riddled with internecine squabbles that the Kaz could find no central authority with which to deal. Talan, restrained by the discipline of Orian reason, suggested that the Kazi expansion into the Orion arm had been too rapid for the empire to control properly, that the Kaz were thinly spread in the region, and that a few less valuable places had therefore been temporarily overlooked. In his opinion, this state of affairs would not continue indefinitely. Eventually the Kaz would address these omissions, clean up these untidy spots.

In the meantime, Riga served as a precarious haven for those few beings who thought to escape the Kazi yoke, a collection of exiles, outlaws, refugees, fugitives, derelicts, and general flotsam uneasily squatting upon that semifriendly shore.

"Seek out the humans," Talan said, back in those better days on the homeworld when he had thought Ayyah might take up her father's lifelong battle against the expanding Kazi empire. He still had faith in humans, for all they had rejected him and sent his diplomatic mission home in disgrace.

"Great rebels exist among them," Talan had explained. "Don't be misled by the collective mind. The individual is often at odds with the group. These noncomformists become adept at finding ways to work among the cracks and flaws of an organization." He could have been bitter, and was not. He left a giant image for his daughter to live up to.

Ayyah's experience of humans was limited to one. Bill Anderson had been Talan's friend and also his adversary early in Ayyah's life, a thoroughly disagreeable person and one, she had to admit, who had required considerable effort to control.

Ayyah could not imagine herself making a human friend. But she could see where the right human rebel might be useful. No rule of logic or nature required one to love one's instruments.

The day before scheduled planetfall, she took her petition to the captain. Surprised to be stopped in a bare corridor by one so low in both status and stature that she was scarcely visible, intrigued by the small one's audacity, *Gan Gorfed*'s captain, bending to match his height to hers, showed himself to be sympathetic to Ayyah's request. He had no great enthusiasm for land-based bureaucrats anyway, he said. Their sole purpose, he pointed out through halting syllables of Sindharr, was to make the movement of ships and ships' personnel as difficult as Riganly possible.

He instructed her carefully on how it might be done. If he had been a faster thinker, he might have wondered why Ayyah was so anxious to escape official notice.

On the other hand, chances were that wondering, he still would not care.

When *Gan Gorfed*'s shuttle set down inside the fenced compound of the reception area and the crew went into the main building to deal with officialdom, Ayyah stayed aboard and out of sight, as the Rigan captain instructed. Entry control was often lax, he said, and if she got caught out, she could always let on that she did not understand what was required.

Everything Rigans did, they did with a characteristic absence of urgency. The pilot returned eventually and moved the shuttle into a holding shed to await the customs official's pleasure. There Ayyah left the vehicle and took refuge among big, dusty crates and barrels and huge chunks of machinery lining the walls.

The fence meant to contain a rhinoceros won't hold a snake. The fence around the reception area was built by Rigans with Rigans in mind, and while Rigans are big, powerful folk, they lack a little in the matter of agility. The fence was heavy woven wire held up by thick, three-meter-high poles of local wood. Under cover of night, in the shadow of the shed, Ayyah dug her nails into the wood, climbed a pole, and dropped lightly down on the other side.

The port city occupied a wide plain delimited in the south by a series of sharp cliffs on top of which the Lord High Regent's brooding castle stood in a circle of light. The castle was over four thousand years old, unchanged in that time except for the glittering chrome-plated trim added to battlements, casements, and doorways. No one had ever accused the Lord High Regent of good taste.

Above the castle, a wide swath of Riga's night sky lay empty of stars.

The eerie blank blackness surrounded by a glowing aura made a spectacular sky. It was caused by a dust cloud less than two light-years away, and that cloud was the reason Ayyah had suffered all the indignities and discomforts of her trip to Riga.

Near the end of his life, Talan had become almost frantic in his efforts to collect and sort as much information as he possibly could for those who would take up the battle against the empire. His eyesight was poor by then, and his voice was a harsh rasp. At the very last, his mind began to fail him, and his thoughts became scattered, often incomplete. He fought even this as long as he could. Ayyah came to admire her father's courage.

She took away from the leafy grove where Talan went to die the last shreds of data he was able to leave. Less than a year later, the Kaz descended upon Orion.

Those last scraps were only hearsay. There had been no time to verify rumors of a nest of Terran pirates building a refuge near one of the suns buried within the ArGald Nebula near Riga. There was only gossip overheard where people who made their livelihoods between the stars came together, in customs sheds, in the anterooms of traders' offices, in the bars and taverns of the spaceports, stories of madmen who dared Kazi space and preyed on Kazi ships.

"Be wary of the savior mythology," Talan had cautioned in earlier lessons. "It exists among many peoples. In this legend, an unbelievably powerful, charismatic individual rises suddenly from humble beginnings to redress injustice, overcome oppression, and reestablish basic morality. The vanquished seek relief from their subjugation in fantasy."

Fantasy. Now the Oriani were a conquered race also, and as subject to wishful thinking as any less disciplined people. She was a living example, chasing a wild hope without either the resources or the knowledge to catch it, having modestly cast herself in the savior role, ready to lead her people out of darkness into the promised land.

Doubt could paralyze. One must not recognize doubt.

The port city was a collection of large, roughly cubic, permacrete buildings of various sizes dropped randomly onto Riga's coarse black soil like some giant child's abandoned blocks. Rigan architecture was solid but graceless and lacking imagination. People and vehicles found what ways they could among the buildings.

The soil felt harsh underfoot. The angles of the city were unrelieved by vegetation. Nothing grew there.

Ayyah knew little about Rigaport as it existed in modern times. History suggested it had been a barbarous place before the Kaz. She had no reason to suppose it had improved. Her safety here would depend more on her wits than on rule of law, and although she had little of commercial value in the carryall she wore on a strap slung over her shoulder, a thief might have to remove it from her body before he discovered the fact.

Few of either people or vehicles were about in the night. Ayyah wandered the streets a long time before finally finding an individual leaning against a wall with his massive jaw hanging slack and his little eyes firmly fixed on extragalactic space. He peered down at her when she spoke to him, first in one language, then another. His eyes squinted almost out of existence, then he heaved himself off the wall and shambled away without speaking.

The second person she found was a female, much smaller than any male, almost dainty by Rigan standards, hurrying along on some apparently urgent business. The female was willing enough to talk, regarding Ayyah gravely with her tongue protruding from between long teeth in her efforts to understand, but they soon discovered they had no common language. It seemed an impasse until the woman grabbed Ayyah by the arm, a gentle enough action for her that almost took Ayyah off her feet, and pointed the Orian toward an open doorway from which light spilled out. She gave Ayyah a little push, sending her stumbling in that direction, and hurried off.

Lacking a better plan, Ayyah continued along the way indicated.

The doorway could be the doorway into any Rigan building, except that the wall to the left of it was graced with hand-lettering in the graphics of a dozen languages declaring repeatedly that the name of the place was the Offworlder and almost anyone's credit was acceptable.

The room was of generous Rigan dimensions, brightly lit near the center, fading to dim at the periphery, with a high counter running the length of the far wall where business of some sort was obviously done. A Terran and a young Sgat were behind the counter. Gaming tables of various sorts occupied part of the middle space, and some of them were in use, but most of the area was taken up by clusters of lonely people spending time. They were grouped roughly by race, but with a lot of scatter.

An interesting variety of heads turned when Ayyah went in. Activities stopped, and conversations died as she passed; she ran a gauntlet of inquiring and not overly friendly faces as she made her way toward the counter. The sense of hostility she got from them made the hair on the back of her neck prickle. It took conscious effort to keep her hackles flat and her tail still.

One could scarcely blame the denizens of the Offworlder for the paranoia that flourished among them; they expected one day the doorway would be darkened by the Kazi army, and then their last refuge would be no more.

Though it looked the more approachable of the two behind the counter, the squeaks and trills of the Sgat's native tongue were unknown to her, so Ayyah addressed the Terran with words her father had taught her in childhood, and which she had not had occasion to use often since then. They lay awkward in her mind and came out ill formed and hesitant. She was conscious of sounding inept, which did nothing to ease the way.

"I look for—seek—the human having a name MacDonald."

"Yeah?" the Terran behind the counter said. His face was closed against her. He was not going to offer any help. That was immediately obvious. The Sgat stretched its vermiform body to its full height, leaned over the counter, and twittered at her. The Terran aimed a slap at it. The Sgat collapsed in on itself and the blow went overhead.

"Shut up," the Terran said. The Sgat squeaked with annoyance.

The exchange told Ayyah much about the relationship between the two, and strongly indicated that the information she wanted was here, but offered no clue about how she might persuade the Terran to part with it.

"It is consequential—important—I should discover—encounter—find—the human MacDonald."

"Yeah? To who?"

"I hold not understanding of what you ask."

Ayyah was conscious of activity in the room behind her and of footsteps approaching. Judging by the sound and spacing, they were human.

"I'm telling you it ain't important to me," the man behind the counter said. "So why don't you just hustle your tail out of here before you find it's in trouble."

An unkempt Terran with a strong scent leaned on the counter next to Ayyah and said to the man behind it, "Why don't you get me a beer, Alex?" When the other went to do his bidding, the man turned to Ayyah. "Don't you mind Alexei. He's just naturally unfriendly." He took the glass from the glowering Alexei and turned his back on him, hooking his elbows on the counter top. "My name is Tomas Lopes. You're Orian, aren't you?"

"Yes."

"Come on over to the table and talk to me a bit. Can I get you something?"

Ayyah sorted through the question, trying to understand its significance. "I need presently enlightenment regarding current location of the human MacDonald."

Lopes absorbed this with pursed lips, but did not respond directly. Instead he said as he guided her toward a table where two other Earthlings waited, "I never thought I'd actually see an Orian. I thought the Kaz pretty well got them all. You're a pretty rare bird."

"Bird?"

"I mean there aren't many—never mind. Sit down, why don't you, and tell me what you want with MacDonald."

Ayyah declined the proffered chair, which had a solid back guaranteed to make sitting unpleasant for any creature with a tail, and pulled a small stool over instead. One of the other humans grinned. "Hey, Tomas, what've you got there, a pussy-cat?"

Tomas Lopes held up an apologetic hand. "Don't pay any attention to that loudmouth. He doesn't mean any harm. He's just naturally stupid." The one so described continued to smile, as if incapable of taking insult. Tomas Lopes went on. "The thing is, you see, I might be able to help you out."

It seemed a very strange thing for Tomas Lopes to say. Ayyah struggled for words. "I require—need—no help going out. Help needed is to find the human MacDonald."

"Yeah, well, okay."

"You hold this information?"

"Could be. The thing is, why do you need MacDonald?"

"I hold—have—a work for him."

"You've got a job for MacDonald? Why him? Wouldn't one of us do?"

Ayyah hesitated. Tomas Lopes was presenting himself as a pleasant, concerned individual whose only motive was to be helpful. But there was a smell of excitement about him that was out of keeping with his feigned casual interest. The other two humans were frowning, trying to understand what Tomas Lopes was doing, but they had not interrupted, so one might suspect that Tomas Lopes was their leader. The concept of leaders and followers was one Ayyah had difficulty with, but she accepted it intellectually as a relationship common among humans.

So where was this leader leading? To some scheme of his

own, she was certain. The only way that came immediately to mind in which Tomas Lopes could wrest gain from her mere presence involved the Kaz, and Ayyah thought wisdom would dictate that she withdraw from this association at once, while withdrawal was still an option.

Wisdom had precious little to do with her present enterprise, and she had not ever imagined that the search for MacDonald would be so simply concluded as walking into an odd place such as this and asking for him.

Tomas Lopes had hidden plans. So be it.

The language was becoming easier as her use of it stirred old lessons.

"Perhaps also another is satisfactory," she said. "The need is of fast ship, best navigation, and bold spirit. I would go into Kazi space."

"You sure you want to do that?"

"Yes."

"It sounds pretty dumb to me. But that's your business. I can take you to MacDonald."

"Expression of appreciation," Ayyah said.

"Eh?"

Ayyah searched her memory for the proper term. "Thank you."

"Oh. Yeah, sure, you're welcome. Now if you'll just wait here a moment until we go settle our bar bills with Alexei, we could get started right away."

Ayyah remained seated while the humans walked away with studied casualness. When they were two or three tables away, their conversation took on an urgent concern. They obviously did not expect Ayyah to be able to overhear. They were not accustomed to the sensitivity of Orian ears.

The one called Ching seemed most alarmed. "You out of your bleating head, Tomas? You're not really thinking about taking that thing home?"

"Would you stop clucking? I'm about to make your fortune. You could give me a little help."

"But the Kaz . . ."

"Yeah, exactly. The rewards have been posted for a century. And Kazi credit spends as good as any, better than some."

"MacDonald isn't going to like this," the third man said.

A small being in an orange robe slipped furtively through the doorway into the night, unnoticed by most of the Offworlder's clientele. Ayyah hoped Tomas Lopes's business with Alexei would be settled quickly. She did not think the nervous creature had her best interests in mind.

Thissah the Roothian made his living by being available. He hung around the Offworlder, fetched and carried, ran errands, found people and things, and took careful note of comings and goings in Rigaport. He scurried around like a nervous salamander, seemed always to be there when someone thought to look for him, and was all but invisible otherwise. He looked innocuous, a diminutive, thin-skinned, big-eyed version of a Rigan in a bright orange robe a bit grubby around the hem. His greatest ambition seemed to be survival in a world that was too rough and abrasive to be comfortable.

He managed better than most people realized, and sent his credit home to be held in trust in the Temple of the Immaculate Saint of Roo. The priests stole a portion of it. He knew that, and considered it the price of safekeeping while he built up a reserve against the time he would return to Roo and start his family.

That time was near. The years had taken their toll. He could not delay much longer, even though the reserve was not as large as he would have liked. He intended to live well on Roo and raise many children.

He was surprised to see the Orian come into the Offworlder, but he did not question the turn of events that had sent him this windfall. The saint provided for those who kept the faith, and in his own way, Thissah had been faithful.

He hung around long enough to see the Orian in the company of some Terrans. They were in the port often, those Terrans, but did not live there. They sometimes sent Thissah in search of items that were not exactly on the legal products list. He knew them to be pirates and had hoped, by persistent association with them, to find out where they went between visits. Unfortunately, they were careful about hiding their trail, and so far, he had been unable to acquire that valuable bit of information.

With the Orian, he had no need to delay. She was valuable where she was.

Thissah slipped out of the Offworlder and into the Rigan night. He traveled close to the walls and skittered across open spaces after carefully looking left and right for possible observers. No dangers lurked in the empty streets. Apprehension was a matter of habit.

His destination was a ground-floor room in a large building near the edge of the port city.

Greenish light leaked out around the edges of the coverings over the windows. That was a relief. The ugly one was awake to receive his news.

The Kazi squatted on a short bench, busy at some incomprehensible Kazi business, when Thissah entered without knocking. It turned from the complex instrument before it and regarded Thissah for a moment with the light glinting off the myriad planes of its shiny black eyes. Then it reached down for a small device, which it hung around its abbreviated neck. A flat, thin, metallic voice emerged from the device.

"Why are you here?"

Advance Base 4,903

Advance Base Number 4,903 served as a supply depot, staging area, and training center. Although nearly a million Kaz were stationed on Advance Base 4,903, the main construction on the surface was the port and docking facility. Everything else was underground, in a maze of tunnels and rooms cut into the stabilized earth, like an overgrown rabbit warren or a giant ants' nest.

Within the largest and most central of the underground rooms, the broodmaster dismissed the brood. The young were ready to molt, restless and inattentive. They would absorb nothing of their lessons until the molt was done, so the broodmaster let them follow their instincts to seek the warm, quiet, humid place provided for that difficult time.

Scrabbling and bumping into one another, minds already blunted, the youngsters left. When they were gone, the whole jostling, fidgety mob of them, the broodmaster paced along the uppermost of the half-dozen benches cut into the circular wall that gave the place the look of a small amphitheater, a domed, stepped bowl so familiar to it after the passage of a dozen broods. Could it be so many, could the time be so long? The soft greenish light, brought in from the surface by optical cable and spread evenly by controlled scattering, was starting to fade, indicating the beginning of the slow sunset above. The planet turned slowly on its axis.

Normally at the end of a long day, class and teacher would have gone to feed and sleep. But the broodmaster itself was unsettled.

It had no reason for its unease. The current brood had given it nothing to worry about. Right from hatching they had been a

robust lot. Of twelve twelves, ten twelves of them had survived
the vicissitudes of life so far. Most would molt successfully.

It paced as it awaited the messenger sent by a member of an
earlier brood.

The messenger arrived promptly, young, lively, its youthful
carapace gleaming in the fading light like polished anthracite. It
entered the amphitheater with a properly respectful body attitude, overlain with elements of tension. Its smell was one of
anxiety. It raised its forelimbs in the correct greeting of lower
rank to higher and then dropped them quickly, waiting for permission to proceed.

In the nonauditory language of the Kaz, that told the broodmaster this individual had information it considered important
and urgent. With an attitude of attention, a receptive smell, and
a raised, half-open foreclaw, the broodmaster told the youngster
to go ahead.

The messenger nodded its acceptance. It had news, it said,
from the intelligence gatherer on Riga, of an Orian.

The broodmaster expressed its surprise too forcefully. It disturbed the messenger almost to the point where it would forget
the rest of its story.

The young one recovered itself and went on. The Orian had
been in the company of three Earthlings known to be part of a
band of pirates working in the region of Riga. The Earthlings
had been under surveillance for some time in hopes that they
would lead observers to their nest. The direction of the nest from
Riga was now known. If the broodmaster could see its way to
assigning a few vessels to the region to conduct a search, pref-
erably scoutships, which were swift and difficult to detect, it
seemed likely both the pirates' nest and the Orian could be in
Kazi hands forthwith, Broodmother willing.

An Orian? the broodmaster asked. It had almost forgotten the
sign, the time was so long since it had seen or said anything of
Oriani. *You are certain of this?*

*The intelligence gatherer believes the information to be reli-
able,* the messenger answered.

The broodmaster settled back on its legs to consider the matter. The intelligence gatherer sent strange news indeed. The
matter was worthy of contemplation.

Of all the soft, warm creatures the empire had encountered,
Oriani were among the most dangerous. During the progress of
the empire down the Orion arm, they were the ones who had

come nearest of any race to organizing effective resistance. They were clever people, careful planners. At their strongest, they had been able to achieve a number of small successes, balking Kazi plans in the Ellgarth Cluster, organizing the Interplanetary Community, fomenting dissent on a few worlds near the periphery of the empire, diverting energy and resources.

The broodmaster passed some of these thoughts on to the messenger as a way of ordering its own mind.

I do not know much of these people, the messenger said.

A strange people, with strange ways, with an evil that clung to them. They were called the "eaters of eggs" and "cub killers," creatures that deliberately and routinely fouled their own broods, the broodmaster answered. The revulsion it felt was deeply seated and unquestioned. It was as repulsed by the thought of an Orian wandering about loose as the average human would be by the thought of a maggot sandwich.

But they fought well, defended themselves well, it continued. *Soldiers feared them, right to the end. The end, of course, was inevitable. Orion is a Kazi world now, though its dry deserts are of minimal value.*

I was taught, the messenger signed, *that the Oriani were dead.*

Yes. The broodmaster nodded. *So were we all. Teaching histories rarely mention it, but some old records describe starships fleeing Orion crammed with refugees desperately seeking to escape their fate. Most agree that the Empire Fleet destroyed all the refugee ships before they cleared the Orion system. A few express doubt. The presence of an Orian on Riga is not wholly impossible.*

Where one is . . . the messenger began, but did not complete the thought.

Others must be, the broodmaster finished for it. *Be assured, where the others are when they are Oriani, plots against the empire will be hatching. Eat. Rest. I must think on this awhile.*

The messenger left at once. The broodmaster was still deliberating when darkness overtook it, and like all members of its race, in the dark it slept. When the light dropped below a certain threshold level, it stopped moving, stopped thinking, stopped all but the most basic biological stirrings. Throughout the underground complex, Kazi activity paused while night ran its course.

When the light returned, the broodmaster picked up its

thoughts again, exactly as it had left them, with scarcely a sense of a passage of time.

But something had happened during the night, for the broodmaster awoke knowing what must be done. First it found the messenger and directed it to return at once to Riga with instructions to the intelligence gatherer that it must track the Orian very closely. Broodmother willing, the one would be the key to the many. It would, it promised, do what it could to assemble the search team the intelligence gatherer requested with all possible haste.

The broodmaster's place in the Kazi hierarchy was such that it could do this, and it would not be obstructed so long as it did not interfere with the activities of others higher up in the organization. A broodmaster had considerable latitude in an otherwise rigid society.

It saw plainly a danger to the empire here. A Kazi's first duty was always to the empire. Some time ago the broodmaster had trained a brood of soldier commanders. It would call them now, to fill its need. It would go to Riga itself, to direct the operation.

But first it would go to its brood and pass on its information as best it could, given the condition of its charges, and it would try to impress upon their molt-dulled brains the importance of the Orian, of Oriani. For it felt older and frailer than usual this morning, and much in need of the rest that was to be denied it. Possibly the stresses of the journey to Riga would be the death of it.

It would undertake the journey nonetheless. It believed the matter to be that important.

Broodmother willing, it would be given the time to alert the area commander.

Pigpen

Ayyah was not unduly impressed with the pirates' stronghold.
The humans called the asteroid Pigpen, and the name seemed
appropriate insofar as Ayyah understood the nature of pigs. Located on a minor satellite of a small, young star, as a refuge it
had some advantages. With one side fixed facing the primary,
the asteroid was half hidden in a dust cloud that made an approach to it dangerous unless the way was known. So Tomas
Lopes insisted.

It was unknown to the Kaz, uncharted, but was not far from
at least two major lanes of commerce.

"The Kaz have not found this place?" Ayyah asked.

"Nope," Tomas Lopes answered. He was much less talk-
ative since they had left Riga, busy at the controls of his vessel,
shutting it down after the landing. His companions had steadfastly declined to answer questions.

"You know the reason for this?"

"Maybe they just aren't looking."

"This is not a state of affairs one would expect to continue."

"Folks sleep light on Pigpen," Tomas Lopes said.

Three interconnected domes, huddled together in a shallow
crater, were visible from the landing area on the side of the
worldlet remote from the sun. Tomas Lopes assured her twenty
or so humans had exclusive use of the dome at one end. A dozen
horned Brodenli claimed dominion over the dome at the other
end, and no one felt inclined to argue. The larger dome in the
middle held a mixed bag of folk of various shapes and sizes who
got along together surprisingly well.

"This surprises you?"

The humans were occupied with the machinery that connected
a flexible tunnel between ship and dome, and Tomas Lopes did

58

not answer. Then, during the brief walk, which seemed long, through this flimsy construction when she could feel the void just beyond the wobbling, frail wall sucking heat and life away, it was Ayyah who had nothing to say.

At the entrance to the dome, the man called Ching turned to her and grinned. "Scary, eh?" He seemed pleased that she should be frightened.

Tomas Lopes conducted her around the dome's interior with proprietary pride. The people she met were all human, of about middle age with a scattering of younger ones, and uniformly astonished by her existence.

The facilities were primitive, consisting of one largish common room in which the gray curve of the dome showed plainly, furnished with an unpleasing clutter of inflatables, salvage and rudimentary handicraft, several bedrooms similarly furnished, and the kitchen. The floor was bare permacrete, badly finished. The lighting was erratic, bright in places, shadowy elsewhere. The whole place had a temporary air about it, as if the entire population might pick up and move at any moment. Modern conveniences appeared to be represented only by an island of interdome communications and a sensor monitor installed in the center of the common room.

A murmur of machinery pervaded the dome; fans sighed.

There were no windows. Tomas Lopes shrugged. "Nothing to see."

It was not very clean. It lacked both comfort and good humor. Ayyah felt confined, caged. She wondered if some other group of tidier brigands might not better serve her needs.

A pointless question. Tomas Lopes would be unlikely to honor a request for transportation elsewhere.

She was not given much time to explore alternatives in any case. Shortly after her brief tour of the place, the lights above the dome's airlock indicated that the lock was cycling and a sudden tension took hold.

"Here he comes," Tomas Lopes announced.

The one called Ching and a couple of others took up positions beside Tomas. Another male and a female hustled a somewhat bewildered Ayyah into the kitchen and closed the door behind her. Curiosity suppressed a tendency to resist this less than gracious treatment. She wanted to see what these strange creatures were up to.

"We're ready, Tomas," they called.

Beyond the door, Ayyah heard the female identified as Ursala Sinclair ask, "You sure you want to do this?"

In the kitchen behind Ayyah, a pleasant voice said, "Hi."

Outside, Ursala Sinclair continued. "MacDonald doesn't like us dealing in sentient life. He's likely to be a bit pissed."

"I'm counting on it," Tomas Lopes answered. A false note in his voice suggested he was trying to sound more confident than he was.

"What's going on?" the voice asked. Ayyah turned to meet a friendly young man in gray coveralls busying himself at a counter.

"I am not informed," Ayyah said. "Perhaps you would tell me."

"I'm just the technician. I look after life support. They don't tell me anything."

"Life support?"

"Environmental apparatus, you know what I mean? Acme life support and recycling, model IV, two-year money-back guarantee not valid in Kazi-held space. Pretty good system, actually. All those little necessities of life—water, air, heat, food—they don't exist here naturally. We got to make them all or ship them in."

"Yes, of course," Ayyah said. "The energy comes from where?"

"Solar panels on Nearside, the side facing the sun. Speaking of food, would you like a sandwich?"

Ayyah was hungry but wary. "Explain please what this is."

The technician blinked and rubbed a hand over his chin. "Uh, bread, peanut butter, a little jam, maybe, like that."

"Butter is an animal product?"

"Uh, yeah, but peanut butter isn't. It's ground-up peanuts. Legumes? Plants? We grow 'em as part of the recycling process. Nitrogen recovery, eh?"

He brought a round plastic container for her to see. It looked not promising, but smelled good, if unfamiliar. "I think I would like this sand-which," she said.

"Would you two knock it off?" Ayyah's male escort snarled. "I'm trying to hear what's going on out there."

"Ah, lighten up, Sven," the technician said, handing Ayyah the sandwich.

Peanut butter was odd stuff that stuck among her teeth and

glued her tongue to the roof of her mouth, but it had a pleasant, smooth fragrance, and she was very hungry.

The lock finally completed its cycle and the inner door opened. It was thick metal, set tightly into a heavy metal frame, a high-silled, narrow oval, a minimal door such as might be found in a submarine, designed to be the smallest useful opening in the dome's skin. MacDonald would be happy to get a little distance between himself and Delladar Oll. The lock was a tight fit for three of them and a kitten, and the Lleveci's aloof stiffness made him uneasy.

Oscar Achebe was the first through. "Uh-oh," he said. It was not an auspicious sound.

MacDonald followed him into the dome and looked around. Lopes and his henchmen were waiting expectantly in a tight little group by the lock door. Something was up. MacDonald felt certain he wasn't going to be pleased.

Instinct warned him not to make an issue out of it. "Hey, a reception committee. That's nice. Tomas, this is Delladar Oll. She'll be staying with us for a while." He bent and set Cat down on the floor.

Ursala Sinclair, immediately distracted, cooed appropriately. "What's his name?"

"Cat," MacDonald answered.

Lopes was taken aback. Ching was making a try for Oriental inscrutability, but his worry was plain. Obviously, they thought Delladar Oll was a bodyguard. A Lleveci warrior was an obstacle to be reckoned with. Better he shouldn't enlighten them. MacDonald had the feeling he was making points even though he didn't know what the game was.

Ursala flashed a supercilious, I-tried-to-warn-you smile at Tomas and reached down to pick up the kitten. Cat evaded her with a haughty sideways step and went on about the important business of exploring. Whatever was happening, MacDonald felt Ursala was out of it. As calmly as he could, he introduced Delladar Oll around, wondering all the while how to take advantage of his little surprise. A clue or two to what it was all about would be a big help.

Sven Svensen came out of the kitchen and headed for Lopes. "What's taking so long?" he asked before he had properly assessed the situation. Then his eyes widened at the sight of the Lleveci.

"Were you in a hurry about something, Sven?" MacDonald asked, trying to keep his appearance amiable, hoping for a hint.

Sven shook his head, attention fixed on the warrior. He sidled up to Lopes and gave him his what's-happening? look. Lopes raised his hands, palms up, trying to show less concern than he obviously felt.

The moment of impasse was shattered when the kitchen door swung open and someone came out, with a flustered and apologetic Miranda Corbett in pursuit.

MacDonald turned as the door opened. He met the Orian's saffron eyes head on.

Oscar let his breath out with a soft whistle. Even the taciturn Lleveci produced a grunt of surprise.

"Oh, my God," MacDonald said.

He backed up a pace and rubbed his hand over his face.

"You're eating peanut butter," he complained, annoyed at such a commonplace under such circumstances.

"Sand-which," the Orian agreed.

A pause of singing tension and held breaths ensued while MacDonald stared at the figure before him. The Orian returned the favor with frank curiosity. Cat left off exploring and trotted over, tail erect, full of goodwill. The Orian seemed unsettled by the kitten. She stepped back before bending to examine it more closely. You could almost imagine they were mother and very small child.

Without turning, MacDonald called Lopes to him with a crook of his finger. "Okay," he said with menacing softness. "Explain."

There was some murmuring among the ranks. It dissipated quickly, for the coming confrontation was the most interesting thing that had happened on Pigpen for a handful of years, and no one wanted to miss a word. MacDonald was aware of having for once the company's undivided attention, and it made the hair on his neck prickle. Undoubtedly, most of them were aware of Lopes's plan, whatever it was. He and Oscar were the ones who had to play blind.

Lopes didn't answer immediately. Sven Svensen jiggled uneasily.

"Sven?" MacDonald asked.

Svensen shook his head. "This is Lopes's show."

Delladar Oll sized up the situation and moved to a position just back of MacDonald's left elbow.

"I think you'd better tell me what's going on here, Tomas," MacDonald said. He didn't raise his voice. Instinct and Fleet training agreed: He should give every indication of being in control. People most often took one at face value.

"Maybe you want to talk this over in private?" Lopes suggested.

"Nope," MacDonald answered, as Lopes knew he would. "I want to talk it over right here." One point for Lopes. MacDonald had to risk a public discussion or give the appearance of being unsure about the outcome.

Lopes smiled his acquiescence to absolve himself of all responsibility for the consequences, took a deep breath, and plunged in.

"That's an Orian," Lopes said. The party in question watched Lopes intently and listened with pricked ears, but seemed not unduly alarmed by the proceedings. Cat sat happily between her feet and was washing himself.

"That's the part I already figured out," MacDonald answered shortly.

"The bugs'll pay your weight in credits for one of those alive."

"I see."

"It's been a damned long time since we've got any real money around here."

"So you decided you'd do something about it."

"Well, yeah, I did."

"Would you mind telling me where you got this . . . person?"

"Riga. Rigaport, actually."

"Riga."

"Yeah."

MacDonald turned to the others. "You people approve of this?"

A few nodded. Most shrugged noncommittally.

MacDonald turned back to Lopes. "Tomas, for a moderately smart man, you are abysmally stupid at times."

Lopes bristled but managed to control his temper. "I suppose you want me to let her go, eh?"

Finally MacDonald understood what Tomas was doing. Every living being there dreamed of departing Pigpen with a king's ransom in credits to live in dissolute luxury on some benign world amid spring rains, gardens, and dancing girls. Everyone on Pigpen dreamed of being somewhere else, of moving to some more amicable ambiance the moment his fortune was made. The making of fortunes was all that held the group together, their only point of common interest. The Orian was a way to bring the dream a little nearer. If MacDonald demanded they release their prisoner, giving up a fortune practically in their hands, bad feelings would be generated. Pigpen's inhabitants were already grumbling about the poor hunting lately. Lopes, opposing Mac-Donald on the release of the Orian, would get a lot of support from people who were not averse to a change in leadership.

Being leader was a precarious position, held largely by mutual agreement, with little honor and only those privileges the office-holder was able to appropriate by force of will, subject to change without notice and without recourse to parliamentary formality.

MacDonald's education and Fleet training gave him a slight edge in assuming the office. Tomas saw himself being every bit as good a leader as MacDonald was, perhaps better. MacDonald was very much aware that he occasionally had qualms of conscience, which sometimes forced him to allow a prize to slip through their fingers lest innocent bystanders get hurt, and he knew it damaged his popularity.

Lopes's universe was simpler, divided into Them, who had all the good things in life, and Us, whose job it was to take those things away from Them. No innocent bystanders populated Tomas's world. Ching and Svensen, and maybe a couple more, wholeheartedly agreed with him.

MacDonald knew that Lopes had long believed that all he needed to effect a change of leadership was an incident, an issue to gather the uncommitted rank and file behind him. He had one now, a test case.

"You want me to let her go?" Tomas asked again.

Rule number one in any contest: Keep the opposition off balance. MacDonald surprised Lopes, and a few others, by shaking his head. "I don't think it will do much good at this stage."

Throughout the exchange the Orian stood quietly just outside the kitchen door.

MacDonald turned to her, feeling she ought to have some say in this; also hoping to demonstrate to one or two of the brighter human minds present that she was a person in her own right rather than an object of commerce.

She was slight, even for one of her race, a little over chin

high with her forward posture balancing the long swinging tail.
She had silvery gray fur and tufted ears.

He was uncertain about how to proceed. In thirty years, in
the Fleet and out of it, of bashing around most of the known
worlds of the Orion arm, he had dealt with a variety of races
and had learned to feel his way around any number of alien
conventions, but he had never dealt with an Orian before, or
even known of anyone who had. Knowing that the Kaz had
applied their policy of extermination to the Orian homeworld,
he had assumed the race was extinct.

It was common knowledge that the Kaz had a particular dis-
like for Oriani. If they weren't extinct, then they were dangerous
to have around.

Suppose a saber-toothed tiger dropped in for dinner.

"Do you speak English?"

"Yes," she said.

"Do you understand what's going on here?"

"Yes."

"Do you have a name?" he asked.

"Yes."

It took a minute before MacDonald realized that was all she
was going to say.

"Well, what is it?" He caught himself sounding irritable.

"My name is Ayyah."

"Okay, Ayyah, you want to tell me what you're doing here?"

The Orian indicated Lopes and a couple of his henchmen with
a gesture.

MacDonald questioned Oscar with a look.

Oscar shook his head. "I don't think so. From what I've heard
of Oriani, there's no way these brickheads could have taken her
prisoner if she didn't want to be taken. They're not that quick
or smart."

"How smart do you have to be behind a blaster?" MacDonald asked.

Oscar shrugged. "I don't know. I never tried it."

"One more time, Ayyah," MacDonald said. "What are you
doing here?"

A tiny flick moved the end of the tail. Had some weird Orian
sense of humor been touched? Or was she annoyed? Bored?

"I wished to find you, MacDonald. The method that presented itself seemed expedient." Her speech had a guttural ac-
cent, and the words were formed carefully, as if she were not

too sure of them, though she seemed to be getting more sure even as she spoke.

"Expedient? Suicidal is what it is. Do you have any idea what you've done?"

"I judged the risk to be acceptable."

"Did you now? To whom? What do you want from me that's worth all this risk?"

"I seek your help to free my homeworld of the Kaz."

Derisive murmurs emerged around the room. MacDonald's single syllable of laughter lacked amusement. "Sure. Why not? All you have to do is ask."

"What're we going to do with her, Oscar?" MacDonald asked. They were in a pair of inflatable chairs in MacDonald's quarters with a bottle of Rigan firewater on the table between them. The narrow bed against the curved wall was a rumpled mess in which MacDonald had previously sought sleep but failed to find it. The kitten had taken over the blankets, easily finding what MacDonald could not, curled tightly around a tummy bulging with handouts from the kitchen.

MacDonald regarded the glass in his hand without much enthusiasm. He had seriously considered getting stinking drunk, but when it came down to actually doing it, he was too worried and nervous to feel he could afford the luxury. He needed his wits about him.

"Did Ayyah tell you why she thinks you're the man who can bring down the empire?" Oscar asked. He took a sip from his glass and made a face.

"It's not that bad," MacDonald said.

"It's not that good."

"She said some stuff about a good, experienced pilot and a fast ship. I don't know how much of it I believe. She's got some scheme cooked up about going to someplace called Rayor. I don't exactly know what that's supposed to do. I'm not sure I want to know. I'm not sure I even like her. Besides, it doesn't have much bearing on the bind I'm in. So help me, I'm going to skin Tomas and eat him."

"I guess you better do that. If Tomas gets away with this, whatever you decide to do about the Orian, it's going to divide the group."

"I have a tremendous urge to pack up and blast away and let them have Tomas. What do you think about Aldebaran?"

"Boring. Besides, you know perfectly well Tomas can't handle the job. Without a strong leader, these people are just so much Kaz bait."

"Do I care?"

"You care. That's why you have a problem."

MacDonald took a big mouthful of his drink and wished he hadn't. The stuff tasted like turpentine and burned going down. He shuddered. Oscar smiled indulgently.

"I've heard it said," Oscar mused aloud, "that Oriani don't know how to lie."

"I'd have a hard time believing any civilization without at least an occasional white lie. Just imagine your significant other swirling into a room in a brand-new dress and asking you how you like it. Are you going to say 'Sorry, dear, it's bloody awful and it makes you look like an old potato'?"

"You've got a point. But then, maybe furry folk aren't vain about their dresses."

"If I put her down on a neutral world somewhere, I'm going to have a mutiny on my hands. The people think they're looking at half a million or so credits all wrapped up in a furry package. Tomas has neglected to mention that collecting it from the Kaz is going to be just about as tricky as juggling nitroglycerin."

"You might point that out to them."

"Mm." MacDonald looked down at the floor. Dust mice had gathered in one corner, a bad housekeeping convention.

"Have you thought about going through with the deal?" Oscar asked.

"You mean actually sell her to the Kaz?"

Oscar nodded.

MacDonald slumped a little in his chair. "I'm not that good a juggler. Besides, I don't think I hate her that much. It would be kinder to drop her out the airlock."

"But that wouldn't solve your problem."

"You honestly think that's what I should do?"

"No. Practically, it's probably your best answer. Morally, it stinks."

MacDonald considered the amber fluid in his glass and discovered that it had not improved any in the time he had been holding it. He set it down on the table. "What chance, do you think, Tomas got the Orian away without coming to Kazi attention?"

"Zero," Oscar answered promptly. "Two-thirds of the people in Rigaport are on the Kazi payroll. The only reason we've been able to come and go without too much trouble is the Kaz don't pay enough for dime-a-dozen humans to make it worth anyone's while to turn us in. There's more profit in overcharging for supplies.''

The door slid open and Delladar Oll came in.

"Don't you ever knock?" MacDonald asked crossly.

The Lleveci said nothing.

"Well, you're in, so come and sit down. Do your people have a taste for alcohol?''

"No.''

"No, thank you," he corrected. I'm getting peevish in my old age, he thought. "I'm sorry," he added. "I didn't have to do that. Tell me something, though. Why were you ready to back me up against Tomas? You had no stake in that game.''

"Thin, nervous, lying eyes?''

That pretty well sums up Tomas, MacDonald thought. "That's the one.''

"Plain reason. Need weapons. You have. He not.''

"Makes sense.''

"Have short time only.''

MacDonald sighed. "I know. I'm sorry. I realize I've been neglecting you, but I didn't know about the Orian when I suggested we come here.''

Delladar Oll thought it over for a beat. "You too busy. Find other source.''

That sounded like pressure tactics. Sources of heavy arms and ammunition were not found on every street corner.

However, it was probably not in his best interests to irritate the client any more than necessary. He could go along with it. Let her think she had him worried. It wouldn't hurt, and she'd feel better.

"Hey, hold on a minute. Don't be like that. Give me a chance to work it out.''

Whatever the Lleveci might have said in reply was lost in an electronic screech from the wall-mounted intercom speaker behind MacDonald. As he twisted around, the screen above it lit with the features of the Caparan who lived in the dome next door. He apparently had something exciting to say, but his voice had slid up the scale beyond audibility.

Oscar was already heading out the door. MacDonald and Delladar Oll followed.

The common room was a bustle of consternation. In the middle of the hubbub, the Orian stood calmly before the interdome communications terminal, apparently translating.

"What's going on?" MacDonald demanded.

"This person says an outlying watcher, a sentinel, has observed a Kazi vessel," Ayyah said. "This person believes the vessel has found something—I do not know the correct translation—elements of a system for finding the right path."

"Navigational markers?"

"Perhaps. It is difficult. Your speakers are not accurate at these frequencies. I believe this person thinks the vessel is coming here."

"Here?"

"That is my interpretation of this person's words."

"Holy shit."

A furrow of puzzlement developed between Ayyah's brows. "Shit?" she asked Delladar Oll.

"Can they make it, Oscar?" MacDonald asked.

"Excrement," the Lleveci replied. "Human curse."

"If they've found the markers, I don't see why not," Oscar said.

"Holy? Of godlike qualities?" Ayyah persisted.

"Let's not wait to find out," MacDonald said.

Delladar Oll shook her head to show she was not going to answer any more of the Orian's silly questions.

People were just standing around babbling at one another, looking stunned, doing nothing. MacDonald bit his lip. He had to get them moving. He had to get moving himself. He shouted directions over the hubbub.

"Evacuation plans, everybody. Get spaceborne and scatter. Ursala, you take the technician. I'll take the aliens. Don't stop to pick up your purse. Go, people, go."

Thissah

A fiercely contested game of Rocks and Sticks was in progress on one of the Offworlder's center tables. The pair of cursing Higant playing looked as ready to eat one another as to complete the game, and the patrons were hotly intent on the match, anticipating blood. Thissah the Roothian slipped away unseen. The shouts of the spectators egging the contestants on followed him into the Rigan night.

Holding his robe tight to his body, Thissah spared a glance to the sky. Above him, stars, and to the south the ArGald Nebula rode above the Lord High Regent's castle, apparently undisturbed. Otherwise, the night was empty. Nothing had changed.

And everything had changed. The pirates had vanished from Riga, and in the Outworlder proprietors and patrons mourned the loss of custom and the loss of friends. Thissah considered himself lucky that he had prepared for his departure before this. He would not find much work here for a while.

In fact, his luck was running so high he was certain some disaster must be poised to overtake him to balance the score. Chance favored the vigilant spirit. Still, it was chance. Scraps of overheard conversation had alerted him to the new opportunity even as he gathered his few possessions and transferred the last of his credit to Roo: a few words across a table, an innocent question asked of a bank clerk, a discussion over beer of the Kazi raid on Pigpen with the participants quietly applauding the pirates who had escaped the empire's strike.

He heard two particularly interesting things: a merchant asking about an unusual furry being that had been seen on a way-station in an out-of-the-way region of space humans called the Dragon's Tail—for no reason Thissah could think of even after he had acquired a concept of dragons; and a ship's captain musing privately to his mate over the sighting of the well-known pirate vessel *Harrier* heading hellbent for election—whatever that might mean—in that general direction.

There were two things he already knew: A certain now-deceased human female had maintained a retreat somewhere in the Dragon's Tail, and humans often associated that female with MacDonald, associate of Tomas Lopes, pirate of the ArGald and master of the vessel called *Harrier*.

Added together, these bits of information made marketable news.

Almost. An element of guessing entered into it. The ship's captain was reporting secondhand data, and furthermore, he was known occasionally to stretch the facts to make a good story. The merchant was a wide-eyed Boosh, member of a race new to space, who, in view of its naked, wrinkly skin, would be inclined to find anything with fur unusual.

The trick would be to pass the guess on to the Kazi as the truth.

Early in their association, the Kazi had warned Thissah that lies would be severely dealt with.

Thissah had never been comfortable dealing with his Kazi contact. It always seemed contemptuous of him, and too smart to be reassuring. It out-thought him, anticipated him, understood the significance of his news before Thissah himself understood it, and made the Roothian feel thoroughly outclassed and uneasy.

Thissah skittered across the road to hug the shadows on the other side. The glow in the sky that marked the spaceport and safety seemed very distant. The ragged, wandering passage ahead, too unpremeditated to be properly called a street, presented a good many dangerous corners to be passed.

The Kazi's perspicacity bothered him more than his conscience. But he was not trying to sell it a lie. Not really. Call it an educated extrapolation of the facts. Anyway, in the morning he would be gone, and even an annoyed Kazi would hardly be annoyed enough to follow him to Roo.

Little of the greenish light leaked from the room near the edge of the city. Entering, Thissah stayed close to the door as if anticipating the need for a fast getaway. The Kaz were darker shadows in the gloom, three of them, the intelligence gatherer distinguishable only by the sounding device around its neck. "All Kaz look the same," popular wisdom had it. It was true.

The intelligence gatherer waved its arms at the other two, and that seemed to calm them. Then it asked Thissah, "Why are you here?"

Having three Kaz rustling in the dim light and making the atmosphere in the room heavy with their smell did nothing to make Thissah feel more secure. With a silent prayer to the blessed saint, he plunged in.

"Have newss of the Orian," Thissah said.

The Kazi in the corner perked up right away. Obviously it understood him, though without a sounder it could not reply. Thissah felt a small measure of his composure return. One thing he had learned early in his life was that any creature, regardless of how clever, most easily believed the tale it wanted most to hear.

The Kazi's response was not reassuring. "The last news of the Orian came to nothing."

Dawn found the three Kaz once again debating in the ground-floor room of the massive building near the outskirts of the port city. The intelligence gatherer had been using the room as meeting place and living quarters for some time, and so it was not so poorly suited to Kaz as it might otherwise have been.

Louvered shutters reduced Riga's bright sunlight to tolerable levels, and the packed earth on the floor was moist and cool. A sleeping bench occupied the far wall. Between sleeps, it served as combination desk and sideboard. It was cluttered with the intelligence gatherer's equipment and a stack of computer records.

The local Fleet detachment leader had joined the intelligence gatherer and the broodmaster to assess the attack on the asteroid known as Pigpen. The detachment leader apologized that the raid had not served the empire as well as had been hoped. The raiders had been hampered by the broodmaster's wish to take prisoners. The pirates had been better equipped than expected and more organized and disciplined than was usual in these nests of outlaws. Their pickets had been alert, their sensors effective.

The attack on the pirate stronghold had been successful, the detachment leader pointed out, in that it destroyed a base of operations for the pirates. However, many pirates and pirate vessels escaped destruction.

Fleet specialists had studied the trajectories of escaping vessels, though these were much confused and rendered doubtful by the dust. They analyzed debris, made an on-site inspection of the ruins, correlated their observations with previously obtained data, and concluded that of the fifty or so inhabitants of the asteroid, approximately half had escaped in six vessels, destination unknown.

The broodmaster had only one question it considered important. *What have your prisoners told you? What of the Orian?*

The detachment leader had difficulty suppressing expression of its skepticism. *None of the prisoners admits having seen an Orian. No Orian body was found,* it said, *and no sign that an Orian ever lived on the asteroid has been uncovered. A small amount of hair found in a sleeping place has been tentatively identified as coming from a small domestic animal of Terran origin. It is certainly not Oriani.* Perhaps, the leader suggested, the broodmaster's information was in error.

The informant has been reliable on many previous occasions, the intelligence gatherer said. *If what the Roothian said was true, the Orian would have only just arrived.*

If an Orian was there, the local leader said, emphasizing the conditional somewhat, *it is gone now. If it was there and escaped, the chances of it being found undoubtedly rest entirely on the accuracy of the Roothian's new information.*

The broodmaster reluctantly agreed that the leader's assessment was probably right. *Do you know the place the Roothian described?* it asked.

It is out of empire space, the Fleet detachment leader answered. *Our people are tired. I am tired.*

The broodmaster signed its understanding. Fatigue and age were weighing it down until it felt unable to support its own weight. Still, it had to convince the Fleet detachment leader of the need to pursue the single, slender lead remaining.

However intelligent or civilized, it said, *a frightened creature most often seeks refuge among its own kind. Perhaps the Orian has already told us what we must know.*

You believe there are others? Alarm brought a sharp scent and a briskness back to the leader's gesture.

Where one is . . . The broodmaster did not complete the adage.

The local Fleet detachment leader leaned back on its legs wearily. *The emperor will not be pleased to hear the eaters of eggs are again scheming against the empire.* Its blurred signs showed it also was nearly spent. It continued, *Nor am I. We are too weak in this sector to fight a battle such as we fought for Orion.*

Rigans will serve for now, the intelligence gatherer pointed out. *We have found many who fight for pay. The Roothian can lead them to the place. Let us learn what we face before committing our forces.*

The detachment leader signed its approval of some such plan.

I will have the Roothian brought, the intelligence gatherer said.

The Dragon's Tail

The brightest star in the loose, straggling cluster called the Dragon's Tail is visible from Earth's northern sky as a part of the constellation Draco. Graduates of Navigation 513 knew it well. The thin metallic voice of the Kazi instructor's sounder would remain in MacDonald's memory for as long as he lived.

"Alpha Draconis is your beacon for the entire sector, students. It is suggested you commit the spectrum to memory."

Easy for a Kazi to say. Virtually impossible for a human to do.

The Dragon's Tail was otherwise an unremarkable group of stars, holding nothing of particular value, off the main trade routes, a galactic suburb in which a piratical lady could build a quiet hideaway in a remote part of a planet orbiting an unspectacular sun.

"Tasetoru" was as close as MacDonald's tongue could come to the planet's name. In geology and climate, it was not so remarkably different from Earth. The Tasey, the incurious native people, did not ask why the humans had come there, nor why the lady planted lilacs in her front yard.

Marion was very certain about how the yard should be laid out. She had a ring of motion sensors laid around the house, built a quaint and pressure-sensitive brick walk between the dirt trail that meandered by her property and the front door, and let the thick-leaved local vegetation grow up except where the lilacs were.

Syringa vulgaris is hardy and adaptable, and proved to be unpalatable to the local insects. The lilacs flourished and grew quickly into trees. Thoroughly confused by the unfamiliar rhythms of their new home, it wasn't unusual to find some flowers fading away to seed when others were budding.

75

The lovely scent of lilacs was intimately mixed in Mac-Donald's mind with memories of Marion.

The door of the house still responded to his voice, though he had not been there in almost six months, not since Marion had accused him of trying to run her life and had told him she would prefer he found someone else to bully. The house had its own power supply and was fully automated, so even the ivy in the windowsill was fresh and green. It looked for all the worlds like Marion had just stepped out for a moment.

The pain he had been able to push into the background clamped down around MacDonald's heart. He set Cat down in the funny little house that was half local architecture and half Welsh cottage, left Ayyah and Delladar Oll to find their way around under Oscar's guidance, and went out into the yard to be alone for a while.

He found the place beneath a tall, leather-leaved native tree where, when the lilacs were newly planted saplings, he had put his spade down, taken Marion's away from her, kissed the smear of dirt on her nose, and said for the first and last time in his life, "I love you." She had burst into smiles and tears all at once. "Ah, my reticent great oaf," she had said, laughing and crying. "I thought you'd never get around to saying it."

A year later, the trees had grown tall and had put out their first flowers. One evening when Tasetoru's pale sun, setting, glinted like a base alloy of gold among the leaves, Marion said, "If the Kaz get me, old dear, you've got to promise you'll look after the lilacs."

He had sworn to do it, amid all those protestations of mutual immortality people inevitably make at a time like that.

He had forgotten them, not given them a thought until this moment. He felt as if he ought to apologize.

He was still there, sitting on the sun-dappled lawn beneath the neglected trees, when Oscar came to find him.

"Old loves and new graves. We've lost a lot of good people, Oscar."

"It's the way it is in this business. We all got into it with our eyes open." Oscar cradled a low-hanging blossom in his hand and bent to inhale the heady fragrance. "Which doesn't make it easy."

"I never meant to hurt her. I worried about her."

"I know."

"It's so strange to be here without her. I thought I'd be able to handle it. Now I'm not so sure. I keep thinking I'll go in and she'll be there. She would have loved Cat. She was such a pushover for anything small and helpless. She was forever rescuing things.''

"It's over, Mac. Time to start thinking about what we're going to do next. Got any plans?''

"Plans?'' Sitting by the lilac trees, MacDonald felt ready for a rest, a pause, a quiet interlude. He thought about chewing on a grass stem in traditional fashion until he remembered that this was not Earth, the ground cover was not grass, and chewing on it could conceivably have all sorts of unpleasant consequences. "No plans,'' he said. "Except maybe rest up a bit. Try to regroup. The pack, what's left of it, is pretty well scattered. I don't know.''

"I don't think our guests are going to like that. Our warrior friend is already getting impatient to go after the weapons, and Ayyah is trying to persuade me that the only moral and practical course open to us is to go hunting for that place she calls Rayor, which doesn't happen to be on the charts.''

"To tell you the truth, I've got a feeling Ayyah is a little more than two jets short of a blast. You've got to think that way about anyone who thinks they're going to dig up some magic to make the empire go away.''

"She sounds acutely rational most of the time.''

"Madmen often do, I'm told. I admit I don't have much experience of mad Oriani. Anyway, I don't think we'll go roaring off into the dark looking for Atlantis, or Krypton, or Amber, or Rayor, or any other mythical place.'' MacDonald leaned back against the trunk with his hands folded behind his head. Above him, white clouds drifted along in a blue sky. "It's nice out here, Oscar. I don't want to go into Marion's house. I don't want to listen to those two nagging. I don't want to do anything dangerous for at least a year.''

"Okay,'' Oscar said. "But while you're communing with Nature, give some thought to how you're going to finance the bucolic idyll.''

"Eh, what?''

"We're broke, boss. Our reserves went up with Pigpen. Your life savings are in the *Harrier*, and I never had any. So we've got a problem.''

"Blast,'' MacDonald said, and closed his eyes as if that might make the problem go away. "The universe conspires against us."

Oscar shook his head. "We're not that important. The biggest trouble with the universe is that it doesn't give a damn."

"Philosophy I don't need. Money we do. Couldn't you have told me this later?"

"How about lunch instead?"

"Sounds mundane."

"We have to eat."

"Yeah, I guess." MacDonald broke off a few flowers and took them into the house with him. He found a glass and some water and set them with a flourish on the worn blue kitchen table, a pleasant little homey touch.

"That's nice," Oscar said, a tad sarcastically, MacDonald thought.

Ayyah had a completely different view of lilacs.

They represented, she said, "complete ecological irresponsibility." Taken aback, MacDonald could only frown at her, feeling he should defend Marion against something or other.

Delladar Oll left off peering hungrily into cupboards long enough to give a derisive snort.

"Ecological irresponsibility," Oscar echoed. "That's a big mouthful to describe some pretty flowers."

"It does not describe the flowers, Oscar Achebe. That much I am sure is clear to you. It describes the fact of their being here. Anyone could see from casual inspection they are not native to this world. Ecological irresponsibility describes the thoughtlessness with which an alien species has been introduced into this biosphere without regard for the consequences."

"Only Orian," Delladar Oll growled, "make disaster of posies."

"They're not doing any harm, Ayyah," Oscar said.

"You know this, Oscar Achebe?"

Oscar shrugged and turned to the cooker and the important things of life.

"What do you want me to do, Ayyah, dig them up?" MacDonald asked.

"Not say, not say," Delladar Oll warned. "She say yes too quick."

Ayyah's face was utterly impassive. Only a tiny twitch of the tail suggested she had been touched. "It would be well for Lleveci to understand, if possible, that dangers exist other than those that may be shot at.''

Delladar Oll's hand was on her knife when MacDonald stepped between the two of them.

"Knock it off," he said.

"If meaning Orian's head," the warrior answered, "pleasure mine."

Ayyah, for her part, apparently decided further discussion was beneath her dignity and walked away.

She was not, Ayyah told herself, angry. She was astonished. Dealing with alien minds was more difficult than she had ever imagined it could be. Outside, away from the others, perhaps she would be able to think more clearly.

How could they not understand a reality so obvious? None of them was stupid. That lilac flowers pleased them did not make the potential for damage less.

A small thing, surely, considering the larger issues on her mind, but an illustration of a simple reality: They did not communicate well with one another. She found herself in danger of forgetting her father's injunction against assuming superiority to people she did not understand well.

The Lleveci she thought she understood well enough. Delladar Oll was a creature for whom violence was the answer to all obstacles.

The humans were confusing. With nothing to gain, MacDonald intervened in the quarrel between herself and Delladar Oll as if the conflict offended him. Yet during the commotion on Pigpen, she saw much of conflict in the face of great danger, the shouting of opposing orders by all and sundry, much dashing to and fro to collect material possessions with furious arguments over ownership in the face of imminent destruction and with a fine disregard for one another's welfare. The lack of discipline and the lack of rationality disturbed her, and even more disturbing was the implied evaluation of goods over people.

On the other hand, in the midst of crisis, MacDonald had rushed off to his quarters to find the little animal. It was confusing. No consistency could be found in these actions. Where did human values lie?

Where did her own values lie? She discovered she was not displeased with the turn of events, and this was, of itself, disturbing.

Overall, the Kazi raid had probably worked to her advantage. Her limited knowledge of human psychology suggested that MacDonald would be more tractable when removed from his home and his familiar companions. Given choices, she would have preferred a way less damaging to other lives, but the Kaz had not offered choices.

Strange that they should do her work for her.

The arrival on Tasetoru had been interesting. Though the place seemed to hold much meaning for him, MacDonald knew little about it, or the Tasey, except that lacking a proper spaceport, he had to land the shuttle in an open field. Now, having arrived at the building known as "Marion's House," he seemed disinclined to move. That inertia would have to be overcome. Therefore, she was obliged to seek out another strange ally, the Lleveci warrior.

Obtaining Delladar Oll's assistance would be difficult. A natural enmity existed between them. Ayyah had not inherited her father's diplomatic skills. She had none of his instinct for finding the one approach among many that would elicit cooperation from an otherwise unwilling accomplice.

She found a place in the yard where the sun beamed between the trees. A breath of moist, green wind rustled the leaves. Tiny feet padded among the grasses. Insects rustled and chewed. She sat quietly in the sunlight, absorbing its warmth while the busy life of Tasetoru bustled around her. After a time, she went back into the house, her level of tolerance recharged.

Oscar was hard at work at the stove. In the room off to one side of the kitchen, Delladar Oll had found an unoccupied area of floor and had spread various weapons upon it, some partially disassembled, which she was industriously attacking with rags and oil.

"Help with bad work?" she asked as Ayyah approached. "Ha. Not believing. Make dirty hands."

Ayyah thought it over. A certain repugnance attended these instruments, but it could be managed. Attaining even a particle of respect from the Lleveci would make the coming argument more compelling. She squatted down beside Delladar Oll, picked up a blaster, dismantled it, cleaned the contacts and the coils, aligned the optics, replaced the power pack, and reassembled the weapon with smooth efficiency. She was silently grateful to old lessons that she remembered how it was done.

Delladar Oll stopped what she was doing and watched.

"Ha," the warrior said. "Know some danger for shoot at."

"The danger now," Ayyah said, "is that the humans won't want to leave this place."

"Have deal. Honor deal or pretty angry me."

In spite of her curiosity, Ayyah carefully avoided asking what deal had been forged between Lleveci and humans. "The deal can be honored on Tasetoru?"

Delladar Oll hesitated a moment as if deciding whether she was giving away information that somehow might weaken her position. Ayyah congratulated herself for her moment of restraint. The Lleveci would not have answered a question about the nature of her bargain. Such an inquiry would have made her suspicious, possibly hostile.

Delladar Oll ducked her head in the Lleveci sign of negation.

"You are able to pilot the starship?" Ayyah asked.

Again Delladar Oll ducked her head.

"Then I think we must take very great care of MacDonald."

"What do?"

"Perhaps it is time you reminded MacDonald and Oscar Achebe of their obligations."

Delladar Oll's hands worked automatically while she considered the argument. She handled the engines of death as if they were part of her. Ayyah wondered at the intricacies of chaos that brought her to attempt to make an accomplice of one whose whole outlook hinged on conflict and death.

Oscar Achebe came in, interrupting to tell them that if they wanted to eat, they should come to the kitchen and see what they could find. Humans had no manners.

Grave considerations were set aside while they served the requirements of the body. It was fitting, for without life, nothing is. But Ayyah was impatient with the need.

In the end, impatience proved as foolish as any other irrationality. By the end of the meal, Ayyah discovered that her attempt to forge a peculiar alliance had been unnecessary.

When the meal was done and he had cleared the table into the recycler, MacDonald leaned his elbows on the worn surface. The tip of his finger drew invisible circles on the plastic tabletop. Cat climbed into his lap and started cleaning his paws. Of the four species at the table, Cat had been the easiest to feed, happily wolfing down a bit of reconstituted synthetic chicken. Oscar wisely decided the best way to oblige the aliens was to leave them to rummage in the food storage unit themselves to find what they could that was suitable. One way and another, everyone gathered in Marion's rustic blue and white kitchen got fed. With simulated bacon, dehydrated onions, and artificial eggs, Oscar had done well by the humans.

MacDonald hesitated. This wasn't going to be easy. Then he wondered why he cared if the Orian was pleased. Perched on the edge of the chair with her tail bent off to the side, Ayyah watched him intently, ears pricked, as if she were anticipating his announcement.

"We can't stay here, Ayyah," he said. "We have business to do, and we have to get on with it. I'm sorry you got caught up in this. It wasn't intentional on my part. The best I can do for you now is put you down on a neutral world. Your choice of which one, provided it's not too far off our route."

For a moment, the Orian only stared at him. He could almost see the gears going around in her head while she digested something unexpected. "This is not what I wish to do, MacDonald."

"What, then?"

"I wish to go to Rayor."

"Oscar says there's no such place."

"You are mistaken."

"Oh, am I?" MacDonald was doing his best to be amiable and fair, but she wasn't making it easy.

"Yes. Oscar Achebe did not say Rayor does not exist; he said it does not appear on his charts. This is true, but does not lead inevitably to your conclusion."

"Forget the logic lesson. I have neither the time nor the inclination to go hunting for nonexistent—or uncharted—places. It's a big galaxy, lady."

"It is important, MacDonald."

"Why?"

"I cannot tell you this."

"Fine. You can stick it in your ear."

"I do not understand you."

"I guess you do. Or else you think I'm damned stupid."

Ayyah treated him to another moment of penetrating golden stare. "I think you believe I choose not to explain. I would make known to you that I do not have the information you—"

She was interrupted by a bleating alarm warning them that something had crossed the perimeter of the grounds.

In the times MacDonald had been on Tasetoru with Marion—

he had to stop a moment in spite of his concern and let the feeling pass—the alarm had gone off a few times. It had always been one of the shaggy natives, sometimes taking a shortcut across a bend in the trail while ambling his way from one little group of the hump-backed indigenous dwellings to another, sometimes just sitting like a hairy lump under the lilacs. It didn't seem to occur to the Tasey that it mattered if they stuck to the trail—and probably it didn't, since they never caused any trouble or did any harm, except for the alarm startling a body at awkward moments.

So, though he took Oscar and a couple of blasters with him when he went to investigate, he expected to find the brown woolly hump of a Tasey shuffling without haste across the yard.

Or maybe some local wildlife. He had never seen any, but there must be some.

Thissah was way, way down on his list of expectations.

If MacDonald had been asked to list the people he would most like to meet in a quiet corner of the galaxy, Thissah would not have been included. The Roothian had been useful on occasion, but there was a slipperiness to him. MacDonald wouldn't have trusted him on the other side of a door.

And there he was, at the door. For a moment, MacDonald could only stand there with his mouth open and the gun hanging heavy at the end of his arm.

"I'll be damned," Oscar said.

"Hhallo, MacDonald, time iss long, yess? You are not expecting Thissah, I think."

"Uh, not exactly."

"Who?" Delladar Oll asked.

"Thissah. From Rigaport. A Kazi collaborator, I guess you'd call him. An informant of sorts."

"Iss too much noisse, pleasse. Iss making talk hhard."

Maybe it would be easier to think without the alarm bleating away, to figure out what the hell was going on. The Roothian was nervous. Everything about him twitched. MacDonald reached for the panel beside the door to turn the alarm off.

Before he could do it, Delladar Oll pushed past him and slammed the door shut.

"We go. Now, very quick. Yes?" she shouted over the noise.

"Pleasse opening," Thissah squeaked through the door and the din.

"Go where?" MacDonald asked, feeling particularly thick-headed.

"From here. Kazi friend here. Come how? Kazi soldiers close. Send small one for not scaring. Yes? Need other door."

"Now you tell me," MacDonald said. He scratched his head and thought about it for a minute. Thissah pounded on the door. "If you're right, another door wouldn't help much. I don't think everybody would be coming politely up the front walk."

Oscar opened the door a crack. Thissah was still there. He looked up hopefully. Oscar slammed the door shut and set the locks.

"There's two coming up the walk right now. Rigans, armed. This door ain't going to hold them for long."

"Steel core," MacDonald said. "Stronger than you think." He was thinking furiously, trying to remember what Marion had told him about the construction of the house. The building shuddered. The bad guys were trying to blast their way in. "Keep away from the windows," he warned, not knowing how much of that sort of thing duraglas would take.

Delladar Oll had a weapon unlimbered, ready to blast the first creature that showed its head.

"They want us bad enough, they'll burn us out of here," Oscar worried.

"Yeah, I guess. Could happen. The construction is mostly Hi-D resin and wood. And you wouldn't believe the ceremony you have to go through to get a little lumber on Tasetoru. You're not allowed to cut a living tree," MacDonald said, but it was just chatter until his head started working. One possibility had come to mind. "Grab your weapons and come on."

The rest of them followed, without argument for once. The kitchen entrance to the utility room let them into a dim, dank underground place full of the pipes and wires and machinery of a modern home.

"I think we might be able to make it up the aqueduct," MacDonald said. "I just hope they aren't too familiar with the construction of Tasey houses."

"Assuming, of course, none of the bad guys are Tasey."

"Have you observed the locals closely? They've got all the ambition of a bunch of giant cotton balls. They'd make lousy mercenaries. You couldn't hire them to roll downhill."

MacDonald was working at a panel set into the wall and held with flush-mounted fasteners rusted into place. They probably had not been moved since the house was built. Ayyah came to lend a hand. "I am who the Kaz seek," she said. "If I surrender to them, they will be satisfied."

"You want to do that?"

"No. Many lives depend on this not happening."

"Including yours." The clamps were free. MacDonald looked around for something he could use to pry the panel out.

"Yes, most certainly including mine." Ayyah dug her claws into the surface, braced her foot on the wall, and pulled the panel free.

"Doesn't that hurt?" MacDonald asked.

Ayyah didn't answer, only regarded the narrow earthen passage before them. The pair of rough pipes attached to one wall had leaked a little. The floor of the serviceway was muddy. She hesitated.

"Move, stupid Orian," Delladar Oll growled.

"What's going on?" Oscar asked. He looked puzzled.

"The water comes from a pond behind the house, just over the rise. If I'm remembering this right, the serviceway has an access just short of the pond," MacDonald said.

"But you don't know."

"I don't know. If you've got a better idea, I'd sure like to hear it."

"I wish I did," Oscar said.

Delladar Oll pushed past Ayyah and led the way into the passage. The others followed in good order. When it was MacDonald's turn, he realized someone was missing.

"Cat," he called.

A plaintive, worried mew came from between the furnace and the autovac tank. He hurried back to rescue the kitten.

The serviceway was short, ending where a plastic-lined opening had been let into the roof. Another panel closed it, but the fastenings, it seemed, were on the outside.

In spite of Oscar's assurances of its indifference, MacDonald was becoming quite convinced that the universe did indeed, and with malice, conspire against him.

Delladar Oll's blade attacked the earth around the lining. Ayyah's nostrils dilated and her head twisted back the way they had come. Her ears were up and her tail rigid.

"What?" MacDonald asked.

"Smoke," she said.

Delladar Oll dug harder. After a few minutes, MacDonald could smell smoke, too. He was at the end of their single-file line. No one could get close enough in the narrow passage to help the Lleveci. His fingers worked against his palms in frustration. There had to be something he could do. The smoke was getting thick.

Oscar looked back over his shoulder. "Weren't you the fatalist?" he asked.

"Burning to death is the hard way," MacDonald answered.

With a cry from Delladar Oll and a rush of falling dirt, an opening appeared above, with a shaft of sunlight and a wandering plume of fresh air. Ignoring a fit of incongruously delicate sneezes, Ayyah was already digging the Lleveci out from under the fall.

They climbed out onto the grass and breathed. The grassy shore of the pond gave way to the ranks of trees and a little rise of land that separated them from whatever was going on at the house.

"I hate to bring this up," Oscar said after a while, "but the bad guys are between us and the shuttle."

"One thing at a time," MacDonald said, because he had not yet figured out what he was going to do about it.

"A closer assessment of the problem would be in order," Ayyah said, and started across the grass without waiting for the others to agree. It was as good a move as any.

"Not too damned close," MacDonald warned.

Soon they lay on their bellies at the edge of the ridge. MacDonald parted the leaves in front of him. At the bottom of the slope, Marion's house was burning, the roar of the flames audible through the trees, smoke billowing out into the forest. He could just make out dark forms prowling the grounds as near to the flames as they could tolerate the heat.

The lilacs were charred ruins. Many of the more distant native trees had lost their leaves and were beginning to smolder. A full-fledged forest fire seemed entirely possible.

"Count six Rigans," Delladar Oll said.

MacDonald was angry. He didn't trust himself to say anything. His teeth clamped down on his lower lip. His fists clenched. He wanted desperately to hit something, anything, to lash out, to redress the balance of justice. He was furious at being chased again, furious with his helplessness to do anything but run, furious with the destruction. How could they? Marion had loved that house so much. He wanted to go screaming down there and rip the scaly bastards limb from limb.

Beside him Ayyah said, ''Anger will not serve you now.'' She probably didn't know how random the emotion was. She could be its object as easily as anything else. The interruption of his black mood was provocation enough, given the humor he was in.

Cat was smart enough to seek refuge. He was riding in Oscar's shirt, having decided his usual conveyance was too dangerous this time.

Innocently, Ayyah continued. ''Perhaps you would benefit by imagining the lady's response to any foolish sacrifice on behalf of a ruined house.''

He was going to hit her. He was turning, fist ready, but she was quicker. Her hand touching his wrist, gentle and fleeting, startled him. She seemed not to like the contact. ''Look,'' she said, her gaze directed past him.

Just outside the flickering light cast by the fire, a wide circle of shaggy brown mounds, singly and in clumps, had assembled as if by magic, for their approach had been soundless and their presence unobtrusive. The Tasey sat on the grass that wasn't grass making a ring as near as the fire's heat would allow to the region of ruined trees.

''Lord love a duck,'' Oscar said, following the line of Ayyah's sight. ''There sure are a lot of them.''

''You understand what is happening here?'' Ayyah asked.

MacDonald shook his head. Who could say what a Tasey thought, if anything? They had no features to betray the workings of the mind, and they offered no audible opinions.

''Haven't got the foggiest.''

''Fog?'' Ayyah asked.

''Maybe we should see if we can get to the shuttle,'' Oscar said.

MacDonald looked up at the sun slanting redly through the smoke and the leaves. His fury had subsided to a smoldering spot about that color in the depths of his soul. ''Let's wait for dark. If they've wrecked it, the time won't make any difference. If they've posted a guard, darkness might help.''

''Smart warrior blow up,'' Delladar Oll remarked.

''Well, you better hope the Rigans aren't that smart, because it's the only way we've got to get off this planet.''

* * *

The thought of remaining indefinitely on Tasetoru did not sit well. Nor did the realization she was helpless to alter the circumstances. Ayyah was not accustomed to feeling helpless.

At least she could be grateful for tolerable night vision. She was able to avoid the thickest bunches of dew-wet leaves.

Full dark arrived before MacDonald was willing to move. Then Delladar Oll led the way cautiously through the night-shadowed trees. The humans stumbled noisily over roots and ran into branches and grumbled. A stealthy approach would be impossible.

"How come we haven't seen any?" Oscar whispered in spite of the danger. "Where are they?"

They had circled from the meadow behind the house through the forest almost to the pathway in front without encountering any sign of the Rigans.

"I don't know," MacDonald whispered back.

The fire had subsided to a ruby glow among the trees. Ayyah tested the air. The smell of the smoke had changed from the sharp scent associated with active flames to the darker note of smoldering bed of embers.

"Can you hear them?" MacDonald asked her.

His dark rage had diminished into an icy calm. This was the first time he had condescended to ask her for anything, or treat her in any way except as an obstruction to his otherwise perfect plans. Some slight hope was raised of finally achieving acceptance.

"Be still. Be silent," she said, and they did as she asked. It was a degree of cooperation, a step in the right direction.

She listened to the living, breathing night.

A rustle of wind, a slither in the grass, small movements, a rattle of leaves, a tiny shriek as some small thing ended its life in the clutches of some larger thing, a brush of twigs against a bulky body, the many, many unidentifiable pats and ticks and twitters of life going about its business. And something else.

"I hear no Rigans," she said. "But I hear rhythmic movements. Beings lighter than Rigans."

"Rhythmic movements," MacDonald echoed skeptically.

"Yes."

"I'm going to have a look."

MacDonald left the path and pushed his way through the undergrowth, moving as quietly as he could. Curious, and also concerned about the welfare of one essential to her plans, Ayyah followed. She was not yet convinced he was over the blind anger she feared could possibly send him plunging madly into battle with the Rigans. Such a derangement of responses she did not understand. She watched him closely, warily, uncertain about what she would do if the madness should take him again.

He hesitated where the forest suddenly ended. She came up beside him and saw what he saw.

Tasetoru's large, ringed moon had risen. The house was a glowing ruin, painting surfaces with reddish light. Hordes of shaggy Tasey milled around, intensely industrious in the fire-damaged area. They had laid charred logs out in a pattern on the ground and carefully, reverently, avoided disturbing the pattern while they worked. Off to one side, a group was tugging the body of a Rigan along toward an open hole apparently prepared to receive it. They tipped the body into the hole, then almost filled it with earth, standing on the mound above and pushing the dirt in with short flat feet, like burrowing animals.

Another group arrived towing a sapling on a runnerless sledge. The young tree was garlanded with bright bits of colored material. Bumping and nudging, they got it into the hole and upright. Then they pushed more dirt down around it. When the tree was planted, all the Tasey gathered into a series of rings around it. While an astonished Ayyah and an equally astonished MacDonald watched from the shelter of the undergrowth, they began a shuffling sort of dance, circling first one way and then the other.

There were five other decorated young trees in the burn.

Ayyah's first response was a feeling of responsibility, as if she had committed a criminal act that resulted in the deaths of the Rigans, and it sickened her. Her second was a fit of revulsion toward creatures who would kill people to feed trees.

"Well," MacDonald murmured beside her, "it does solve the problem."

She wanted to get away from him and his passions on the one hand and his cold-blooded acceptance of murder on the other, to get away from all of them, to be alone for a while so she could sort out her feelings and get them under control.

Such luxuries were not to be had. "We better get going," MacDonald said. "Before the Rigans' friends show up, or the Tasey lose track of exactly who was responsible for killing their trees."

The Illah Valley

In a record containing miscellaneous, unrelated scraps, Talan
had written, "The irrational brute, the primitive self, forever
lurks just beneath the surface of the civilized man. One must be
wary, lest it erupt and destroy all that has been gained since
ancient times, ruin all that is to come."

The uncivilized brute was refusing to stay submerged. Ayyah
found herself irritable and restless and ill at ease, annoyed with
herself for her lack of progress and further annoyed for being
unable to control this feeling. Considerable effort was required
to maintain an outer decorum to cover the inner disquiet. The
polished, mannerly surface felt particularly frail that day.

The four of them and the animal crowded into the *Harrier*
undoubtedly had much to do with her uneasiness. They were
too close together, bumping one another, breathing on one another. Anyone might feel the strain. Still, Delladar Oll could
keep her elbows tucked in and her voice pitched to a reasonable
level and thus grate less harshly on the tolerance of her fellow
passengers. A little restraint would be gratifying.

Instead of making herself unobtrusive, the warrior seemed
determined to occupy as much space as possible. She had developed an angry red color, and her mane fuzzed out like some
indignant beast while she waved her long arms and yelled.

"You leave nowhere? Not smart."

"There's a damned lot of space in this universe," MacDonald
said as reasonably as anyone could expect him to under the
circumstances.

Occasionally Ayyah had wondered if humans knew anything
whatever of discipline. At the moment, she could only admire
MacDonald's self-control.

"The chances of someone coming upon it by accident are

90

damned close to zero,'' MacDonald continued. ''That barge is safer at an anonymous point in space than it could possibly be if I parked it in the most closely guarded place you can imagine. Even if someone knew of its existence, you think about looking for an object with no dimension bigger than fifty meters somewhere among the stars. You wouldn't find it in twenty lifetimes.''

MacDonald also was stressed. It showed in tight facial muscles and a tendency to react too strongly to stimuli. The loss of the base on Pigpen was a serious blow, and little things like food and fuel and a place to live no doubt loomed large before him. His need for financing was urgent, which would explain his tolerance of the irritating Delladar Oll.

The distress caused by the loss of the building called Marion's House on Tasetoru was more difficult to understand. By Ayyah's reckoning, the loss there was much less, the material loss confined to one small structure, and the lost lives, though undeniably lives, were those of MacDonald's enemies, for whom she expected him to have not much sympathy. Yet he seemed wounded and angry about it more than for the greater material loss and greater number of casualties experienced on Pigpen.

Both of those events worked in Ayyah's favor. At least, she thought they did, robbing MacDonald of physical and psychological ties. Humans had an expression, ''Nothing to lose'', which often preceded reckless actions. From the human perspective, her plans, or truly, her lack of them, must appear to be reckless.

The humans did not have the weight of the ancestors at their backs, nor the bleak prospect of annihilation ahead.

Oscar Achebe worked the controls of the little ship. He went about his business with a refreshingly calm, cool demeanor. Catching her eye, he said, ''Don't worry too much. We'll get you to a neutral world. Real soon now.''

Disturbed that her worry was on her face, Ayyah took the pilot's chair, momentarily vacated by MacDonald who was busy checking some gauges on the back wall—bulkhead—and bickering with the Lleveci. Having MacDonald's friend favorably disposed toward her would be beneficial. ''The barge will be difficult to find?'' she asked him.

Oscar Achebe spared her a glance before returning his attention to the instruments. ''Well, like Mac said, there is indeed a damned lot of space in the universe. On the other hand, Mac is just about the best navigator you're going to find anywhere in the Orion arm. On another hand, he's talking about some very heavy accuracy here. If we miss it by one part per million, we miss it by half a light-year, give or take. On still another hand—"

"You have an inordinate number of hands, Oscar Achebe."

"Yeah." He smiled at her, teeth flashing white. A display of teeth was a friendly sign in humans, though a sign of hostility in almost every other race of animals known. She was making progress.

"Anyway," Oscar Achebe continued, pointing to one of the instruments in front of him, "on this other hand, here we observe a perturbation on the mass sensor showing an object almost exactly where MacDonald said the barge would be." He leaned back in his chair and called over his shoulder, "Got the barge on sensors." He smiled at Ayyah again. "Maybe that'll give 'em something to do besides argue."

"What does this barge contain that makes it so important?" Ayyah asked.

"Heavy arms and ammunition liberated from the Kaz," Oscar Achebe replied, with no idea of the position he was putting her in. Indeed, he seemed entirely pleased about it.

"I do not wish to be a party to trade in weapons," Ayyah told MacDonald firmly. She stood toe to toe with him in the narrow aisle behind the passenger seats. She would have been more comfortable with more distance between them. Delladar Oll had stopped complaining when the barge came up on visual. Relieved, MacDonald had been trying to return to his station when Ayyah intercepted him.

"You're not a party to the trade," MacDonald answered shortly. "You're an innocent bystander, and a bloody irritating one at that. If you want to stop standing by, I'll ask Oscar to hold after the next jump and you can get off."

"Oscar Achebe would agree to this?"

"I don't know. You'll have to ask him. I don't think he'd fight me about it. As matters stand, you're not exactly an essential part of this enterprise."

"Tomas Lopes seemed to think I had value."

"Tomas and I don't think the same way about such things."

"This I do not understand. You would oppose your own people to protect me from Tomas Lopes's scheme. Yet you claim to be willing to leave me to die in space. If my death would serve you, you could have left me on the asteroid. This is a most curious lack of consistency.''

"Ayyah, I've had about enough static from the passengers. I'm not going to engage in a philosophical debate. I'm running this show, and we're going to do it my way. Period. Is that clear?''

"Quite clear, MacDonald. But—"

"No freaking buts.''

"You want to maybe stop fighting and give me a hand with the coupling approach?'' Oscar asked, a little louder than was his wont.

"You could leave a living, sentient being to die in space?'' Ayyah asked.

"I could. You'd better believe it,'' MacDonald answered.

"Perhaps so. Yet I find it difficult.''

MacDonald shook his head and abruptly pushed by her without further ado.

Somewhat unnerved by the brushing contact, Ayyah picked up the kitten from one of the passenger seats and sat down to collect herself. Obviously MacDonald was not going to pay attention to her protests. Ayyah could see nothing she could do at this stage that would dissuade him. Her conscience should have rested more easily than it did.

MacDonald dropped into the navigator's chair. "How's the fuel?''

"So-so,'' Oscar told him. "We'll get to Llevec. After that, we'd better start looking for a gas station. Gee whiz, you're tough, boss.''

"Can it. She'll hear you. Our resident indignant moralist has ears like a rabbit's.''

More than you know, Ayyah thought, finding it within herself to be amused. The kitten settled itself in her lap and was making a very small, contented, buzzing sound. Nonplussed, Ayyah did not know what to do about it, so she left it alone, lying on her legs as if it belonged there. The sensation was not all that unpleasant.

She was unhappy that she had been unable to divert MacDonald from this most hazardous enterprise. All other considerations aside, she needed MacDonald and she needed his starship. She had lost control over both, and did not immediately see how she might regain it.

A bump and clatter announced the mating of the *Harrier* to the barge. In a few moments, they were under way again.

Llevec was a Kazi world recently absorbed into the empire. Neither Oscar Achebe nor MacDonald suggested they would get in and out of Lleveci space undetected. It was, MacDonald assured them, simply a matter of timing.

Required to give her fate into human hands, Ayyah could easily, if she allowed herself, wish Oscar Achebe's "real soon now" neutral world had appeared earlier. The survival of the individual was a deeply seated instinct, not easily put aside.

"You afraid," Delladar Oll had said contemptuously, early in the proceedings.

"To know no fear is to know madness," Ayyah had answered.

The warrior had laughed in her open-mouthed way.

The *Harrier* was now in synchronous orbit above a small chain of islands in Llevec's Middle Sea. The barge was clamped underneath it. In the seat next to Ayyah, Delladar Oll held a small sensing device in her restless hands, waiting for the sign that a certain section of the planetary sensor net had suffered a sudden, inexplicable failure. The *Harrier* was then to drop the barge into a descending glide, and somewhere along the path ground-based Lleveci would take remote control of the little on-board engine and guide the barge to a landing at the appropriate place.

Learning of the plan, MacDonald shook his head. "That seems like a rough way to treat some moderately delicate machinery."

Delladar Oll reassured him. "Barge land in snow." She gave him that information as if parting with a mighty secret.

"If everything goes exactly right," he had cautioned.

"It be right."

That assurance was given before the Kaz showed up.

"I'm reading two ships coming up on the port quarter, under power, closing fast," Oscar said.

With the *Harrier* drifting in orbit, there was nothing much for the pilot to do. MacDonald moved over to the navigator's station and examined the board over Oscar's shoulder. "I don't suppose they're friendly."

"I don't suppose."

MacDonald turned to Delladar Oll. She cuddled the little device close to a small ear almost lost in the bushy mane.

"Come on, lady," he said. "We've got to get rid of this thing."

The Lleveci gave no sign of having heard. She remained intent on waiting for the signal.

"Got 'em on visual," Oscar said.

Straining to see past the humans, Ayyah made out a pair of pinpoints on the screen, unidentifiable but growing rapidly. MacDonald started back to the pilot's station. "Stand by for engine start," he said.

"No," Delladar Oll objected.

"Yes," MacDonald answered. "If you think I'm going to sit here and be shot at, you've got another think coming." He continued to Oscar, "I'm going to cut the barge loose in five—"

The sharp scent of human fear alerted Ayyah. She turned to see the tip of Delladar Oll's crystal blade directly under MacDonald's chin. Any movement on his part promised to be acutely painful.

Embarrassment wilted her ears. Intent on trying to see the instruments and second-guess the pilot, she had missed the warrior's sudden move. Delladar Oll had been quick. She should remember that warriors were trained for just such things.

"You wait," the Lleveci said.

Oscar was on his feet, but Delladar Oll warned him away with a minuscule movement of the knife. That gave MacDonald room to talk without immediate damage. "Do it, Oscar," he said.

"I kill, Achebe," Delladar Oll warned.

"Me, too?" Oscar asked. "You think you've figured out how to fly this crate, is that it?"

"Move it, Oscar," MacDonald insisted.

Oscar said, "We've got a pair of Kazi fighters coming at us. If we don't get moving, we're all dead, and your people don't get the merchandise anyway."

Ayyah forced her recovery. Embarrassment, she reminded herself, recalling childhood lessons, is an egocentric emotion engendered by the failure of reality to match the internal image of the perfect self.

The Lleveci's attention was divided between MacDonald and Oscar Achebe. MacDonald chanced backing away.

Preoccupied with that maneuver, Delladar Oll was unaware of Ayyah's unobtrusive movement. The Orian managed to get a hand clamped onto the wrist of the knife hand. For a moment, in the silent, static struggle of tense muscles, Ayyah began to doubt she had the strength to hold the Lleveci. Then, slowly, the knife was lowered. Delladar Oll glared furiously.

"Sidallut," she spat.

"You know nothing of my ancestry. Know this. Dead, we are useless to your people," Ayyah said. "Suicide ill becomes a warrior."

The Lleveci looked surprised. "You think to know language of hills?"

Ayyah didn't answer.

"Dying, cowardice, both not serve duty," Delladar Oll agreed sourly. "No right thing here."

The device in the Lleveci's other hand gave off a brief, plaintively wavering bleat. Her change of mood was dramatic and immediate.

"Now, MacDonald, now," she directed, as if nothing serious had occurred between them.

"No time, Mac," Oscar said. There was a gentle nudge as the engine cut in. *Harrier* was no longer drifting. Ayyah watched the Lleveci closely to see if further intervention would be necessary. Strangely, with the incident she had gained some stature in the warrior's eyes. She could only hope she would not be required to jeopardize it.

MacDonald spared a glance for the two females. They seemed to be keeping each other busy. Good. He was free to think about flight paths for the few seconds it took him to reach the pilot's station. He had it half worked out in his head; he could picture the trajectory in his mind, superimposed upon the green and silver landscape below, even while he tried to see the sensor panel with one eye and the engine monitor with the other.

"We have to go somewhere," he said. "Down is as good a way as any. It might even throw them off for a second or two. A shallow hyperbolic course could get us to just about the right place to drop the barge on our way out. Maybe they'll chase it."

"Not likely. They expect the planetary sensors to be tracking," Oscar answered. "And they're getting bloody close."

"Let's give it a try. Acceleration in thirty seconds. Strap in. This could be wild."

"You're weird, sir," Oscar said.

"You always say the nicest things."

"Honey tongue Achebe, they call me. Do we really need the money this bad?"

"Yeah, we do. Everything's so bloody expensive these days."

"I think we're not going to make it."

"I owe you a good scare for calling the *Harrier* a crate."

"You're doing a job of it, believe me."

"If we get out of this, remind me to give Ayyah a big hug and forget all her carping on the morality of the arms trade. That furry paw clamping down on the knife is one of the nicer things I've seen in my life."

"She'll be very unhappy if you do. If you don't kill us first with all this chatter. Barge away."

It could have worked. *Harrier* had an advantage in speed, and her passengers had an advantage in the amount of acceleration they could tolerate. High-g turns tended to make Kaz unconscious and flat.

The damned barge did him in. When there was no time to do all the mathematics, one had to guess. MacDonald realized a fraction of a second too late that he had underestimated the degree to which loosing the barge would disturb *Harrier*'s course. He had planned to take her across the fighters' path just out of range of their weapons, forcing them into a tight turn and therefore gaining a few precious seconds for the little ship to build up speed.

They passed the fighters a shade too close. An alert gunner got a salvo away. *Harrier* staggered. She began to skitter capriciously all over the sky. MacDonald fought with the steering controls.

He wrestled her back the way the fighters had come to force them into a complete 360-degree turn.

"We're losing air from the aft cargo bay," Oscar said.

"Evacuate it and seal it off."

Once that was done, steering was easier, for all the good it was doing. The engine monitor was nothing but bad news.

"Losing power," MacDonald informed Oscar. "Internal systems on battery."

It didn't help. The arc of the planet drifted gracefully up to meet them. *Harrier* was falling, and MacDonald couldn't stop her.

"Where're the bad guys?" he asked.

"Coming around now. Looks like they're going to stand by above and watch us burn."

"We're not dead yet," MacDonald said.

"Atmosphere, Mac," Oscar warned.

"No vernier control," MacDonald answered. "I can't get her tail down. We're going in belly first. Crash harness, everybody."

Harrier bounced on the wisps of air like a rock skipping on water. It felt as if she were being slapped around by a giant hand.

"Ready with reverse thrust, as much as we've got. I'm going to keep her as flat as possible," MacDonald said, fighting the controls with one hand, the buckles of the harness with the other. "We'll shed energy to the air."

"It's going to get hot in here," Oscar said.

"Mm."

It did get hot. As the air got thicker, the scream of the wind outside grew louder, until it was a hundred hurricanes rolled into one. The ship glowed. Her proud colors blackened and boiled away. Only her aerodynamic shape and the contribution of her faltering engine prevented *Harrier* from becoming a meteor high in Llevec's sky. MacDonald's heart ached. Even dying, she was a good bird.

After what seemed like a long, tense time, Oscar shouted over the howling air, "Aircraft, tracking."

"Piss all I can do about it," MacDonald said. "Start looking for a place to belly down. An ocean would be good."

"I can't swim," Oscar complained. He called up orbital maps of Llevec onto the navigator's tank. *Harrier*'s path was a curved orange trace across it.

"Can you bounce?" MacDonald asked.

"No, I'm not much good at that either."

The decision was taken out of their hands when the engine quit. It coughed once when MacDonald tried a flying restart and then declined to show any further sign of life.

"What've we got?" MacDonald demanded with a certain urgency.

Oscar sucked in a breath and tried to keep the quaver out of his voice as he inspected the computer's projection of a ballistic course. "Mountains," he said. "Or forest. Choose one."

"That's it?"

"A river. In a bloody deep valley."

"Oh, boy. Let's see." Oscar transferred the graphic to MacDonald's screen. It didn't look good. "Okay, the river it is. I would like everyone's fervent prayers that the drogue will deploy."

"Too much speed," Oscar said.

"Too few choices."

The drogue popped open with an explosive snap, a wide mesh canopy of tough polymer fibers. *Harrier* staggered as if she had run into a wall and threw her passengers brutally against their harnesses.

The chute began to shred almost at once and, as it did, to dance and swirl erratically behind the ship, yanking her every which way.

A tatter snagged in the topmost branches of a tall tree. The branches snapped like straws, but it was enough to spin the ship and drop it as if it had bounced off a step. MacDonald cut the drogue loose to give himself steering, but it wasn't enough. Bits of tree flailed at the battered ship. A great rent opened in her side. Her people were helpless to help her.

With a banging, screeching, sparking, thundering crash, *Harrier* was on the ground. The heavy engine continued to slide a bit after the nose had stopped and folded her up amidships like a moth-eaten accordion.

In the terrible silence that followed, MacDonald pulled his bruised face out of the pilot's control board, blinked a couple of times, and concluded he was alive. It was a mixed blessing. He felt decidedly mangled where the straps of the harness had dug into the flesh.

He put one hand on the broken board in front of him. "You're a tough old dame," he told his ruined ship.

Beside him, Oscar groaned.

"You okay?"

Oscar was a moment answering. "Yeah, I think so." He was holding his elbow and wiggling his fingers to make sure they still worked. "Breathing isn't too much fun at the moment."

"What happened to the aircraft?"

"Damned if I know. Sensor board's dead."

"Okay, let's get out of here. Gently. She's not stable." Mac-

Donald freed himself from the crash harness and moved carefully among heaved and buckled deck plates to help the passengers. The aft bulkhead had a definite forward bulge, and he wondered about radiation, but those sensors, like all others, were gone. The drip of cooling fluid, on the other hand, was an undeniable and obvious health hazard.

He could feel the deck tremble under his feet. Oscar lowered the hatch. *Harrier* swayed. They both stopped moving and held their breaths until the ship settled down.

Ayyah was bleeding from a cut above her eye. She was already up and helping Delladar Oll. The Lleveci looked dazed.

"Are you hurt?" MacDonald asked her.

"I live," she answered.

"Can you walk?"

"Yes."

"Good. Outside, then. One at a time. Carefully. If she starts to slide, we've had it. Don't touch the skin. It's hot. Get well clear. If the engine goes, it'll make a mess for quite a way around."

Ayyah crossed the deck as if she were walking on eggs. Even so, as she started down the hatchway steps, the deck tilted.

When she was clear, MacDonald sent Delladar Oll, who was inclined to stride purposefully in denial of her fear. There was a little grating sound below as she cleared the hatch.

"Okay, Oscar," MacDonald said.

"Mac, I—"

"We don't have time to argue about it. Go."

Oscar went. MacDonald was not far behind. Out on the stony slope, he craned his neck to look back at his charred ship balanced on her broken belly on the hump of a huge boulder. Behind, a black, smoldering scar marked her passage through the forest. In front, the rocky bank angled down toward the river.

Something was missing. "Where's the damned cat?" he asked.

He hesitated a moment then started back toward the wreck.

From his place closer to the river, Oscar called, "Mac, wait. Don't be . . ." but MacDonald was already climbing cautiously back through the heat shimmer into the broken ship. ". . . stupid," Oscar finished without force. "It's just a damned cat. You don't even like cats, you idiot."

Inside, MacDonald smiled. Oscar was a good man and absolutely right. Still, he couldn't just leave the little critter. The wreck swayed under his weight. His breath stopped when he heard a crunching screech. A few pebbles bounced down the side of the boulder and rattled into the scree beyond.

It took him a moment to find the furry bundle huddled in a corner. "Come on, Cat," he said, swooping it up. He could feel movement under him. More pebbles bounced as he eased cautiously down the step with Cat under his arm. He came toward the others faster than was prudent on the stony ground, waving them on as he ran.

Behind him, metal screamed as it was rent apart.

The whole group stopped. They couldn't help pausing to watch. It was like the death of some noble animal.

Harrier slid slowly forward with tragic grace. She seemed to hesitate a moment on the brink as if fighting her fate, then she tipped and fell and slid, rumbling, until she hit the water with a great thundering detonation of steam.

MacDonald urged them on, shouting above the roar, pushing roughly, running. He expected to feel the deadly heat of the exploding engine on his back at any moment. He stumbled on the loose gravel and wished for Ayyah's easy lope.

He wouldn't let them stop until they rounded a bend in the riverbed and all they could see of *Harrier* was a plume of steam rising skyward. The anticipated explosion did not occur.

Then the aftershock set in. Oscar sank down on a convenient rock because his rubbery legs would no longer hold him up. Nearby, Delladar Oll, her face blanched almost completely white, paced tight, nervous circles. Only the Orian seemed unaffected, squatting down on her haunches in an attitude of rest with her tail wrapped around her feet as if she were merely waiting patiently for the others to recover.

MacDonald, in pain, walked away from them toward the water, still carrying Cat. His body hurt, but it would heal. It was the spirit that was wounded too deeply to allow him to be sympathetic, too deeply to share.

He could only stand at the river's edge, looking out over the water toward the black forest rising on the other bank and blue mountains beyond, the kitten's body still in his hands.

After a while, Oscar came. MacDonald held the wee furry thing out for his friend to see. The tail hung limply down on one side of his hands, and the head lolled lifelessly down on the other, the little eyes tightly closed as if in furious sleep.

He couldn't look at Oscar and maintain any sort of control.

He squatted down with his head bowed and moved stones until he had made a shallow depression. He laid the kitten in it and started piling stones above it.

"Mac, I'm sorry," Oscar said.

MacDonald stood up holding a rock so tightly he thought he might possibly break his hand.

"God, I miss Marion," he said.

"I know." Oscar looked down at the gravel. He didn't have anything comforting to say.

"It's too damned much," MacDonald continued with quiet intensity. He looked past Oscar at the smudge of steam rising into Llevec's sky. All his wordly possessions were represented by a fading column of water vapor. All the pain of all the years welled up.

He threw the rock at the water. "My career. Then my home. And now my ship. The freaking Kaz damned near killed us. They wreck everything." He looked down at the little pile of stones. "It's just too God-damned much."

Oscar's hand rested on MacDonald's shoulder.

"It's time to start hitting back," MacDonald said.

Oscar shook his head. "Fighting the Kaz is like fighting gravity. It's something you just have to live with, around, in spite of."

"Yeah," MacDonald answered. But he was not agreeing.

"We'd better get moving," he said finally. "We've made enough noise and smoke that someone's bound to come to investigate. It'd be a good idea to be somewhere else when they do."

Ayyah watched the humans from the bank where she and the Lleveci were left and told by Oscar Achebe to stay. She had heard about Terran rituals of death but was surprised that the animal was afforded the honor. She could hear little of the conversation above the rush of the river and the crunch of stones as Delladar Oll paced restlessly.

The Lleveci stopped pacing long enough to ask Ayyah, "What they do?"

"Mourn," Ayyah said.

"The animal?" Delladar Oll asked with incredulity.

"That, among other things. It seems humans have it in them to respect some few lives other than their own."

Ever ready to take offense, Delladar Oll turned to glare at

Ayyah, undoubtedly taking the comment as a slur upon the Lleveci race. Ayyah met her sharp eyes calmly, offering no sign of malice.

"Useless beast," the warrior complained.

Ayyah had no argument with that.

A silver dot appeared in the sky above the river valley and swooped suddenly by them with the ear-shattering, roaring whine of jet engines close to the ground.

The noise hurt. Ayyah flinched as if physically struck. Her ears flattened tightly to her head.

"Kaz," Delladar Oll shouted over the noise. "We go."

Rullenahesad

The Kazi security team investigating the crash of a starship in the Illah river valley found the blackened wreck partially underwater.

The leader posted its Lleveci conscripts as lookouts around the site while the Kazi technicians worked. The Lleveci would keep careful watch. Mountain warriors reputedly treated collaborating Lleveci no differently from their Kazi masters. Lleveci might be casual about Kazi priorities, but they had sense enough to worry about their own lives.

The technicians clambered over the wreck, studying their instruments. The leader commandeered a hand lamp and waded through the shallow water toward the open hatch. The hatchway was partially collapsed, but remained open enough for a Kazi.

The space within was dark. Swinging the circle of its lamp, the leader could see that the passenger compartment had suffered little damage. The supports and restraints were obviously designed for bipedal creatures of about four Kazi masses. All were empty. No bodies. Undoubtedly one or more survived.

Back outside, it took note of the position of the sun. They would have to be done there before nightfall rendered Kaz vulnerable far from the lights and security of the city. It signaled the technicians to gather and report on their progress.

The ship had heated badly during its passage through the atmosphere, they pointed out, and all identification had burned away. They believed the design to be Terran. Electronic systems had suffered heat and water damage, so on-board records were most probably lost. They asked for time to take samples of paint and metal for analysis in the laboratories in Rullenahesad and to recover the records in case some part of them proved to be readable after processing.

The leader signaled its agreement and urged them to be quick. While it waited, it went carefully along the gravelly riverbank, seeking some sign of the survivors, downstream a hundred meters or so, then back and upstream, around a bend in the river.

It was about to return to the ship when an odd little pile of stones caught its eye. It did not immediately see how running water could arrange rocks in such a tidy heap. Curious, and yet conscious that the sunlight was filtering through the trees on the opposite bank and threatening night and helpless immobility for Kaz, it undid the pile, not knowing what it might find.

The Kazi governor on Llevec balanced on extended hind legs, braced its forelegs on the windowsill, and looked out over the small city known to the locals as Rullenahesad. Lleveci cities were all small, most of them hardly more than villages. Lleveci windows were high off the floor, and if one was endowed with a long, flexible neck, perhaps it made sense. The governor had no neck to speak of and would have been happy to do without a window at any height. It spent too much time in this above-ground office these days. It would not have called the feeling it got from all these open rooms agoraphobia, exactly, more an uneasy sense of being in the wrong place, a feeling it was trying to overcome by periodically subjecting itself to an overdose from the third-story window.

Below it, the tunneling machine that should have been at work preparing new Kazi quarters in the city was lying idle. Again.

Built to be Llevec's spaceport, Rullenahesad lay on the high prairie steppe that divided highlands from lowlands on this continent. It had an ample supply of landing pads, shuttle bays, warehouses, cargo handling facilities, passenger terminals, and so forth. But when the Kaz made Rullenahesad into the de facto capital of the world, some serious shortages became apparent: housing for a burgeoning population of civil servants and bureaucrats, for example, and office space, and suitable accommodations for Kazi overseers.

The crowding caused a certain amount of confusion, which was by no means lessened by the sullen obstructionism of the native people. Building had begun in an attempt to alleviate the shortage, but progress was marvelously slow. The governor was certain the leisurely pace was deliberate, and had attempted to speed it up by making the well-known and well-respected Lleveci leader Yalla Rullenahe personally responsible for the situation. Yalla Rullenahe had only flooded the governor with endless reports about the lack of skilled labor, the failure of the kilns to deliver cement, not being able to get optical cable, and the shortage of lumber since many of the highland mills had burned down and those that remained were suffering from the raids inflicted by mountain warriors upon those the warriors deemed collaborators.

Reprocessing Yalla Rullenahe was a mistake. Everyone in the city had gone into mourning, and the workers were only now beginning to return to duty.

The Kaz could only wait. To consign the entire construction industry to reprocessing, as satisfying as it might be, would be counterproductive.

The governor dropped to the floor and went over to the bench that allowed it access to the top of the desk. Several days earlier it had asked to have the desk cut down to Kazi size to make this silly business of the bench unnecessary. A workman had come promptly, deposited some tools on the floor, and as promptly disappeared, never to return.

Feeling irritable, the governor sent for its Lleveci aide.

The aide came in, neck crooked deferentially.

The governor waved an angry foreclaw at the tools. "The workman has not returned."

It would have liked to have expressed its feelings on the subject more adequately, but the sounder had the same flat, uninflected delivery regardless of the wearer's mood. That was one more small irritation.

The aide's head bobbled unhappily at the end of his neck. "The carpenter has been reprocessed," he said.

"You did not obtain another."

"You did not ask for another."

The clenching of the governor's forelegs tight to its body and its flat stance would have warned another Kazi of dangerously short patience. The posture meant nothing to the Lleveci.

Controlling itself, the governor made the sounder say, "I am now asking for another, and as many others as may be needed to accomplish this tremendous task. Am I understood?"

"Yes, Governor."

"Further delay will be your personal responsibility."

"Of course, Governor. As you say. If it please you, sir, the security team leader awaits your pleasure, sir."

"Send it in." The governor settled itself on the bench with

its back to the window. But it was still conscious of the sulking city beyond the glass.

It was frustrated by semi-invisible opposition. In the uplands, at least, the Kaz met honest resistance; the mountain tribes made no secret of their hate for the new order, rules and rulers alike. In the lowlands, the majority had meekly become cooperative servants of the empire on the surface, but underneath, resentment festered and made strange things happen.

It had reacted too strongly to the silly business of the desk. It knew that. Word of the incident would be all around the city by nightfall and would amuse the beastly creatures at their evening meal.

The security team leader's scent as it entered was of puzzlement and dissatisfaction, its attitude one of apology. The governor was ready to forgive in advance, in gratitude for the opportunity to be able to communicate Kazi to Kazi with one who would not endlessly say one thing and mean another.

The team leader made its greetings in proper form and began its formal report.

The team found nothing significant, but laboratory results are yet to come, it said.

The governor asked about the barge. The security leader's attitude of apology deepened. The aircraft had not tracked it, since the pilots assumed the sensor net would provide that information. The barge dropped into a shallow glide path. Available data suggested it was a type commonly used by the military. Barges of that type bore a small engine to provide a measure of steering control and to soften landings. Trajectory suggested the high mountain ranges of this continent, but it could be anywhere on the planet.

Commonly used by our military? the governor asked.

The team leader signaled yes.

The governor requested the specifications and queried the computer terminal on its desk for a list of losses of which the barge might possibly be a part. The computer offered only one, twelve twelvedays earlier, a consignment of weapons to the Terran garrison, taken, it was assumed, by pirates. The governor was not reassured. No good could come of heavy weapons in the hands of the highland rebels.

An intensive search should be mounted immediately. Unfortunately, it did not have enough of its own people to spare. To send Lleveci would be futile. Even the most reliable of them were afraid of the mountain warriors. They would give the governor a superficial effort at best. At worst they would surreptitiously aid and abet whatever was going on up there.

The governor issued instructions to the military commander on Llevec to listen carefully to its intelligence network for signs of the barge. It was about to dismiss the team leader when the other indicated it had something further, which might or might not relate to the wrecked starship.

It described the body of a small creature found within a grave of stones. It was not a creature any of the Kazi team members had seen on Llevec, and the Lleveci claimed not to know of anything like it. So far, the leader said, the creature remained unidentified, but it was clearly too small to fit the appointments of the vessel.

What do we know of Lleveci funeral customs? the governor asked.

This one knows nothing, the leader responded. *Possibly the sociologists would be better informed.*

Inquire, the governor instructed. *Tell me what you find.*

Alone, the governor pondered its alternatives. Though its intelligence network was extensive, the governor had serious doubts about reliability. Even among lowlanders a century away from tribal life, Lleveci had a deeply ingrained sense of tribal loyalties. They would happily accept the empire's favor with one hand and hold a knife poised in the other.

How fortunate they had only two forelimbs.

The best it could do, the governor decided, was to send its recommendations to its district supervisor, by the fastest ship available, that a substantial military force with heavy equipment be put down on Llevec immediately; first, to recover the barge with all possible dispatch; and second, to solve the problem of the upland rebels once and for all; and that a team of electronics technicians be made available to determine what caused the sensor net failure and find those responsible.

Though it had expressed its concerns as forcefully as it was able, the governor did not expect a favorable response. The Kaz were thinly spread in this sector. In the governor's humble opinion, which it kept to itself, the empire had expanded much too quickly in the area after the fall of Orion. The empire's success had always been the result of careful, patient progress backed by long-term planning. Patience was the great Kazi virtue. The empire could outwait rebellious populations, for generations if need be, until the intolerable notion of Kazi control became the mundane fact of everyday life.

To abandon that dependable tactic and proceed into this region with such unseemly haste was wrong, so the governor believed.

The governor's body expanded with a deep intake of alien air, which it let out slowly. What was done was done.

A few days later, it was surprised and gratified to receive the information that a starship had been dispatched from sector headquarters and that the 44th Battalion of the Army of the Empire was aboard.

The Hidrillah Forest

Ayyah washed the bloody patch on her forehead for the second time just before the party left the river, lying on her belly on the bank and using quick little handfuls of the icy water, her lips pulled back with distaste, an unconscious show of sharp teeth. Her face was beginning to swell, almost closing one eye. The grimace hurt and warned her she was making an unbecoming display. She willed it away in spite of the unpleasant water.

They had been following the Illah upstream. Ayyah discovered that for once, she and Delladar Oll agreed on one thing. This was not a wise course beyond their first urgent need to put distance between themselves and the wreck before official investigators arrived. It was an obvious place for searchers to look and, in any case, would get the group nowhere. The farther north they went, the Lleveci pointed out, the deeper and steeper the river valley became.

She squatted on the streambank with her tail wrapped around her legs and tried to find some warmth in the thin Lleveci sun. MacDonald and Oscar Achebe sprawled beside her on the bank.

"Now what?" MacDonald asked. His dull voice suggested he did not care very much.

"The simplest solution for Oll will be to leave us. By herself, she won't have any trouble disappearing. We're the ones who stand out in a crowd," Oscar Achebe said.

"This will not happen," Ayyah assured him. "Lleveci honor forbids it. Honor is a very real thing to a warrior, almost tangible. MacDonald is owed for the service he has done them."

"What service?" MacDonald asked morosely. "It was a business deal, and I don't even know if I delivered."

"Lleveci see this differently. Delladar Oll will look after you to the best of her ability," she said. "You would be unwise to try to argue her to your way of thinking. Her patience as shepherd will be not great. This is not considered warrior's work.''

''What about you and me?'' Oscar Achebe asked.

''Unknown,'' Ayyah admitted.

''You seem to think you know the Lleveci pretty well,'' MacDonald said as if he doubted her expertise, though she had given him no reason to do that.

''I have studied many cultures.''

MacDonald only grunted in reply. Ayyah did not know how to interpret that unfriendly sound.

Suddenly Delladar Oll was standing over them, the erect hairs at the crest of her mane exhibiting impatience. ''Go now,'' the warrior said.

Since Delladar Oll had located herself on the ground and found herself on familiar terrain, she began to act like the leader of the party. Oscar Achebe didn't object, and MacDonald, deep in some despondent emotional state, was in no condition to oppose her. Ayyah could find no real harm in the warrior taking the initiative, yet it made her uneasy.

She did not look up. The Lleveci culture was full of small signs given large importance. To look up at another with bent neck was a sign of subservience. Ayyah did not want Delladar Oll to imagine she was in any way subservient. She looked steadfastly at the water. ''The humans require rest.''

''Rest long if soldiers come,'' Delladar Oll replied. ''No time for rest.''

''A few minutes will be no great risk, and the Terrans will travel better for it.''

''You all at once Terran expert?''

Ayyah didn't answer. The disposition of knowledge seemed to engender hostility in all her companions.

''Orian, you altogether shut up every time not liking what happening. No good. Much annoying.''

Again Ayyah did not respond—not, she told herself, because she was deliberately baiting Delladar Oll, but because such a statement had no sensible answer.

''Where are we going?'' Oscar Achebe had taken the role of peacemaker.

Delladar Oll pointed at the forest.

Regarding with misgivings the dark mountain rising before them, MacDonald groaned. ''Up there?''

In answer, Delladar Oll scrambled up the narrow trail worn

in the rock where animals came to drink, and waited for the others.

Ayyah followed, climbing the rocks in a couple of easy leaps, tail extended for balance. The humans scrabbled and slipped, cursing and grumbling, boots clattering on stone. Ayyah braced herself, leaned down, and offered MacDonald her hand. It was a considerable concession from her. He waved her away irritably.

Before them, the forest stood like a wall, dark and damp, the narrow smooth stems rising branchless for fifteen meters or so before spreading out into an umbrella of leaves. Beneath the closely ranked trees, shrubs and bushes fought for light and air in the cramped spaces. Long thin green strings of moss hung down from the high branches and many-colored lichens coated the lower stems. Every errant ray of sunlight was captured, every possible space occupied.

The rank overabundance of vegetative growth, the dim green light, and the moldy smell reminded Ayyah of KD2434 and the dying colony huddled there. A sense of failure welled up. She pushed it away. This was not the time to indulge in emanations from the primeval self.

"You got quite a bang on the head there," Oscar Achebe said. "You okay?"

Puzzling through the question took a moment. "I am not seriously damaged," she said.

"I've seen friendlier-looking jungles."

"I have not seen a friendly jungle."

"In forest, not see from air," Delladar Oll said. She started away along the game trail. The outworlders could follow or stay. She had no time to listen to complaints. There was a degree of impatience in the hand that pushed the branches aside.

Ayyah trotted comfortably along, matching the Lleveci's long strides. Soon the Terrans were left behind, as was her intent. Once out of the range of human hearing, she said to the warrior, "The Kaz will be looking for the crew of the downed starship."

"Obvious," Delladar Oll replied.

The sky was invisible through the leaves, but the changing quality of the light on the forest floor suggested that sunset was not far distant.

"Night will be soon?" Ayyah asked.

"Afraid dark?"

"No. You are planning to take us where?"

"Know forest well. Young me hunt here. One ridge, one valley morningwise, village of Ollsad. We go there."

"I believe that plan to be ill advised."

"So?"

"The Kaz recruit spies among Lleveci?"

"Lowland maggots only. Mountain people, no."

"No lowlander ever comes to Ollsad? No villager ever leaves the village? Such a secret will be very hard to keep."

Delladar Oll stopped abruptly, turned to face Ayyah with her mane fuzzed out indignantly. "Think my people not to trust? Think Kaz buy kinsmen? I think I cut you open, Orian."

"I think you ask much of them. I think you put them in great danger. Kazi claws reach out in all directions, even into remote communities—your neighbors, perhaps. Outworlders will be utterly conspicuous, impossible to hide, prime targets for any passing lowlander wishing to earn Kazi favor. The empire does not treat kindly those who give aid and comfort to its enemies."

Delladar Oll started off again, walking fast, following the narrow trail, head bobbing in time with her stride. "Nice talk, Orian. Make big problem. Turning round in head, not go away. Big job, get outworlders safe off Llevec." Her mane had collapsed to its normal state, and she scratched it now with long bony fingers. "I go home. Ask Mother's advice."

"We cannot survive in your forest without food and shelter."

Delladar Oll's squeak was a sound no one from any race would interpret as anything but total exasperation.

Ayyah tipped her ears back to listen for Oscar Achebe and MacDonald. Their grumbling conversation had stopped. Their walk sounded labored, careless of crunching leaves and whipping branches. "The humans tire," she said. "The slope is hard for them, and the air thinner than they are accustomed to."

Delladar Oll growled with annoyance, as if it were Ayyah's fault the humans were ill adapted to conditions she could not change. She leaned her narrow frame against the bole of a tree and, for the moment, became a part of the forest.

When the humans caught up, she told them she was leaving the trail, and they would have to stay close or be lost. MacDonald greeted her announcement with a curious lack of interest.

Oscar Achebe urged him along. "Come on, Mac. I don't think we want to be out here in the dark." MacDonald looked at his friend as if to say he didn't care much, but he made the effort.

The soil was thinner on these steeper slopes, and so were the trees. Delladar Oll set a brisk pace. The humans fell behind again almost at once and started calling to her to slow down. Ayyah waited for them, though not overly confident of her ability to track Delladar Oll through unfamiliar forest. Eventually, in spite of her hard warning, the warrior slowed her pace and gave them time to catch up.

It was early dusk when they reached the edge of the meadow. Delladar Oll held them at the verge.

"Herders' cabin," she announced. "Winter grazing. Herds gone to high pastures, I think. Wait. I check."

The vegetation was tall and a little dusty. The meadow was silent, and the smell of unfamiliar animals, though strong, was at least several days old. "The herds are not here," Ayyah said.

The Lleveci scowled at her. "Wait, Orian. I check."

"As you wish."

Whatever relationship Ayyah had managed to build with Delladar Oll, it evidently did not include trust. Perhaps, Ayyah thought, from dealing endlessly in the techniques and instruments of death, a warrior became unable to trust. Intimate knowledge of how precariously life resides within its fleshy vessel could easily lead to a form of paranoia. The psychology of warriors would be interesting, were there but time to study it.

Moving through the tall grasses and small shrubs that made the border between forest and pasture, Delladar Oll watched and listened and sniffed the evening mists that rose to the top of the grass and dissolved.

Ayyah waited beside MacDonald and Oscar Achebe as instructed, her fur fluffed out against the growing damp while Delladar Oll confirmed what Ayyah already knew.

Satisfied, the Lleveci returned and led her charges to a small building half hidden among the trees. There they found firewood, provisions, and a weapon, primitive but adequate facilities for the short term.

Laying a fire, Delladar Oll tried to explain in her curious English that these forest cabins provided for strayed hunters, lost travelers, and wayfaring strangers, as well as herders, and therefore an elaborate courtesy went with them, including a rule that no one would take more than his immediate needs from them, and would replace what was taken at the earliest opportunity.

"A sensible precaution," Ayyah said, turning her back to the flames and luxuriating in the warmth.

"All Llevec happy for Orian approval." Delladar Oll took the small energy weapon from its place on the wall and announced she would see what the forest would provide for dinner rather than dig into the cabin's stores.

Oscar Achebe joined Ayyah at the fireplace. MacDonald sat on the floor nearby, arms wrapped around his knees. He stared into the fire as if seeking an augury there, and frown lines pulled his eyebrows together. He seemed distant, as if in his mind he occupied some other space.

Perhaps such a state of mind was normal for human beings. Ayyah could not be sure it was not. It did seem unhealthy.

"MacDonald is seriously hurt?" she asked Oscar Achebe.

"Yeah, he is," the human answered. "Not in his body so much, that would heal, but in his soul."

"I do not understand this."

Oscar Achebe raked his fingers through the tight, dark curls on his head. "How can I explain? The ship was—I don't know if there's an Orian equivalent. Tell you the truth, I don't know much about your people. The ship was MacDonald's family, his honor, his reason for living. People like me, we cling to the fiction that some day we'll put all this half-mad nonsense behind us and settle down to some sort of decent life. Flying a starship was all the life MacDonald ever wanted. It's hard for him to face the fact he lost his chance."

"You are coping adequately?"

Oscar Achebe offered her a crooked smile that, in Ayyah's judgment, lacked humor. "I've been better."

He was neither amused nor friendly. The business of smiling was more complex than she had been led to believe.

Before full dark Delladar Oll returned. She had the weapon slung across her back and a dead and bleeding small animal in each hand. Her hands were red with blood, and drops of it fell onto the cabin floor.

She dropped the two limp carcasses onto the tabletop, then dug into a small cupboard to one side of the fireplace for a small steel knife, which she handed to MacDonald. He took it, but looked as if he had no idea why he had it. "What do you want me to do with this?" he asked.

Delladar Oll hung the weapon back on the wall where it belonged. "Figure out." She rummaged around for a container and water to clean herself.

Ayyah went outside.

She sat quietly among the tall grasses contemplating the darkening sky. The air was damp and cold. The pain in her stomach must be from the blow to her head, she told herself. Her revulsion was psychological and cultural, not physical. Every generation of Oriani made anew the conscious decision not to kill animals for food.

The old instincts were not gone, only buried. Much of her disgust might be laid down to knowing that deep within, warm, red meat still had an appeal.

She did not want to believe that very much.

Something moved in the night.

"Danger here," Delladar Oll said.

"Yes," Ayyah answered without looking at the Lleveci. "I have heard the predators hunting."

"Go in now."

"I would prefer to wait until you have finished feeding," the Orian said, and the saying of it brought forth an image of savage, ravenous scavengers, mad with the taste of blood, furiously tearing at a carcass. The primordial appeal of gory flesh vanished with the image.

"We eat."

"Yes."

"You, too."

"I cannot."

The word Delladar Oll used did not exactly mean liar, but something close to it. She pointed with a long bony finger at Ayyah's mouth where the fangs indented the lower lip. "Not say cannot. Can. Say will not."

Her anatomy was something she was born with, not something she had chosen. She could not be held morally responsible for having a carnivore's teeth. Ayyah was in better control of herself now. The flash of embarrassment the Lleveci's words brought forth was quickly suppressed. Calmly she said, "Believe as you wish."

"Starve you, can't fix."

"It is so."

"Stupid Orian, kill yourself, no fault mine."

"Agreed."

Exasperated, Delladar Oll turned away.

"Warrior," Ayyah commanded. Even in the dim moonlight, Ayyah could see the Lleveci stiffen with annoyance at herself for stopping.

"You need not contend with me," Ayyah told her.

Delladar Oll grunted, neither agreeing nor disagreeing.

"There is no contest here. We pursue the same objectives. We are much alike, I think."

The Lleveci hissed, thoroughly insulted. Gathering up her indignation, she stalked across the field to the cabin. Plainly, she did not intend to go hungry to soothe any finicky Orian's ruffled feelings.

Alone in the dark, Ayyah reviewed her actions and found them wanting. At present, Delladar Oll was as important to achieving her goal as MacDonald was. A way would have to be found to reduce the friction between them.

Llevec's small, distant moon crawled across the sky. When sufficient time had elapsed that she thought the others had finished their meal, Ayyah went inside, hoping to find a little warmth on a cold, alien night.

Delladar Oll rose at first light to find the Orian had come in during the night and was sleeping curled up in front of the fireplace with her fur fluffed out, trying to absorb what heat remained in the dead embers. For the first time it occurred to the warrior that Ayyah would be finding Llevec a bit too cold for comfort. Some bit of sympathy was touched. She had been cold and hungry herself on occasion, though if anyone had asked why she was rummaging in a cupboard for a blanket to spread over the sleeping Orian, she would have said that if the alien got sick, she would be ten times the problem she already was.

The Orian's head rose during this operation, and the yellow eyes looked up, absorbing the incident without judgment. Then they closed again, and the head dropped back to rest on crossed forearms. Delladar Oll left to begin her journey through the forest.

It was midafternoon before she reached Ollsad. The village was quiet, the population about its summer's work. The men had long since left the streambank; it was occupied now by a group of young children and their teacher, who were exploring the art of setting fish traps in the cold water.

However busy they might be, the villagers were always alert, and so by the time Delladar Oll had crossed the stream, an Aunt on sentry duty was aware of her arrival and had come to meet her.

The Aunt agreed to carry a message to the chief elder, and Delladar Oll retired to her parents' home to await the elder's reply. It came quickly, so again her visit was cut short by a summons to the house in the center of the village.

By the elder's fire, Delladar Oll learned that the barge had landed safely, not far from its intended objective, high on the Korall glacier, and that its cargo was being distributed to the defenders of the mountain passes.

"You have done well," the elder said.

"No, Mother," the warrior answered, happy to speak again to one of her own and leave the awkward inadequacies of an alien tongue. "There are problems. I need your counsel."

A physician was dispatched to the herders' cabin, on the fastest mount available. Other matters took more discussion and planning. The circle around the elder's fire grew ever larger as Mother called her advisors, both military and civil, and as she sought the opinions of those in the village who had experience of humans. Experience of the Kaz was available in abundance. Few adult Lleveci had escaped at least one brush with the invaders.

Slowly, carefully, a scheme was hatched. Over the evening meal served around the fire, it was refined and polished, with long necks beginning to sway in agreement. By the time the members of the circle were drifting one by one to their homes and their own beds, the consensus was that it was workable, fitting, and worthy. Other people in other places might have thought it reckless, foolhardy, supported by a risk out of all proportion to the gain. The warriors of Ollsad considered it no more than MacDonald had earned, no less than the Kaz might learn to expect from the proud people of the high valleys.

Furthermore, it was an expedition that would appeal to the adventuresome spirits of young warriors kept too long idle, waiting to move against the enemy. One swift thrust to the Kazi gut, and gone, just to remind the invaders that the warriors had not forgotten them.

The advisors drifted home and remembered being younger.

Finally only the elder and Delladar Oll remained by the fireside with the bones of the meal and the dregs of the wine.

"Speak to me of the Orian," the elder said.

"Lluruent," the warrior answered, referring to a large, slow reptile they both knew. It spent most of its time basking in the sun. When approached, it roared and puffed itself up with a great display of ferocity, but it was actually helpless to defend itself. A child could kill one with a stick. The meat was edible but not much appreciated, being soft and tasteless. Its name was a term of contempt among Lleveci.

"This is not what I understand of Oriani," the elder said.

Delladar Oll held her tongue.

"When I was very young," the elder said, "people spoke of Orion as the sheathed sword. When I was not so young, I heard it said it cost the Kaz more to take Orion than they bargained for, that they could have had a dozen other worlds for the price.

"Possibly what I heard was exaggerated."

"I do not know Oriani. I know only this Orian, who is mad."

"How so?"

"She speaks of schemes to defeat the Kaz. All alone, with only MacDonald's ship to carry her deep into Kazi space. As if a thousand billion others have not dreamed the same dream and found it futile."

"As I dream, my daughter?"

"Mother, I did not mean . . ."

"What does the Orian dream?"

"She speaks of a world that is not on Kazi charts. She thinks to find some magic there, I guess. It is a dead dream now, with the ship wrecked."

"It is not necessarily so. Come," the elder said. She rose from her seat by the fire with difficulty. She was tired, and it showed.

She led Delladar Oll into the back of the house, where tradition gave way to technology. There, in a room bright with lighting panels, among the best equipment current information science had to offer that warrior clans could afford, the elder called star charts onto a big screen.

"Show me where the Orian dreams there is a lost world."

"Hey, Mac," Oscar called from the cabin door.

MacDonald roused from his lethargy, vaguely curious about what Oscar wanted. The bed was a woven lattice of what looked like rawhide hung in a wooden frame and wasn't all that comfortable anyway.

Oscar was standing in the doorway staring across the meadow.

Ayyah had joined him. MacDonald looked over her head in what seemed to be the right direction.

The beast was large, the offspring of a mating between a dinosaur and an elephant, shrunk down to give a shoulder about two meters high and then modified by adding, a silly afterthought, the typical long, thin, Lleveci neck. The Lleveci rider stopped it some distance away. He called and gestured to them, but they couldn't understand what he was saying.

"Maybe you'd better get that little gun of Oll's," MacDonald said.

"No," Ayyah objected.

Oscar slipped inside and picked the energy weapon off the wall. "I hope you know how to run this thing," he said when he returned to the doorway.

"I trust you," MacDonald said.

"Oh, boy."

Ayyah stared at MacDonald as if she wanted to see through his skin. "You cannot damage this person who is innocent of wrongdoing."

"Everybody's dangerous to us right now. You know that as well as I do."

"You will shoot this one to elude an imaginary danger?" Ayyah placed herself between gun and target, facing Oscar.

"Ayyah, damn it," Oscar protested.

"If these people wished us harm," Ayyah pointed out, "surely they could assemble sufficient numbers to be certain of achieving that goal."

There was a small silence, during which the rider dismounted and approached with the outspread arms and bobbing head that would have signified, if they had better understood their hosts, nonhostile intent.

"She has a point," Oscar said.

"Bear in mind any well-intentioned wayfaring stranger carrying the good word to the nearest village could do us in," MacDonald said.

"I don't think I can shoot an innocent bystander because of that. Besides, this guy's pretty brave. He doesn't know what the hell we're saying, but he's coming on anyway. If he had murder on his mind, you'd think he'd find a safer technique."

It was a good argument. To be honest with himself, MacDonald didn't think he would be able to shoot the guy either.

The refugees backed into the room and allowed the Lleveci to approach.

He was carrying a largish bundle. In the patch of sunshine on the floor by the open door, he unrolled the bundle and laid its contents out for the others to see.

Ayyah, ever curious, was the first to approach. She examined the objects and tried out her few words of mispronounced Lleveci, to the newcomer's delight.

"This one is a physician," she said.

"You sure of that?" MacDonald asked.

In response, Ayyah squatted in the patch of sunlight with her tail around her feet and let the Lleveci examine the bloody mess over her eye.

When it came his turn, MacDonald had to admit that the doctor did as much as anyone could expect with patients whose physiology he understood scarcely at all.

When MacDonald went to find her, Ayyah was sitting in the meadow with her wound turned toward the noon sun. The shaved patch over her eye showed her gray skin, with the cut the doctor had neatly glued together making a black line through it. She acknowledged his presence with a tilt of ears.

He and Oscar had been trying to think of some course of action, and they had produced between them a depressing dearth of possibilities. Without much hope, he trudged through the tall grass to see if Ayyah had thought of anything.

Before he had a chance to say more than "Hello," he became aware that the meadow was ringed with Lleveci riders.

"I see them, MacDonald," Ayyah murmured.

They were full maned and well armed; blasters and long-barreled laser rifles were much in evidence, in addition to more traditional weapons. The warriors looked all too capable of taking care of themselves in a fight.

MacDonald hardly had time to work up a good sweat before Delladar Oll separated from the warriors and rode toward him. The others followed, leading pack animals and spare mounts.

He had some of his nerve back by time the Lleveci pulled her mount to a halt nearby and slid down over the animal's shoulder.

"What's this all about?" he asked crossly.

"Having plan, MacDonald."

"And the plan is to scare the outworlders to death, is that it?"

Delladar Oll frowned, then bobbed her head in a Lleveci-style shrug. "Make camp. Then talk," she said.

The warriors were as efficient as they were fierce. In short order they had unpacked their animals and staked them out to graze, then set up a couple of temporary shelters of tightly woven fabric stretched over bent steel frames that, unlike their permanent buildings, were colored with muted greens and brown, and blended into the scenery and became invisible. They laid a fire, stalked and killed some unfortunate forest beast half the size of a cow, and had the meat roasting before the outworlders had time to get used to their presence. MacDonald was suitably impressed.

From the packs, Delladar Oll presented clean clothes to the humans. Oscar's wide shoulders threatened the tunic's seams, and the leggings on both of them had to be rolled several turns at the bottom.

"I don't think we're quite the right shape," Oscar said.

MacDonald shrugged. The stuff was clean, and that was a big advantage. A lot could be forgiven on that account.

There was also a package of spiced biscuits made of ground grain. Delladar Oll handed this to Ayyah with a degree of resentment that was palpable. It looked as if she still thought the Orian should have the courtesy to make do with the food available.

"Mother says perhaps Orian find this agreeable."

Ayyah nodded her thanks and tucked into one of the biscuits immediately.

"Now what do we do?" MacDonald asked.

"Leave here. Long ride. Two days."

"On one of those?" he asked, regarding with a jaundiced eye the scaly animals tearing up the thigh-high grass.

"Yes."

That explained the clothes. They were suitable for riding. MacDonald made no effort to hide his misgivings. The beasts had thick hides and surly expressions.

He had even more serious reservations about the plan.

Inside the cabin, with his elbows on the map of the port city of Rullenahesad spread over the table and as many curious Lleveci as could fit inside looking over his shoulder, he said, "We can't get away with it. The spaceport's crawling with Kaz, and like you said, there's no way to tell which Lleveci are loyal to the Kazi regime."

He said that and meant it. Nonetheless, a little spark came back into his outlook. Any plan, even a stupid, hopeless one, was better than none. He asked Oscar with a look.

"I don't see all that many alternatives," Oscar said. "We can't hide in the forest forever. Someone's bound to come by sooner or later, and we definitely stand out from the natives. And if we could, what then? Are we going to spend the rest of our lives watching the trees grow? I'm not even sure I like these trees. They're peculiar-looking things."

"Ayyah?" MacDonald asked.

"We need a vessel. This is the only source."

MacDonald raised his eyebrows as if in disbelief. But he wasn't completely unhappy with what they were saying. He was more than willing to be convinced. "I've never been inside a Kazi ship," he warned, and realized much later only Oscar understood the warning, and Oscar was willing to disregard any hazard if it would get him away from the planet. The man truly didn't like those trees.

Delladar Oll continued as if she hadn't heard. "Has condition."

"Ah," MacDonald said. He had been expecting some such string attached. Life rarely offered something for nothing. "But I'm all out of guns."

"Condition is: Take Orian where she wants. Mother wishes."

"Eh, what?"

Delladar Oll didn't bother to repeat herself. She let him chew it over at his own speed.

"Do you realize she doesn't even know where she wants to go?"

"Yes."

"Forget it. The deal's off. Tell your mother no way."

Night fell quickly in the Lleveci mountains. In the cabin, MacDonald and Oscar Achebe chose to make their dinner from the bones of yesterday's meat. Delladar Oll ate her evening meal with the warriors, leaving the outworlders to fend for themselves. Ayyah took two of the Lleveci biscuits to a small rise in the meadow where she could be alone for a time. She was feeling the stress of the constant presence of the others and their endless gnawing away at dead things.

A short distance from the knoll, the warriors' fires winked in the dark. In the black shadows of the forest, night birds called.

The air was cool. Ayyah shivered. She would endure it. There was much to think of, and she needed the solitude.

The Lleveci plan was audacious, perhaps desperate, possibly workable, but pointless without MacDonald's cooperation. She needed to turn him from his stubborn refusal to consider it. But how, when she knew so little about him?

Oscar Achebe, a shadow in the dark, left the cabin and crossed the meadow, intent, it seemed, on visiting with the warriors. It would be interesting to know what he would get from the visit, having no common language. Observation of the interaction was not possible. She had other business to attend to. Ayyah left her private knoll and returned to the building.

The fire inside had burned down to embers, but the room was pleasantly warm. A small chemical lantern glowed on the table where the map still lay spread out. With a short length of tree stem cut flat on either end serving him as a stool, MacDonald sat with his chin in his hand staring at the chart.

"The scheme could work, MacDonald," Ayyah said.

He looked up and frowned at her. "Look at you," he said. "You're shaking. What were you doing out there in the cold?"

"I wished time to think. I took valuable assets from my community when I left. I owe better use of them than to end my days on Llevec."

"Not much you can do about it."

Ayyah tucked her tail to one side and backed close to the fire. The heat was worth any amount of smoky smell sticking to her fur. "Oscar Achebe said you always wanted to be a pilot, nothing else. This is so?"

"Yeah, I guess. Even when I was a kid, my mom could always get me to do my homework by reminding me starship captains needed their schooling."

"Homework?"

"Studies."

"Yes. The Kaz were on Earth then?"

"Hell, yes. Way back to my grandfather's time, I guess."

"Humans commanding starships is allowed under Kazi rule?"

"Until recently. Until six weeks before I was due to take command of the *Great Bear*. Weren't enough bugs to do everything. But they got feeling nervous about unreliable humans overhead with guns. Also Earth was losing a lot of high-tech talent whenever ships put in to neutral ports."

"As it lost you."

"Well, yeah. I don't suppose it was that much different for other people."

"How?"

MacDonald's thoughts grew distant. He stared past Ayyah into the flickering red coals. "It was a long time ago. I jumped ship at Ioror. Not very romantic or honorable."

"Leaving the Fleet was so simply accomplished?"

"I had help."

Ayyah sensed a delicate balance between them. A wrong word would drop MacDonald back into his taciturn black mood. She could only hope the right one would win her the insights she needed.

"The helper must have been a person of determination and courage," she said.

"He was. Martin Halloran was a damned good captain. He knew more about how to make a starship dance than I learned from all the books I ever studied and ten years of practical applications. I liked him the first day I met him." MacDonald continued to stare at the fire. He was hardly talking to her anymore.

"He had to retire in a few months. He didn't want to turn the *Great Bear* over to a bug, any more than I wanted him to. I had just transferred over, getting to know the ship, when the word came.

"We had a two-week run out to the Arkkyne Sector and back, and then a bug was going to take over. I was still in shock, I guess. Halloran called me into his cabin and said we were probably going to have a bit of engine trouble about the time we reached the Ioror Asteroid. I remember him so well, leaning back in his chair, grinning over the desk. 'Hell of a place,' he said. 'Every time we put in to Ioror, somebody gets lost. A little point I thought you ought to know.'

"Quite a few of us got lost that stop. Me included. Halloran told me to leave the port as soon as I could and good luck, and he shook my hand, even though he was going to have to go home with the rest of the crew and take the blame for a massive desertion. I heard later the engine trouble showed up again and the *Great Bear* fell out of Earth orbit and crashed into the Pacific. The crew got off, but Halloran went down with her. She was a good, solid ship."

"You left Ioror immediately?"

He looked up at her. "As immediately as I could. I was pretty damned lost and helpless. The Port Authority only wanted us somewhere else before the Kaz came looking for us. I'd never done sweet bugger all outside of the Fleet. I didn't know how to deal with civilians. Then I met this guy called Achebe who took a shine to me and got me a berth as navigator on a ship bound for Riga. It was a rusty tin can hauling petroleum products, a flying bomb, but we made it."

Ayyah turned to toast her other side. "But you were Fleet trained and served with the Fleet a long time?"

"Man and boy, fifteen years, eight months, and an odd number of days." Facing the fire, Ayyah could not see his expression, but she heard the bitterness in his voice.

"Matters of loyalty do not disturb you?"

"They might, if the Fleet hadn't become just another Kazi tool. Loyal to what, the great and glorious empire?"

"Within the system as it existed you functioned exceptionally well for fifteen years, eight months, and an odd number of days."

"I don't know how exceptional. Don't believe everything Oscar tells you."

"Then you left your career, your homeworld, your family."

"No family." A curious note entered MacDonald's voice. Ayyah thought perhaps what he said was not entirely true.

"You spoke of a mother."

"She was dead by then."

"Your father?"

MacDonald snorted and shifted restlessly. "We weren't on speaking terms."

"You know a reason for this?"

"He didn't approve of the way I lived my life. Why do you care, anyway?"

This subject was not a good one. Mention of his male parent put MacDonald instantly on the defensive. Perhaps Oscar Achebe would have more information. Ayyah changed direction.

"Something changed that you felt compelled to rebel against the Kaz?"

"If you mean did I suddenly get religion and realize in a blinding flash that I had spent all my life till then serving the evil empire and I must now atone for my sins, no, nothing like that. The command I thought was in my hands was yanked away. Halloran was a man I respected and he died. A couple of straws that broke the camel's back. I guess I always loved the Fleet and hated the Kaz. Pop never understood that.''

"I do not understand the camel."

"It's just an expression. And why am I telling you all this stuff anyway? You figure on writing my biography?"

Ayyah shook her head, human fashion. "I think not. It has a drab and lifeless ending."

MacDonald's cheeks puffed out indignantly, but Oscar Achebe came in then, and the mood was lost. Ayyah went out to talk to Delladar Oll.

She found the Lleveci by the embers of a campfire. The warriors had retired, and she was alone. She started at Ayyah's approach.

"Call you come, or end up knife in gut," she said crossly.

"I will remember this." Ayyah squatted down on her haunches and watched the fire with the Lleveci. After a time she said, "Humans often speak first and think later."

Delladar Oll grunted noncommittally. Her quiet moment had been ruined. "Oscar say MacDonald lose heart. Wrong. Lose spine," she said.

"I believe this to be temporary. In any case, he can be managed. Toward that end, learning more of his relationship with his estranged father would be of value."

The Lleveci looked at her skeptically.

"Fatherhood carries much meaning for humans. MacDonald is vulnerable concerning his father's disapproval. I suggest you speak to MacDonald again. Remind him that your scheme is the only way off Llevec for him. Remind him that Oscar Achebe is in favor of the plan. Speak to him of the wasted effort of many teachers. Speak to him of the courage of one called Halloran."

Delladar Oll grunted again and turned back to the fire. Ayyah returned to the warmth of the cabin.

The *Kokkon*

"Tell me again," MacDonald said unhappily, "why we're doing this."

They were crouched in the undergrowth just beyond the perimeter of the landing area. In this comparatively wild region, the city had not approached the landing field too closely.

"Because the Lleveci chief—head—whatever she is—offered to let us find our own way home if we didn't want to go along with the plan. Besides, Delladar Oll was about to abandon us right there in the forest," Oscar answered. "And somebody, thank God, made you see the light."

The Lleveci warriors looked to their arms and gabbled quietly together. Ayyah, crouched in the weeds a little apart, had become almost invisible. MacDonald regarded her with a jaundiced eye. She had taken advantage of him in a moment of melancholy, and he was going to settle accounts with her at the first opportunity. Assuming he got an opportunity. Considering the activity around them, it seemed less and less likely.

"It's absolutely insane, you know," he told Oscar.

"I know."

"A couple of smart guys like us should be able to figure a way out of this mess on our own."

"You'd think so."

"I take it you haven't had a stroke of genius."

"I guess not, or we wouldn't be here."

Delladar Oll signaled impatiently to them to keep their voices down.

MacDonald and Oscar sat down side by side flat on the unyielding dirt and kept quiet. It was a chance for them to catch their breaths after a nerve-wracking passage through Rullenahesad sneaking down alleys, hugging shadows, and dashing across streets.

Before them rose an apparently impenetrable fence.

"Fifty years ago this would have been a force field," Oscar whispered. "Things are going downhill."

"I am meagerly grateful for technological decay," MacDonald whispered back. "It doesn't seem to make a lot of difference from this point of view."

The ultrasteel mesh was new, high, and electrified. Within its boundaries, artificial lighting made the area almost as bright as day. The ground for fifty meters or so beyond the fence was barren, without even vegetation to cover its nakedness. Beyond the empty strip were buildings and cargo handling facilities. The older structures were typically Lleveci, brightly colored with pointed roofs. The few newer Kazi buildings were featureless gray masses often without windows. Among them, cranes raised stark arms. A line of ground vehicles stretched out toward the landing pad, waiting.

Between the buildings and the pad was another stretch of bare dirt, designed to ensure that combustible materials were kept a good distance from any potential disaster on the pad. A mobile crane was being maneuvered into place alongside a newly landed shuttle that crouched on its skids as if ready to spring into the air the minute it finished with this ground-based business.

"Now what?" MacDonald asked when Delladar Oll came his way.

Around the shuttle, a scattering of people moved with brisk efficiency under the lights, mainly tall narrow Lleveci forms, but with several squat, dark Kaz among them.

"Turn out lights. Kaz no good in night," Delladar Oll said in response to MacDonald's question.

"I don't do so good in night either," MacDonald pointed out. "Your moon leaves something to be desired as a source of light, you know."

Delladar Oll turned to look at him, but the shadows were too thick for him to make out her expression. It would be her usual exasperation at his stating the obvious. He was sure of it.

"Orian can. Follow her."

"The Orian has a name."

Delladar Oll didn't answer. If she knew that her disregard of Ayyah as an individual irritated him, she plainly didn't care.

She was busy watching the activity inside the fence, trying to pick out a pattern in the movements of the workers.

MacDonald persisted, trying to discover something of her intentions for the immediate future. He didn't like flying blind. He didn't like being treated as a mere appendage to the enterprise.

"So what do we do?" he asked skeptically. "Just walk in and ask them if they'd mind turning the lights out for a few minutes while we make off with the shuttle?"

"Just so. Few inside Kaz. Most Lleveci. Use Lleveci easy."

One trouble dealing with aliens was that many normal psychological devices went down the tubes. Oll understood nothing about sarcasm. The warrior stared through the fence, not looking at MacDonald. "Too bad lowlanders gutless maggots. Easy clean slime-eating Kaz off Llevec, one season, maggots had guts."

"This is not so," Ayyah said from her slightly remote position. She did not turn to talk to them. "You do your kinsmen an injustice. Where there is resistance, there would be more Kaz, and more, as many as needed, until the resistance collapsed under the weight of them."

"No kin lowlanders," Delladar Oll said.

"The act of denial changes nothing," Ayyah answered.

"Maybe we should argue about it some other time," Oscar suggested.

"No argue. Orian knows nothing."

"Any idea how we get in?" MacDonald asked to change the subject.

"Kaz provide. Assall Oll find way. Follow."

One of the other warriors nodded acknowledgment of Delladar Oll's brief order. He took the lead, following the fence from bush to shrub for a while, then angling off toward what appeared to be a group of residences. MacDonald scrambled to his feet and hurried to keep up, with Oscar right behind. Neither wanted to be left to fend for himself in Rullenahesad.

A short distance farther on, Assall Oll halted the group in the shadow of a wall, motioned for silence, and pointed toward a large mound of compacted dirt. A concave light-gathering mirror was mounted on top. A wide tunnel sloping downward opened into the side. Soft, greenish light glowed within.

Assall Oll raised his blaster and melted the mirror. The snarl of it seemed dangerously loud.

"Should we be making such a racket?" MacDonald whispered.

Delladar Oll dismissed his worry with a bob of her head. "Bring guard," she explained.

"Oh," MacDonald said, not entirely approving. The Lleveci watched the opening intently.

A dark, many-legged form appeared in the tunnel. Assall Oll raised his weapon again.

"No," Ayyah protested.

She was ignored. The Kazi fell, smoking.

Assall Oll urged them forward. The group entered the tunnel, Lleveci necks bent into a U, humans hunched over, the Orian leaning forward with her tail up to maintain her balance, to avoid the low ceiling. The warriors led the way, the outworlders trailed behind. At an intersection of tunnels, the group halted while individuals were dispatched in each of three directions. There was more blaster fire. The three returned.

"I think we should get out of here," MacDonald said. He was not the least bit comfortable with what was happening. "They're bound to have sensors in operation."

"Just so," Delladar Oll agreed with equanimity. "Time not much."

"What are we looking for?"

"Power source."

Another intersection. The scouts went out and returned. The Lleveci chattered excitedly among themselves. MacDonald's spine prickled with the anticipation of innumerable Kaz closing in from behind.

They took the lefthand branch. In short way it opened out into a largish, egg-shape room.

The room was cluttered with machinery. The Lleveci fell upon the equipment with fiendish enthusiasm. Sparks flew. Most of the lights went out. More Lleveci chatter, more sparks.

Suddenly it was dark.

Utterly dark. As dark as a hole in space.

A palpable darkness that swirled in close.

Moist warmth pervaded the darkness. MacDonald hadn't noticed it before. The mildewy smell of Kaz was nauseatingly strong.

A dim hand light bloomed among the Lleveci. Welcome because it gave the eyes a place to focus, it was woefully inadequate illumination. The warriors started back the way they had come. MacDonald hurried after them, fearful of losing sight of the small light, stumbling blindly along. He caromed off the wall near the entrance of the tunnel.

A small furry hand took his and guided him to a hold on a muscular tail that felt as if he were holding a hairy snake.

"Mac!" Oscar called.

"Here." MacDonald fumbled until he found Oscar's hand. This unlikely train followed the Lleveci. Seeing them in his mind's eye, MacDonald had to suppress a giggle. He wasn't normally given to fits of giggling. Your nerves are showing, boy, he thought.

The warriors moved quickly, without hesitation, bypassing some openings more felt than seen in the darkness, choosing others by means MacDonald could not guess at.

A little farther along, the group edged around a pair of stalled Kaz, invisible statues in the black, apparent only when touched, when the flesh crawled at the contact. The Lleveci carrying the light paused long enough to plunge his knife once into each of them. MacDonald felt a shudder run down the tail he was holding.

"I don't like this," Oscar said. "I think I'm discovering I'm a bit claustrophobic."

"I don't like it either, Oscar Achebe," Ayyah said. "These violent people make unpleasant allies."

"They seem to know what they're doing," MacDonald said.

"But what they do is not right. They destroy for the sake of destroying, kill for no reason."

"Ayyah," Oscar said, "sweet, gentle philosophies will not get the Kaz off Orion."

Ayyah did not answer. Her tail grew tense under MacDonald's hand.

The tunnel was angling upward, and around a sharp bend there was a glow of light.

The warriors stopped. Clipped-mane Lleveci were working in the lighted room ahead, passing the tunnel mouth from time to time, intent on their business. Enough light washed back into the tunnel to make MacDonald feel confident of letting go of his guide. Delladar Oll moved back to speak to her charges.

"Wait here," she said.

"Now what?" MacDonald asked for the second time in an hour.

"Wait," Delladar Oll said.

MacDonald waited because he couldn't think of anything else to do, not because inactivity pleased him. He was in the dark in more ways than one, and he didn't like it.

One of the workers hesitated in the tunnel mouth, peering into the dark, aware of something amiss. By the time his moment of confusion was over, he was surrounded by two dozen warriors with drawn weapons. Warriors and workers moved out of sight, into the room. After a long, tense silence, Delladar Oll came back into the tunnel to get her outworlders.

The workers stood in a line with their backs to a wall. Waving guns, the warriors faced them. Much sharp Lleveci dialogue went back and forth, but no one seemed satisfied with the outcome. Dials and meters lined the walls of the room. A computer terminal stood near the center. The large window looked out over the field.

A worker was chosen, yanked out of the line, and questioned sharply. She was the picture of abject misery. Her head ducked this way and that. Timing it to a this-way swing, the warrior whacked her on the side of the neck with his blaster. The worker howled. MacDonald winced. Ayyah started forward. MacDonald held her with a hand on her arm.

"They know what they're doing," he said.

She turned and looked at him, into him, as if she were studying his internal anatomy. She shook her arm out of his grasp, less than happy.

"This is what you wanted, what you insisted on," MacDonald said.

"You hold me responsible for this brutality? And for this, you assault me?"

MacDonald looked at his hand and her arm. "Assault?"

She continued to stare at him.

"We aren't going to walk in here and take a starship without encountering some opposition. There's no other way, Ayyah."

Ayyah moved away from him as if from a contaminating influence. He could see her withdrawing into herself, distancing herself from an ugly, sinful world.

"You're going to have to make up your mind," MacDonald said.

Ayyah spoke from her internal space. "I find difficult the choice between these lives and other lives."

"You've already chosen."

She regarded him gravely. "You are perceptive, MacDonald.

And having chosen, one should not regret the necessary. Yet the voice of decency cries within ."

"Nobody said it would be easy."

She seemed unnerved by their moment of almost-rapport. "This nobody was quite right. It is not."

The wounded worker crossed to the computer terminal and poked at it for a moment. On the field, the lights went out.

In a beat, some other, lesser ones came on.

Much more excited Lleveci chatter ensued. The wounded worker's head bobbled frantically, and she sounded close to hysteria. Finally she was shoved roughly back into the line.

A warrior unlatched the window and swung it wide on its hinges. She unslung the laser rifle she had been carrying across her back, settled herself in the casement, and began potting away at the lights. She was remarkably accurate, considering the distance.

On the field, the ground vehicle nearest the shuttle had made a sharp turn and was heading in their direction. The Kaz on foot were hustling along, too. MacDonald began to think seriously about lines of retreat.

Light after light exploded and died. It was getting dark out there.

"Come," Delladar Oll said, urging everyone toward an open doorway.

"What about her?" MacDonald asked, jerking a thumb toward the marksman still busy at the window. Delladar Oll did not answer, just gave him a push toward a flight of stairs leading down. Another time, he would have resented that. In fact, he did resent it. He had a strong urge to turn around and push her back.

A heavy wooden door at the bottom let them out onto the field.

A clipped-mane Lleveci outside looked as if he might have thought to stop them, but a few sharp words from Delladar Oll and a glance up at the window above where the marksman's form was neatly silhouetted against the light discouraged him. He stepped aside.

They jogged out onto the barren ground. It had become too dark on the field for human eyes to guide a man accurately. Few of the emergency lights were still working. MacDonald stumbled on a crack in the tarmac. The Kaz on foot had come to a dead stop.

"You have to admire Delladar Oll's ingenuity," MacDonald said as Oscar huffed up alongside. "Darkness as a weapon is something my tactics course neglected to mention."

"You could see why Kazi teachers might not want to bring it up," Oscar answered.

Some of the Lleveci workers made halfhearted attempts to head them off, but when Delladar Oll fired her blaster right at the feet of one of them, spraying him thoroughly with hot mud, Lleveci opposition crumbled. The workers milled around aimlessly and kept out of the way.

Then they had to deal with the vehicle. Only one was on the move. Either the others were unmanned, or the drivers had decided they didn't want to become involved.

The warriors had been firing blasters at the wheels without significant effect. The vehicle swerved, heading directly toward them. The group scattered, except for one warrior who held his ground. He stood directly in the machine's path, legs spread wide, elbows braced against his sides, blaster steady in a two-handed grip.

"Oh, ye gods and demons." Oscar groaned.

"Get out of there, you damned fool!" MacDonald shouted, forgetting the warrior couldn't understand him, much less hear him.

Ayyah had turned and was running toward him. She was fast, but even her speed was insufficient. The warrior fired into the windshield at nearly point-blank range. Then the wheels rolled over him. Ayyah dived and rolled to get out of the way.

"Orian idiot," Delladar Oll complained.

The vehicle continued on its way, curving off on an erratic course.

"He didn't have to do that," MacDonald muttered to no one in particular. Delladar Oll gave the stunned human a solid push in the center of his back.

"Go," she ordered.

MacDonald whipped around, fists clenched, ready to do battle. "You just quit that!" he barked.

"Finding spine, MacDonald?" the Lleveci asked. She seemed amused. "Go now. You, me, fight later, yes?"

The warrior's crumpled body lay abandoned on the field. Ayyah was bent over it, but MacDonald did not doubt the man was dead. "Go. Let living live," Delladar Oll demanded. "One died well." MacDonald tried to swallow the taste of bile in the back of his throat.

He stumbled over the crane's extended leg and confronted the shuttle with its hatch open to form a ramp, a Kazi adaptation to what otherwise was a Lleveci ship. The lights were on inside, and the hatchway was full of shifting Kazi forms in silhouette, armed and nervous, trapped in the shuttle by the darkness outside but perfectly functional within.

On the roof of the building they had just left a searchlight bloomed. Its bright circle began questing over the field. On another building, another came on, and elsewhere, another and another. The defenders were getting organized.

"Do you remember some old saw about being caught between a rock and a hard place?" Oscar asked.

"It seems to me I do."

"Now what?" Oscar asked.

"That's my line," MacDonald said.

"The cargo hatch is open. You think we could get up the crane?"

MacDonald regarded the long arm of the crane with its triangular bracing. "I guess we'd better try. The Kaz aren't going to give us too much time to debate."

When he told her what he and Oscar planned to do, Delladar Oll nodded her approval, handed each of them a weapon, and assigned half the warriors to follow. The other half would stay and keep the Kaz in the hatchway busy.

"Be careful what you shoot at," MacDonald warned. "If we damage the shuttle, we are in serious trouble."

"Not pass Kaz, all dead anyway," Delladar Oll answered reasonably. Too bloody true. He wished she hadn't said that.

The tall, thin Lleveci warriors slipped through the service opening in the roof of the crane's cab with no trouble, but it was a tight fit for MacDonald, and even tighter for Oscar's wide shoulders. For a while it seemed Oscar would be permanently stuck in the hole, and he reacted less than kindly to the others' efforts to help him through. His vigorous curses made it plain he did not appreciate leaving a portion of his skin on the edge of the opening.

Blasters snarled below. A distant sound of motors came in on the still air.

The bracing on the crane's arm made a tolerable ladder. From the top MacDonald could look straight down along the cable into the open hatch, or back across the field. There seemed to be a flurry of activity near the edge of the field, which gave him a renewed sense of urgency.

A spotlight found them. A missed shot sprayed them with hot sparks from the crane's metalwork. They slid down the cable faster than was comfortable. The rough twists of wire abraded hands and ankles. Crouched in the empty cargo hold trying to get his bearings, Oscar complained, "I'm not going to have enough hide left to hold me together pretty soon."

The hold was dark except for a small light over a ladder at the far end, so MacDonald felt secure in assuming no Kaz were around. Unfortunately, he also realized he couldn't communicate with his troops. He could only touch one of the warriors on the shoulder and point up the ladder. The Lleveci got the idea immediately and passed it on.

In the lighted passageway above, MacDonald paused to recall the layout of a typical Lleveci small craft, staring up at the air ducts, cables, and plumbing overhead to aid his memory. The Lleveci warriors didn't wait for instructions. They divided and swarmed through the vessel, weapons at the ready. MacDonald called Oscar and followed the group going forward, having no hope of controlling events.

They met no one by the time they reached a junction. The Kaz seemed to have gathered on the flight deck with the intent of holding off the raiders until help arrived from outside.

They might just be able to do it, too. MacDonald couldn't imagine help would be long arriving. One thing about fighting the Kaz, no matter how many you beat, there were always more on the way. They sensed one another's trouble.

A few feet ahead the passage opened onto the flight deck, and no door closed the entryway. The Kaz, now aware of someone coming from the rear, had the advantage of being able to fire down a hallway free of obstructions. The raiders had to be wary of instrumentation and controls when firing back.

A Kazi appeared at the end of the passage. MacDonald and Oscar dived one way, the Lleveci the other, into the arms of the intersection. The blast scorched the wall behind them. It seemed as if they had gone as far as they could go without committing suicide. One Kazi could hold them off forever. They were going to be of minimal help to those outside unless they could find some way to get onto the flight deck other than down the murderous passageway.

"If I held you up, could you get the grate off that duct?" Oscar asked.

MacDonald eyed the pipe in question. "It's pretty narrow."

"I think a Lleveci could make it."

"You might be right."

The Lleveci didn't think so, or didn't understand. They declined MacDonald's invitation signaled across the main passage.

"Maybe we could cut the cables, turn the lights out in there, too," Oscar suggested.

"And risk losing all the controls. We'd make this shuttle into a very expensive reprocessing bin with us already inside."

"Man, we don't have a lot of time to think it over."

"I know."

A tall Lleveci dashed across the main corridor, firing toward the flight deck as he went. MacDonald had a vision of melted circuits and charred microprocessors. The Lleveci slid to a stop beside him and chattered at him, trying to tell him something, but MacDonald couldn't make sense of it. The warrior shook his mane in frustration and grabbed MacDonald's arm, leading him impatiently down the side passage. He stopped before a panel in the wall that was secured with a series of flush-mounted clamps. The Lleveci started releasing them, and MacDonald, having got the message, helped.

The Lleveci produced the hand light and crawled through the hole they made. MacDonald followed as best he could, cramped in the narrow space between walls, unable to see much in the dim light, and obstructed by tangles of wires, pipes, optical cables, bracing. They moved through the bulkhead for a short distance, the Lleveci stopping occasionally to shine his light on the symbols stenciled at intervals on the inner wall.

When he found what he was looking for, he handed MacDonald the light and extracted a hand laser from among his clothing, set the beam to the narrowest setting, and applied it to the wall opposite the one they had entered.

The laser whined, the hard composition of the wall complained with snaps and crackles, and the Lleveci swore when splatters of the hot material sprayed back at him. MacDonald could see what the fellow was up to, but it seemed to take an age. When the Lleveci finally put his foot to the cut piece and pushed it out, MacDonald thought that surely a dozen Kaz would be ready and waiting with blasters drawn.

It had not been as long as it seemed in the cramped space between walls, and they came out in a small alcove off the flight deck that must have served some other purpose once but was now fitted with an array of Kazi-size acceleration couches. The Lleveci used the laser first to literally cut the legs out from under the unfortunate Kazi defending the corridor entrance and incidentally burn a deep trench into the deck. MacDonald fired at the one turning from the hatchway to see what the commotion was, and prayed the hatch control mechanism did not go with it.

With the fighting open on three fronts, the ten or so Kaz remaining had no chance to win, and the Lleveci offered them no chance to surrender. The terminal slaughter was the kind of thing that could make a man sick to his stomach.

Later. The reinforcements were getting damned close. Nausea would have to wait.

Delladar Oll pushed Ayyah up the ramp. The Orian had a gun hanging limply from one hand, a sheathed knife in the other.

MacDonald ran for the pilot's station. "Get your people aboard fast," he told Delladar Oll.

"Not all coming," she said.

"They come or they're dead." They might be dead anyway, he thought, along with the rest of us. He didn't know if the shuttle's engine would fire cold. "Get them laid down on the floor or braced on something. This could be a rough ride."

The bridge grew crowded with excited Lleveci, bumping and chattering. "And get them out of here," MacDonald added.

Oscar slid into the navigator's chair. "There's a hell of a mob of Kaz out there headed our way," he said.

"What do you know about Lleveci engines?" MacDonald asked.

"Absolutely nothing. You're supposed to be the expert."

"Too bad. Okay, hatch closed. Firing sequence starts now. Space or glory, people." The engine rumbled and shuddered and settled down to a comforting roar.

A moment's hesitation and the shuttle started to lift, gathering speed slowly, as if it were a painful effort. Everyone breathed a sigh of relief, which turned into a gasp when the little vessel suddenly jolted sideways and yawed down toward the horizon. The Lleveci chatter grew in pitch and volume. They were good people facing dangers they knew and understood, but aboard a spacecraft they were out of their element, helpless and nervous.

MacDonald fought to get the shuttle headed skyward again while Delladar Oll, with a perfectly lousy sense of timing, demanded, "What?"

"Projectile of some sort," MacDonald answered. "We're being shot at."

"Damage?"

"I don't know. It couldn't have been a solid hit, or we'd be ass over teakettling right into the ground."

Delladar Oll looked puzzled but didn't interrupt again.

The sky in the forward windows was black and star-studded. The whine of atmosphere against the hull had faded away. MacDonald took a deep breath and leaned his head one way and then the other to stretch the tense muscles in his neck and shoulders.

"So, we're up," he said. "In a very short time, the Kaz will have fighters after us. Anyone have an idea how we're going to find this alleged starship before we get shot down?"

"Have you changed the set course?" Ayyah asked. She seemed to have recovered from whatever ailed her below. She had rid herself of the gun but still had the sheathed knife in her hand.

"Nope. We're flying by the seat of my pants right now."

"Then the course that is set must have taken this shuttle from the ship to the surface. It should not be so singularly difficult to reverse it and find the ship."

MacDonald looked up at her and smiled. "You're a smart girl, Ayyah."

The frankness exhibited briefly below was gone. Ayyah regarded him with that neutral, enigmatic expression that only rarely changed. "I am not a girl of any sort," she said.

MacDonald shrugged and decided not to go into it. "What are you planning to do with that?" he asked, indicating the knife with a nod.

"I am planning to give it to Delladar Oll in honor of the one who died."

At the sound of her name Delladar Oll looked up from the group of Lleveci who had adamantly refused to leave the flight deck, seeming to feel more in control of things if they could keep an eye on the pilot.

She came over, and Ayyah offered her the knife, hilt first.

Delladar Oll studied the carved handle for a moment before accepting the gift, then turned her fierce eyes on the giver.

"How you know to do this?" she asked.

"I have not done it correctly?" Ayyah was more inquiring than apologetic.

"Too much know our ways, Orian," Delladar Oll said, but there was a new element of respect in her voice.

Oscar interrupted to point out a monitor that was flashing an alarm. "We're losing air," he said. "The hatch seal is leaking."

Thinking a brigand's life did not offer many moments of quiet repose, MacDonald asked the computer for a rate. "I think we'll make it," he said.

"I'd be happier if you knew."

"The alternative is to return to the surface."

"Hmph." Oscar grunted. "Some alternative."

The ship's shuttle bay hung open, so someone must have been expecting this—or some—shuttle.

Mating the Lleveci shuttle to the Kazi ship took a little doing. It wasn't all that good a fit, and MacDonald felt a bit awkward at the controls. He was also feeling a bit breathless, but that might have been as much psychological as physiological. The thump and clang that greeted success was rougher and louder than it should have been. MacDonald concluded the operation with a renewed respect for Lleveci pilots.

The shuttle bay doors closed around them and the bay began to pressurize, if the shuttle's monitors could be believed. Everybody took a deep, reassuring breath.

The pressure was rising above a standard Lleveci atmosphere. Kazi normal, one might suppose.

"Incoming wind," MacDonald warned the Lleveci, who gathered around the hatch with weapons at the ready. He cracked the hatch door to help equalize the pressure. Air whined as it seeped in, and with it came the smell of Kaz.

Two Kaz arrived through the lock from the ship. One wore a metallic sounder, and the tinny voice said as it approached, "We are pleased you are prompt in return—" The sound broke off as the hatch dropped and the Kazi realized that the armed warriors pouring out were not the Lleveci it was expecting.

It died, with its companion, an instant later, and the sound of the blasts echoed in the bay. The air filled with the stench of burning flesh.

"Quit that," MacDonald said, alarmed. "If you miss, you'll rupture the hull."

Delladar Oll offered him a head-bobbing Lleveci shrug. "Not miss. Dead is dead. No choice."

"We've got to get out of the bay," MacDonald said.

"Wait at lock. Kaz come through, we shoot. Soon all gone."

MacDonald shook his head. "We've got minutes, or less. When they realize on the bridge something is not right down here, all they have to do is evacuate the bay, and we've had it. The ground will be in contact any moment. I expect the Kaz have as good a sense of survival as anyone, which means immediately the pressure starts to drop, the outer lock gate won't operate. At best, we'll be trapped in a shuttle with a leaky door."

To her credit, Delladar Oll acted the moment she understood the danger. The lock would only take a few at a time, but since the pressure in the bay was equal to that of the ship proper, the lock cycle was mercifully short. Even so, the last were barely inside when the outer gate slammed shut under automatic control and clipped off the end of the last warrior's sash.

The battle for the starship was much simpler than the fight for the shuttle. There were only half a dozen low-ranking Kaz aboard to supervise the off-loading, and the Lleveci made short work of them. A squad of warriors made a compartment-by-compartment search for others while the rest joined their leader and her offworld friends in a head-scratching session on the bridge while they tried to figure out how they were going to manage the Kazi vessel.

It was ridiculously hot. The humidity was so high that the metal surfaces felt damp. MacDonald wondered briefly how the Kaz managed to keep their ships from corroding away around them.

Sweat ran off his forehead and stung in his eyes. The greenish light illuminating the alien appointments made the bridge look like a stage set dressed for Halloween. Flashing red alarms—the ground trying to contact the ship, no doubt—added a frantic busyness to the scene. Everything was too small, too close, compressed and crowded, and the ceiling was too low.

"I can't fly this thing," he complained. He looked up at the navigation display and banged his head on an overhead projection for the third time. His curses filled the cramped space of the bridge.

"The only alternative available is to remain here," Ayyah said.

MacDonald grunted annoyance. The heat wouldn't be bothering her too much, but the moisture in the air would be lethal over a period of time. Her fur was already beginning to look limp. She probably was no more comfortable than he was, but she refrained from complaining. That was some kind of object lesson, he thought, and resented her for it. It improved his humor not at all.

"It's like trying to work in a freaking shoe box. I can't even read the charts." He was leaning over the bench in front of the pilot's console, pecking away at the keyboard, trying to make some sense of the system, though he didn't expect to have much success. He raised his head with great caution to see what effect he was having on the monitor.

"Here's something," Oscar said.

He was squeezed into a corner that would have fit a Kazi just fine but left Oscar scarcely room to breathe. In front of him was an open cupboard; its door had been removed by the diligent and most careful application of cutting tools from the engine room. The same Lleveci who had burned his way through the shuttle bulkhead had done this more delicate work. Questioned, Delladar Oll informed MacDonald that this person, Ellid Rullenahe, had been a designing spacecraft engineer before the Kaz but refused to design for the invaders and so had left his home city and fled into the mountains.

"So not all lowlanders are gutless maggots," MacDonald said.

Delladar Oll's head cocked on her long neck made her look lopsided. "One here, one there."

"Come and take a look at this, Mac," Oscar said.

MacDonald stood up carefully, hunched over with one hand on his head to protect the sore spot on his skull. He left the hand there to ward off further bumps while he crossed the tiny bridge.

Ellid Rullenahe chattered excitedly beside him, oblivious to the fact he was not being understood. Oscar didn't try to wiggle out of his cramped position; he handed up a few sheets of something almost like paper, but more the color and texture of the stuff of wasps' nests. It was covered with Sindharra characters.

"It looks like the original shipbuilders' specifications," he said.

"Could be, all right. How's your Sindharr?"

"Better than yours, for sure."

"You're right, so get to it. See if you can find some operating instructions, like how to make this flying sweat box go, and how in the name of seven hells we can turn the freaking temperature down."

From various slots and compartments and drawers, Oscar had a pile the size of a small encyclopedia in his lap. "I hope you're not in a really big hurry."

"Oscar, damn, I'm in a hurry. The Kaz are coming. The Kaz are coming."

Later, when he and Ellid Rullenahe had the pages sorted into piles, Oscar said, "Her name is *Kokkon*."

MacDonald was staring with frustration at a display he had managed to get up on the monitor. It looked important, but it was identified with Kazi symbols, so he had no idea what it meant. "Great," he answered Oscar without enthusiasm. "Whatever it means. That's a start. But it isn't helping much."

"It's a broodship."

"Yeah?"

"One of the ships that carries Kazi eggs around. That's why it's so hot and humid. The eggs must be kept at exactly the right temperature and humidity to remain viable."

"So what's it doing here?"

Oscar shrugged. "In for repairs, maybe?"

"That's a pleasant thought, guy. I do love a positive attitude. We've got a ship we don't know how to run, and now you think maybe it's busted."

"Anyway, one thing it does mean is that we can shed a lot of mass by jettisoning the egg containers from the cargo bay. That'll give us a bit more range and acceleration in times of need."

"Fine. Any idea of how to do that?"

"The quickest way would be to suit up, evacuate the bay, and chuck them out by hand. It shouldn't be too hard in free fall."

"Oscar, assorted other problems notwithstanding, I don't think Kazi gear will fit us too well."

"Mm. You've got a point. Let me think about it."

"Later. First find me some way to start the bloody engines."

"Yeah, okay, I think we can do that. Have you got a control there that's labeled with something that looks like a kid's drawing of half a barrel? And one that looks like the Greek letter pi with an upward hook on the bar?"

MacDonald studied the board. "Yeah, I've got those."

"Okay, barrel initiates start sequence. Pi controls engine output. You realize we're going to do this without a checklist?"

"One thing I do realize is that if we fritz around long enough, the Kaz will make it bloody unnecessary to worry about one. I don't think they're going to wait for a full-fledged countdown."

"All right, all right. Let's run through it once, and then we'll put our not inconsiderable lives into your ignorant hands."

"The whole sequence must be in the computer somewhere."

"Probably. You want to wait while I look for it?"

"No."

"Okay then, pay attention."

There followed a period of intense concentration while Mac-Donald tried his best to learn how to get the *Kokkon* safely under way. Ayyah had come to watch and was fiddling with the panel next to him. He ignored her until a display lit at just about eye level to his left. It was a view of space, with a crescent of Llevec's green surface in the lower righthand corner.

"What have you got?" he asked.

"A representation of data from the sensors directed ahead, I believe."

"You know Sindharr?"

"A little to read. Less to speak."

"Some is better than none. See if you can give Oscar a hand." He called over his shoulder in the general direction of the huddle of Lleveci. "We'll have acceleration in a few minutes. I hope. Find something to brace yourselves against. This may not be a smooth, elegant takeoff."

"Mac," Oscar said, "here's a way to get rid of the egg containers. All we have to do is unclamp them—I think we can do that from up here—open the bay doors, and accelerate the ship. They'll stay where they are, and we'll move away from them."

"Mm. Not a bad idea. If we could turn off the artificial gravity in the hold, and if we could be sure of smooth acceleration and proper attitude control, I'd try it. As it is, I'm not sure of any of those things. One thing we do not need is to have one of them crashing around inside the bay until it ruptures the hull or something."

"True. Are you ready to blow us up?"

"As ready as I'm going to get. Call it."

Teeth clenched, MacDonald worked the controls under Oscar's instruction. There was a sudden push backward, and then the gravity-field compensators took over and made down toward the floor again. MacDonald gradually increased the acceleration, pausing after each increase to give the compensators time to catch up. They were extraordinarily slow, which made for a jerking, roller-coaster sort of ride. No wonder Kaz had trouble with sudden changes of speed or direction.

Gradually he learned how to do it, things smoothed out a bit, and he was able to distract himself enough to tell Oscar, "I hope by the time we're up to point five C, you've figured out how to cut in the hyperdrive, or we'll be a long time getting anywhere, not to mention there are likely Kaz in hot pursuit of their stolen ship. Navigation would also be nice. It would help to know where we're going."

"You're a real nag, you know. Try to appreciate my genius."

"I'm trying."

Since the instruments were currently useless to him, MacDonald kept a hopeful eye on Oscar, Ellid Rullenahe, and Ayyah as they continued to study the papers, Oscar frowning with the effort, Ellid Rullenahe chattering away and occasionally demanding Delladar Oll's services as translator, Ayyah with her big ears pricked forward as if listening to the pages would help her interpret the foreign language. As she puzzled out one of them, the end of her tail jerked with alarm. She looked at the page again, to be sure, and then handed it to Oscar without comment.

Oscar's frown deepened. He sucked in a deep, ragged breath. "Mac?"

"Is it important?"

"I think so."

"What?"

"It's not eggs we've got in the cargo bay. Mac, we're carrying a substantial fraction of the Kazi army."

The Broodmaster

In the dirt-floored room in Rigaport, the broodmaster struggled against a growing lassitude. Backed into a dim, comfortable corner of the room it was sharing with the intelligence gatherer, it gathered its strength to receive the messenger from Llevec.

The messenger brought from the governor of Llevec a request for information, along with a computer record containing pictures and an anatomical description of a small furry animal. The records on Llevec did not include data regarding the beast, the message said, nor had inquiries regarding Oriani fauna elsewhere succeeded. The governor hoped the broodmaster could direct its investigation to a source of information.

The pictures showed the creature dead. It had been found on Llevec in a shallow depression under a pile of rocks near the wreck of a downed starship. The starship was of Terran design, the message said, but obviously the creature was Orian, not Terran.

Old memories stirred in the broodmaster, memories of earlier studies, preparing a brood for service in the Terran colony called Centauri. The investigator who prepared the report was mistaken. For all its outward appearance, the beast was Terran, not Orian.

Cats were a useless nuisance. More than that, they were dangerous, with sharp claws and teeth capable of penetrating a Kazi's tegument, which they applied freely. For reasons unknown, humans liked them and protected them. The Kaz on Earth and Centauri had been working at eliminating the animals since the early days of the occupation. Few cats had survived the extermination campaign.

On the asteroid known as Pigpen, technicians found a quantity of hair from a small domestic animal of Terran origin, the Fleet detachment leader had said.

There could not be many cats in this sector.

How many types of small domestic animals of Terran origin would likely be sharing quarters with the pirates? It would query the technicians to be sure, but within itself, the broodmaster was certain.

A Terran ship had crashed on Llevec and killed a cat. Interesting.

MacDonald's Terran ship with the Orian aboard had fled from Pigpen to Tasetoru.

A small Terran animal had slept in one of the humans' beds on Pigpen, but the beast itself had not been found.

MacDonald and his ship and his small Terran animal had escaped Tasetoru, or so it would seem, considering the disaster there.

The Orian was gone again. The trail was lost.

A cat.

It was a frail clue at best. No other clues survived the Tasetoru action. Any outside observer would dismiss it. The broodmaster felt its hopes rise well beyond what it could rationally justify. Justification could come later, if needed. Having thus convinced itself, it commandeered the messenger to pilot its fast vessel and make all possible speed to Llevec. Once more the broodmaster subjected its failing body to the stresses of spaceflight.

En route, it recorded all it knew of the matter and committed to the messenger's care the story of the cat, MacDonald, the Orian, and the perceived danger to the empire of a resurgent Orian nation, for it had begun to feel overwhelmed by its age and its infirmities. Death was close.

For Kaz, nothing could be done about age and infirmity except to pray to the Broodmother and protect the information gathered during a lifetime. Unlike many advanced societies, whose healing arts were fueled by an overwhelming concern for single members, Kazi medicine reflected the Kazi disinterest in individuals. It was primitive at best, impossible at worst. To make even a tiny opening in a Kazi's tough shell was to let the life fluids drain away—a murder, not a remedy.

The broodmaster prayed to the Broodmother and carried on as best it was able.

On Llevec, it was met with confusion. It was almost neglected in the turmoil in Rullenahesad. The Lleveci garrison had lost a starship.

44TH Battalion, Army of the Empire

Just when MacDonald felt things were starting to come together, just when they were starting to make some reasonable, albeit space-normal, speed, just when he felt a glimmer of hope that if all the stars were with them they might just possibly get away with it, Oscar dropped his bombshell.

"A substantial fraction of the Kazi army," he said.

Ayyah had been fooling around with the environment controls on the far side of the *Kokkon*'s bridge, if any part of the constricted space could be called far. The temperature did seem to be easing up a little. Nonetheless, MacDonald's splutter greatly resembled steam escaping from overheated internal regions.

"Army?"

"Yeah," Oscar said.

MacDonald wished he had a free hand; he wanted to hold his head with it. "Why do I get the feeling things are going from bad to worse?" He moaned.

"I think it's because things are going from bad to worse."

"Thank you." MacDonald shut the engines down and let *Kokkon* drift. Delladar Oll was immediately at him, neck bent to bring her face to his level, mane fuzzed out.

"Not stop engine."

"Mm." MacDonald's mind was on other things.

"Kaz come." She parked herself right in front of him. He couldn't see around her.

"Shit, they're riding in the back."

Delladar Oll did not move.

"Look," he said, fighting to be patient in the face of this monumental problem. "We can't make hyperspace until we decipher more of the operations manual. Anyplace away from the Lleveci system is as good as any other for now. We're less

150

detectable to motion and infrared sensors with the engines off. Deceleration in open space is negligible. And we've got this predicament that needs serious bloody attention. Okay?''

Delladar Oll thought it over. Her mane flattened. She went to explain to the other Lleveci. MacDonald turned and sat on the too-short Kazi bench.

Oscar gave him a bleak look.

"Are you sure?" MacDonald asked.

Oscar handed him the paper, a hard copy of the Kazi commander's declaration during a stop in a neutral port.

He stared at the Sindharra script for a long time. "It doesn't make sense," he said finally. "If they're around, where are they? How come we could take this ship away from half a dozen Kaz if there are five thousand or so aboard? How come the warriors didn't find them when they searched the ship?"

The Lleveci still had not acquired enough confidence in the driver to leave the bridge, not so strange under the circumstances. MacDonald rather wished they would express their anxiety by hiding their heads in distant corners. Instead, they crowded around, attracted by the sound of the discussion they didn't understand, making the thick air thicker with the scent of overheated Lleveci. Delladar Oll translated salient bits of the conversation for them. Eventually the nature of the crisis got through to them. Heads swayed at the ends of long necks like a stand of fleshy reeds, and they gabbled excitedly among themselves.

MacDonald speared Delladar Oll with a look. "They did search the ship?" he demanded, and dared her to say otherwise.

After a bit more Lleveci chatter, with indignant heads bobbling perilously close to the low overhead, Delladar Oll reported, "Did search. Only not place for cargo. What call 'hold'."

"Well, it's not likely they'd be there. This is a big ship, but to get five thousand in the hold, they'd have to be stacked like cordwood. It'd be a rough passage, even for Kaz."

Oscar shrugged helplessly. "I don't know, Mac."

"What means 'cord wood'?" Delladar Oll wanted to know.

"A broodship, you said," MacDonald insisted.

"Well, that's what the paper says it was designed for. That's all I know about it," Oscar said.

"You said the heat and humidity was for eggs," MacDonald said.

Oscar shrugged again. He had no answers.

"Yes," Ayyah said suddenly from across the bridge. She joined the crowd around MacDonald, ears up, eyes bright, full of discovery, willing to suffer the jostling of Lleveci elbows in order to share it. "Yes. It could be so. If they were preparing to molt, it could be so. They would need warmth and humidity at the time of molting."

"What do you know about it?"

"I have studied my enemy, MacDonald."

"And?"

"A Kazi undergoes four molts from the time of hatching until adulthood. Most of its education and training occurs between the third and fourth molts, in the juvenile stage. Newly trained soldiers could well be in the fourth molt. They are quiescent at this time, almost dormant, a convenient and efficient time to transport large numbers."

MacDonald was skeptical. "So how long does this molting business take?"

"It varies with the individual. Some days."

"Presumably they've already been in transit some days."

"Yes."

"So anytime now we can expect some thousands of groggy, puzzled Kazi soldiers to start wandering out of the hold?" His skepticism was giving way to alarm.

She pulled back from the group again. "It could be so. If any of our assumptions are correct. If the soldiers are in the hold. If they have been there for a time. If they have not been removed to Llevec."

"This is not trivial, people. It's kind of important to know."

"Any ideas?" Oscar asked.

MacDonald shut his eyes, trying to draw his courage up. "I guess the thing to do," he said with his eyes still closed, "is to go and look. Would it be too much to ask if we have a schematic?"

Oscar handed him several folded sheets of the gray papery stuff. It appeared frail and brittle, as if it should come apart when he unfolded it, but it was tougher than it looked. He located the hold access from the main deck on the chart and started to leave the bridge, stopped, and looked back at Oscar. There was a knot in his stomach that really hurt.

"Are we sure the hold is pressurized?"

"No, we're not," Oscar answered.

"I wish you hadn't said that."

"Want some help?"

MacDonald shook his head. "Someone's got to figure out how to run this bug trap. You stay here. If you can find out how to close the airtight doors, it might be a good idea." The smile was pure bravado.

Oscar looked like he might be going to say something. Then he clamped his jaw shut and bent back to his work.

The hold access door had a view port set into it, at Kazi height. MacDonald got down on his knees to peer through it. It was dark inside.

Alongside the door a bank of colored indicator lights gleamed, each neatly labeled, unfortunately with Kazi letters. He shone Assall Oll's light through the window. He could see part of a railed platform, with a ramp leading up on one side and down on the other. There was no way to see air.

He made his way back up the short corridor. The ceilings were lower there than they were on the bridge. He had to hunch right over and shuffle along. His back was beginning to complain.

He pulled the sliding door at the end of the passageway closed manually and dogged it tight with a bar two feet off the floor. Then he returned to the access door and released the locking mechanism. One of the indicators changed from yellow to red, but he didn't know the significance of that event.

He took a deep breath, a totally senseless precaution, and pulled the access door open.

There was a small sigh of equalizing pressure, but no great rush of wind driving him into an evacuated hold. Feeling a little more confident, he eased his way through the low, narrow hatch and was able to stand upright at his full height on the platform on the other side.

He allowed himself a luxurious moment of stretching his muscles out and another of wrinkling his nose at the overwhelming stench of Kaz. The air was even hotter and moister than it was on the bridge. The hold extended into darkness in every direction from his light. Near him, it seemed filled with a metal latticework, not unlike an overgrown wine rack, forming a series of shelves with narrow passages between them.

He followed the ascending ramp until he came to a frail walkway between two sets of shelves. He hesitated before stepping

onto it, figuring he weighed probably four times as much as the
average Kazi. For a moment, he gave joyful consideration to a
valid reason for getting out of there, back to the relative safety
of the bridge, until such a time as he and Oscar had worked out
how to shut down the gravity in the hold.

He sighed. Who could say when that would happen? With his
free hand clamped tightly on a rail, he put one foot cautiously
onto the walkway, then the other. The flooring held. He was
able to direct his light onto one of the shelves.

It looked dead, lying there with its head resting mouth down
on the mesh shelving and its legs all folded up underneath it. It
lacked the shine MacDonald associated with Kazi hides or whatever, and its faceted eyes looked opaque. He prodded it gingerly
with the tip of a stiff, unwilling finger. It didn't move.

In spite of his time in the Fleet and the years of playing tag
with various Kazi institutions that followed, MacDonald had
never become fully comfortable with Kaz. They didn't look any
better for close inspection. If their blank, rigid faces had some
features, if they had noses, if their mouths were in front instead
of underneath, maybe they wouldn't seem so ugly.

A long, deep furrow had developed along this one's back.
The furrow seemed to be slowly lengthening and deepening even
as MacDonald watched. He was sure it was getting bigger. A
sense of imminent disaster clawed at him.

There were more of them on the shelves on either side, and
above and below and across the walkway, as far and as high and
as deep as the light would reach. MacDonald backed away,
goose bumps all over him. His hair prickled. His knees wobbled
as he scrambled down the ramp and back out of the hatch with
as much dignity as his revulsion would allow him.

"I'm open to suggestion," MacDonald said.

Delladar Oll rattled her mane in an almost human gesture, as
if in astonishment at rampant stupidity. "Open hold to space.
All Kaz dead. Trouble no more."

"You speak of a massacre, not a solution," Ayyah said.

"Kaz," Delladar Oll answered.

"Are they less aware, less living, because of their race?"

"Orian, I care not much. These enemies. Also for you. Plénty
talk free Orion. How you do? Eh?"

"To want my homeworld returned to my people is not the
same as approving of wholesale slaughter."

"Maybe ask please good enough?"

MacDonald edged his way around the quarreling pair, cracked his temple on a duct housing, and swore viciously.

"Oscar?" he questioned softly when he reached his friend's side.

"How much time have we got?" Oscar asked.

"I don't know. I think not much."

"Then I honestly don't know what else we can do."

"Do we know how to open the cargo doors safely?"

"I think so."

"Good. I'll trust you to carry on."

"You will?" Oscar managed a bit of a smile.

"Well, of course. What do I keep you around for if not to look after these little details?"

"I've asked myself that. I've decided it must be that my incomparable beauty really gets to you."

"You think a lot of yourself, don't you?"

"There's a lot of me to think of."

"Too much talk. You talk or you do?" Delladar Oll demanded.

Oscar grinned at MacDonald. "Interesting choices. What do you think, Mac?"

MacDonald grinned back. This peculiar humor often surfaced between them in times of greatest stress. No doubt their passengers found it unnerving. But they were both past worrying about what the passengers thought.

"Guess we do. I can't honestly say I like it, though."

Ayyah had been watching them with ears pricked forward, tail tip twitching. MacDonald didn't have to be an expert in Orian ways to see she was not pleased.

"MacDonald," she said, "I forbid it."

MacDonald turned to face her. His slightly raised eyebrow and trace of a smile could be misinterpreted. He felt none of the previous moment's humor. "Do you?" he asked, altogether too politely.

"Yes."

"Should I ask why?"

"It is unconscionable to destroy five thousand helpless, self-aware persons out of hand."

"Would you like a rough estimate of the number of helpless, self-aware persons destroyed by the Kazi army since the dawn of the empire?"

"This is not relevant. We do not defeat our enemies by becoming like them."

MacDonald had to admit a begrudging admiration for the way she stood up to him. She had guts, nothing but ears over a meter and a half tall, and ready to do battle for what she believed in.

He couldn't give way, regardless. Even if they had not had a Kazi battalion at their backs, a ship with two captains was a study in chaos. And he was godalmighty tired, and they were running out of time.

"Okay, do what you have to do. Forbid all you like. I warn you in advance, I'm not going to pay a lot of attention. This isn't particularly pleasant, but it's the only sensible way to deal with our predicament. If you're offended, I'm sorry, but it doesn't change anything." MacDonald's voice was soft, low-pitched, and cold. He had been holding himself together by force of will. He was very close to the end of his patience.

"Let me tell you something else," he continued. "If I'm going to run this flying Kaz carrier, I'm going to run it. I think I told you once before, I will not take votes. I will not recognize vetoes. If this is not acceptable to you, we will stop at the nearest neutral port and one of us will get off. Do I make myself clear?"

Ayyah's tail had not stopped twitching, but her voice was calm when she answered. "Yes, MacDonald. You have a talent for making your wishes known."

"Good," he said, ignoring the comment. "The best thing you can do is to get back to translating our operations manual. If we don't figure out a way to cut in the hyperspace drive damned soon, the Kaz are going to find us and render this whole disagreement academic."

Obediently Ayyah returned to the cramped corner and the pile of papers.

MacDonald took a deep breath and let it go. In spite of Ayyah's apparent acquiescence, he didn't think he had heard the last of the argument. He turned back to the control board and found Delladar Oll staring at him.

The fierce eyes glared as if she hadn't seen him before, but she said nothing. MacDonald hauled his attention back to the business of unraveling the mysteries of the navigation console while the hair on his neck prickled.

In a few minutes, Oscar plowed through the Lleveci to MacDonald's side. Bending, he flicked a couple of switches on the panel they had previously tentatively identified as the ship's status board.

"That should do 'er," he said.

"Why don't I feel better about it?" MacDonald asked.

Oscar shrugged.

"They're only half made, for Christ's sake," MacDonald went on. "They never had a chance."

"You think we ought to wait for them to get finished?"

MacDonald shook his head.

"I think maybe Ayyah's starting to get to you."

MacDonald didn't dignify that comment with an answer. He had at last made a star field appear on the monitor in front of him, but he couldn't immediately identify the location. There were grid markers along the edges, but he didn't know what they meant.

Suddenly it was more than he could cope with. He slapped his hand down hard on the panel in front of him. "This is insane," he shouted. "Positively insane. We're deaf and blind. We don't know where we are. We don't know where we're going. We don't know how to get there. We haven't got a hope in hell."

Oscar looked up, startled.

Ayyah was coming toward him, with a gray page in her hand. Couldn't they leave him alone for a while? he wondered. He was exhausted, and he had the most godawful crick in his neck from bending under the stupid low ceilings in this stupid Kazi tin can.

"This has something to do with the hyperdrive engines," Ayyah said. "But I don't understand what it is."

In spite of the popular lore about the inability of Oriani to lie, he didn't believe her. There was no place on *Kokkon*'s bridge that Orian ears wouldn't have picked up his outburst. He looked at her. She met his eyes steadily. Still he felt like she was jollying him along like a petulant child. She made him feel embarrassed, which was not to say better.

"Why are you trying to humor me?" he snapped. "You should still be sulking."

"I do not understand the term 'sulking.' "

"To sulk is to be sullen and antisocial from resentment and anger."

"Sulking would be of value to you?"

"Of course not. It's just expected, normal."

"I understand you wish to say that if I were human I would be sulking now."

"Something like that."

She seemed amused. "I am not human, MacDonald."

"You think I'm being childish, is that it?" He sounded childish in his own ears.

"I know nothing of human children. I understand you are stressed near to the limits of your endurance. I understand also that you are correct in saying you must command this vessel. No other among us is capable. We depend on you."

She was gracious in defeat. He felt flattered for some reason, honored, as if her recognition were important.

Oscar cut off his reply. "Sensor reading," he said. "Object approaching."

On the screen, MacDonald could just barely make out a moving pinpoint.

"I should have thought of it," Oscar said. "We just dumped a lot of heat and moisture. Kazi sensors were bound to pick it up. We're in deep trouble, folks."

MacDonald was already at the engine controls. "Find me the firing sequence. Now," he snapped at Oscar.

"I remember it," Ayyah said.

"You only heard it once."

"Once is sufficient."

Time was infinitely precious. They didn't have a hope in hell anyway. "Okay," he said. "Recite."

Cautious acceleration was a luxury they couldn't afford. When the engines cut in, everyone fell onto the aft bulkhead while the field compensators struggled to make down down again.

When he could, MacDonald retrieved Ayyah's papers from among the tangled flesh, handed it to Oscar, and fought his way back to the control board.

"Read it to me," he said.

"We're heading right at them," Oscar pointed out.

"Let's hope they care enough about their soldiers to think a minute before they start shooting. Read."

"They're not stupid. It won't take them long to figure out what we've done."

"I know. Stop chattering and read."

"I don't know if this is right. One mistake and we could end up splattered across the galaxy."

"Read!"

They didn't have enough speed for a proper transition. The drop into hyperspace was gut-wrenching in the extreme and disorienting to boot. Several Lleveci warriors lost their dinners, much to their dismay and that of everyone else in the crowded space.

MacDonald looked up from his work momentarily, speared Delladar Oll with a look that would have made any hawk-eyed Lleveci proud. "Get the mess cleaned up and get your people off the bridge."

For a moment Delladar Oll's mane bristled and she looked as if she were going to argue. Then she ducked her head in a typical Lleveci gesture of compliance.

"My, my, we are getting masterful, Captain," Oscar murmured beside him.

"Knock it off," MacDonald snarled.

"Where are we headed?"

"Damned if I know."

Oscar was silent. MacDonald spared a glance at his friend's worried face.

"Space is mostly empty," he said in a friendlier tone. "With any luck at all, a random jump won't drop us back to space normal inside a supernova remnant or anything like that."

"I feel reassured. But I would appreciate it if we could take the element of luck out of it at the earliest opportunity."

"Me, too," MacDonald admitted. "However, even the supernova is better than the Kaz."

"You've got a point."

Ynacy Station

From its place on a pale green inside wall, the portrait of Peter Allen's grandfather glared down on his grandson. The old man had been stationmaster in his time, and his hair, like Peter's, had become prematurely white. The picture was done by hand in a thick paint that lay in ridges and managed to convey more of the old fellow's personality than mechanically accurate holograms did.

Peter knew very well that his feet were much too small to fit the old man's boots. He tried. He just didn't have that streak of hard fiber—what his grandfather would call guts. The thought of Kazi customers made Peter Allen's guts feel distinctly watery.

His world was one of duralloy walls and enclosed rooms and a nervousness about punctured perimeters. The view from his office window was black space punctuated by stars. Ynacy Station was an artificial environment. Located in a part of space otherwise empty of habitable bodies, it was home to three hundred inhabitants who earned their daily bread providing fuel, supplies, and service to passing vessels regardless of politics or purpose. For the more than two hundred years of its existence, Ynacy Station had never refused service to anybody who could pay in a viable currency.

The population of Ynacy, including Peter Allen, had become accustomed to an exceedingly comfortable lifestyle. They would not want to do anything to disturb the flow of ships.

An apolitical philosophy worked well most of the time. However, they had never dealt with Kaz before. Whether Kazi customers would scare away more business than they would bring was the subject of much of Peter's internal debate.

And if Ynacy refused the Kaz?

The station was unarmed. Any normal ship causing trouble on Ynacy would find itself isolated, blacklisted, with ports closed to it, pirates harassing it, customs officials deliberating at length over its cargoes, its crew refused entry visas.

Would Kaz care about visas and ports and things?

By the time the chief of operations came to ask what Peter wanted him to do, Peter had reluctantly made up his mind. An administrative rule of thumb decreed he should fight no battles he could not win.

"Treat them exactly like anyone else, Bill."

"Whatever you say, Mr. Allen."

Stocky, solid Bill Williams had a way of making his feelings known. It was "Right-o, Pete" when he was happy with what he was told, and "Whatever you say, Mr. Allen" when he wasn't.

Then he fretted and paced and worried and finally, as curious as anyone whose worst fears are coming to pass, Peter Allen paid a visit to bay number four where the Kazi vessel *Kokkon* was docked. The coupling was already attached and sealed, the hatch down, and station personnel busy within. There was no sign of the crew. Peter went to look for Bill.

The windows in Williams's office overlooked the docks. A story and a half beneath them, an unhindered floor stretched twenty meters to the station's outer wall. The wall curved away on either side and upward to a high ceiling all but covered with lighting panels. More panels followed the slope of the wall for about half its height, to make a large, open, well-lit workplace. Men and machines were busy below.

Bill Williams's mood had undergone a complete aboutface. Leaning back in the chair behind his cluttered desk, indicating the activity at number four with a finger directed at the office windows, he said with a delighted smile, "Eh, they're a rum lot, Pete. You figure it. What we got here is an Orian—would you believe an Orian?—two Terrans, and a couple dozen Lleveci mountain warriors in a Kazi ship, with credit on an Eridani bank. A bit odd, I'd say."

No Kaz. For about one second, Peter felt relieved. Then the implications dawned on him. He frowned. If he actually managed to merge his eyebrows, maybe this mess would all go away. Talk about going from bad to worse.

"Damned odd," he agreed, undelighted. "We better check with the bank before the charges get too high."

"Well, they don't want to wait around for that, and I'd say they had good reason. Got a minute? I'd like to show you something."

Peter's schedule wasn't pressing. It rarely was. Worry and nervous tension killed stationmasters, not overwork. He followed Williams through a door in the back of the room that led into the records office, fairly certain he knew what was on Bill's mind.

The records office was a crowded room of desks and clerks busy at computer terminals. "Dig up the Kazi list for me, Sossath," Williams told the Roothian at the nearest one.

The list came up on the screen in Sindharr. That didn't bother Peter. He had learned the language as a youngster working in the bays, when the need to communicate with every kind and type of spacefaring people made a knowledge of Sindharr mandatory. What did bother him was finding the *Kokkon*'s name and registration numbers topping the list of vessels the Kazi empire had expressed an interest in. The empire was offering a handsome reward for information about it.

Many worlds published such lists. Ynacy took notice of them because they occasionally came in handy in dealing with fractious people or slow payments. In all its history, Ynacy had never turned in a ship, but it didn't hurt to let certain folks know such a thing was possible.

Unfortunately, the rumor mill was less discreet. News traveled faster by grapevine than it did by formal methods of communication. Word would get back to the empire that the *Kokkon* had stopped at Ynacy Station.

"Another thing you ought to know about," Bill said as Peter turned away from the screen. "*Kokkon* wants to junk some cargo. The question is, do we want to take it?"

"What is it, and how much?"

"About five thousand dead Kaz. And some metalwork. Probably around 250,000 kilos."

"Five thousand dead—" Peter choked. He knew he had a stunned look on his face. He couldn't help it. Bill enjoyed his rare opportunities to spook his boss, but this was going too far. Sossath's big eyes grew bigger as he absorbed the conversation going on over his head. Peter urged Bill to go between the desks, out of records, and onto the main concourse leading down to the docking area.

He leaned against the smooth wall. He needed its support. In this moment of panic, he couldn't even think.

"You got to admire these guys," Bill said. "They don't do things in a small way."

"They're not admirable, they're dangerous. They're pirates," Peter snapped. He tried hard to imagine how he was going to deal with the situation, but a bloody vision of Kazi vengeance occupied most of his mind.

"Hey, boss, they're on our side, eh?"

"We don't have a side. What we've got is an intensely vulnerable position. If the Kaz show up with guns blazing, you think they'll listen while we explain the principles of neutrality?"

Bill sobered. The message was starting to get through.

"Has that traveling disaster got a captain?"

"Yeah, one of the Terrans."

"You tell him we want no part of his cargo. Then tell Sossath and anyone else who needs to be told that as far as the station is concerned, we have no idea what the *Kokkon* is carrying. Records will show station personnel never entered the hold. If anyone says differently, I guarantee you, heads will roll. What're the odds on taking the *Kokkon* off the record entirely?"

"We've got a Gnathan, the *Nihal*, in bay three."

Peter sighed. Gnathans were inveterate gossips. He abandoned any idea of holding the *Kokkon* until its credit could be verified. When the Kaz came looking, he wanted it gone.

"Does *Kokkon*'s captain know the ship's been listed?"

"Couldn't say," Williams answered.

"It would be decent to warn him. You might point out it would be prudent of him to keep moving."

Williams nodded.

"And, Bill, let's get them away as soon as ever we possibly can."

"Right-o, Pete."

Bill left to pass the word. Peter leaned against the wall and wondered how long before trouble arrived.

The *Nihal* was not good news to MacDonald either. In the bright silence of the station library, he looked up from the obsolete chart before him on the reader and wondered how he could close ever-busy Gnathan mouths. The librarian, a severe woman of scowling intensity, caught his eye and smiled at him hesitantly from behind her desk, as if it were something rarely done. She had been so touchingly pleased to have them express an interest in her historical collection, and so pleased with Ayyah, she had fallen all over herself to find the material the Orian wanted to see. And she kept a watchful eye on them in case there was something else she could do.

MacDonald whispered for Ayyah's ears only, "That woman never had a teddy bear when she was a kid."

"You know of this person's childhood, MacDonald?" Ayyah asked, looking up from her own intense study. "This person's childhood has some bearing on the work at hand?"

MacDonald groaned. He tried to concentrate on finding mythological worlds. With no expectation of success, he asked the computer for earlier maps of the same region and, while he waited for the machine to dig through the archives, asked Ayyah, "If your people really did know Rayor, why haven't they got modern maps?"

"Much was lost in the flight from Orion." Without any obvious outward sign, Ayyah managed to convey her irritation at being interrupted.

"Oh."

MacDonald went back to worrying about Gnathans. After a bit, the computer announced that the chart on the screen was the earliest available. He gave up then, left the sifting of ancient history to Ayyah, and went to see how the work on *Kokkon* was progressing.

Bay three was empty. *Nihal* was gone. Word of the *Kokkon* was already out.

He met Oscar at dockside. His friend had shed the Lleveci rig and looked more comfortable in an open-necked pale-yellow shirt and dark hip-hugging pants. A change of clothes was a good idea, but sartorial elegance was not first on MacDonald's mind.

"How long ago?" he asked with a nod toward bay three.

"Couple of hours," Oscar answered.

"Got an estimate on our work?"

"Tomorrow morning, local, at the earliest."

"Anything we can do to hurry it along?"

"Not much."

"Where are the Lleveci?"

"There's some athletic contest going on in free fall at the hub. They went to watch."

"Okay. There's a bar on the second level that's not bad. Come on, I'll buy you a beer with Delladar Oll's money. My old man believed beer was good medicine in times of stress."

Walking up the carpeted slope of the main concourse, Oscar said, "I never heard you mention your father before."

"We didn't have much to say to one another."

"Where is he now?"

"Dead. Reprocessed."

"I'm sorry."

"Yeah." Damned fool old man, running around with the resistance like an idiot kid, taking potshots at Kaz out of alleys, blowing up public buildings, holding secret meetings to plot the downfall of an empire whose size no one of them could even begin to appreciate. Sooner or later it had to happen. The only surprise was that it was later.

"He was dead a month before I even heard."

"That's sad," Oscar said, pushing open the heavy door to the Pig and Whistle. His curiosity was visible.

"Not really. We weren't friends. Pop figured any human who willingly joined the Fleet was a traitor to his race," MacDonald said. And the old bastard didn't hesitate to say so, he thought. Not even to a fifteen-year-old boy flushed with excitement over the beginning of a new life and the first step toward the realization of an old dream. He had appeared in MacDonald's room in the Academy dorm one evening, red-eyed, rumpled, in need of a shave. He looked over the new uniform with a mouth turned down as if he had encountered rotten fish and said, "I just wanted to see what a stinking, lousy collaborator looked like. I tell you, it's bloody disgusting." He spat on the floor at MacDonald's feet, turned on his heel, and walked out. MacDonald never saw him again.

The Pig and Whistle was reputed to be a historically accurate reproduction of an old English public house. MacDonald couldn't vouch for its accuracy, but the beer was as good as any he'd had in a long time. They found a small pseudowood table in a dim corner.

"What did your mother say?" Oscar asked.

"Nothing. She never argued with Pop."

The beer arrived. Why am I picking at all these old wounds? MacDonald wondered. Ayyah had brought the old man up, back on Llevec. Since then the memories had been haunting the back of his mind. He told Oscar, "When I was commissioned, I got a letter from a lawyer informing me I was cut out of his will."

"He had money?" Oscar asked.

MacDonald shook his head. "Not a freaking dime. It was a purely symbolic gesture. Pop was big on symbolic gestures." This was getting too painful. He took refuge in the beer. With a little foam on his lip, he asked, "How did you make out with dumping our, uh, cargo?"

"Station won't touch it. They want us out of here, yesterday."

"Well, we agree on one thing."

Ayyah was coming across the room with a large folded paper in her hand. When she arrived, she spread it out before them, without preamble, a hard copy of a star chart dated almost two centuries ago.

"This is the place we must go," she said.

MacDonald regarded the ancient data with jaundiced eye.

Pop should see me now, he thought. This is crazier than anything he ever did.

A Sgat twittered into the Pig and Whistle, stopped a moment at the bar to get directions, then headed over to MacDonald's table. MacDonald was a little miffed that it addressed Ayyah, as if she led this insane expedition, but its news was welcome nonetheless.

"Working very hard, I. Making vessel ready now. You go quick, please. Kaz come soon, think I."

"It's gone."

Peter Allen once heard that Terran medicine had gone into serious decline since the Kaz. He hoped treatments for ulcers were still available. He stared out of the office window at the starry void.

"When?" the Kazi asked.

Much of the star field was obscured by the bulk of the Kazi light cruiser *Klact*. The ship was lying in close, so it looked bigger than it was.

"Two days, Terran Standard."

Peter did not think it was an accident that the *Klact* happened to be parked in front of his window.

"Was an Orian on board?"

The shuttle that had brought half a dozen armed soldiers and this one had entered the bay without permission, as if the Kaz owned the place. The soldiers had completely ignored Reception's instructions to leave their guns behind.

"I don't know."

The Kazi rustled impatiently. Peter turned back to it by force of will.

"I do not personally," the station manager said stiffly, suppressing a shudder at the black, blank face before him, "inspect every ship that puts in to the station, nor do I personally interview every crew."

"Your ignorance is most convenient," the Kazi said through the device around its neck.

It was only a meter or so high; Peter could have picked it up in his two hands, except it was revolting and it smelled and he didn't want to touch it and he was afraid of it. It had climbed up onto his desk without so much as a by your leave and now regarded him at eye level. It had introduced itself as the commander of the *Klact*.

"What is known about the *Kokkon* is in the station's records. I understand the vessel took on fuel and provisions. Minor repairs were made to its shuttlecraft, and some small equipment was put aboard."

The Kazi regarded Peter without comment for a moment. The station manager was sure the creature could smell how apprehensive he was. "What equipment?" the Kazi made its sounding device ask.

Peter Allen read from the terminal display on his desk. "Food, fuel, eating utensils, hand tools, Terran clothing, a pressure suit complete with life support, human design, a first-aid kit of standard Terran composition."

"You saw nothing of an Orian?" the Kazi asked.

Peter took a deep breath, holding his apprehension in check. "I told you I didn't. I didn't meet the crew. As it so happens, I never saw an Orian in my entire life. I thought they were extinct."

And that was the absolute truth. Peter hoped the Kazi appreciated it.

"We have news of an Orian."

Bloody Gnathans, Peter thought. They couldn't wait to tell someone. Silently he heaped curses upon Gnatha and all its inhabitants for all time to come.

"You can't believe everything you hear," he said.

"I will speak to the workers," the Kazi said.

"I'd rather you didn't," Peter replied sharply. "It'll upset the crew and disrupt schedules. We have work to do here. You must understand. Many people depend on us." He hoped he sounded reasonable and convincing.

The Kazi drew itself up straighter. It fixed Peter with a glittering black eye. "This station has given aid and comfort to pirates in illegal possession of an empire vessel. You have declined to provide information requested that could lead to the capture of the criminals and recovery of the vessel. Such actions are not in the best interests of this station."

"I don't have the information," Peter interrupted. He heard himself sounding peevish and frightened.

"You deny access to those who do. Be warned. The empire has a very long memory. It knows its enemies from its friends."

Peter Allen collapsed, all the audacity he had, exhausted. "Talk to them, then, if it's that important."

A high proportion of the station's engine mechanics were Sgat. Their many-limbed, vermiform bodies were ideally suited to squirming into tight corners with tools in hand. They were also amiable souls with sunny dispositions who went on the assumption that everyone was friendly unless proven otherwise, which made them popular with customers and with their workmates.

The one who had checked the *Kokkon*'s engines approached the Kazi commander with an openness the Kazi had not previously met in an alien race. The one obstacle to their dialogue was the difficulty with which the trills and whistles of the Sgat tongue were pushed around the syllables of Sindharr.

"Engines good," the mechanic said. "No troubles."

"Where were they going when they left here?" the Kazi asked.

"Know nothing, I," the Sgat answered. "Not much for talk, those. Spend all time, nights, dorm, days, library with old charts."

"Which charts?"

"Know nothing, I. Librarian, maybe?"

"Was an Orian among them?"

The Sgat humped with delight. "Yes. Yes. Most happy, I, for rare occasion. Noble creature, she."

The commander kept silent on the subject of Orian nobility and betook itself along the indicated direction to the library.

The librarian was human, with all the hostility that implied.

She kept her distance from the commander, looking down at it with her lips drawn prissily together, and would say nothing, do nothing, without explicit instructions from the station manager.

"Speak to your manager," the Kazi instructed.

Peter Allen's cheerless face looking out from her terminal screen said, "Give what it wants. Then maybe it will go away."

Rayor

"Orbital insertion now," Oscar Achebe said. "I think."

"Stable?" MacDonald asked.

"How the hell would I know?"

"You're supposed to be the expert on running this bucket."

"Just a minute and I'll look it up," Oscar Achebe answered, patting the stack of paper at his elbow. "Sooner or later, I know I'm going to find all this stuff in the computer somewhere."

"That would be great, if you could just figure out how to run a Kazi-oriented computer."

"Thanks, boss. I could use a little appreciation. After all, we did get here."

"Yes, we did. That's good, I guess."

Ayyah looked up. She was squatting on the deck beside Ellid Rullenahe and Delladar Oll, translating more of the gray pages, when the voices interrupted. She watched for a few moments, uncertain if the humans were quarreling or playful; their games and their battles sounded much alike. Presumably humans knew the difference.

They appeared to be in reasonably good humor.

MacDonald turned toward her, carefully, to avoid banging his elbows. He was surely too big and ungainly for these confined spaces. Feeling crowded herself, she experienced a moment of sympathy she would not, and could not, display.

"There it is," MacDonald said, pointing at the forward view plate with the scrabble of Kazi characters across the bottom. "I hope you're satisfied. Though what in blazes anyone who's afraid of a little rain is going to do down there is beyond me."

Ayyah crossed the deck to see her goal. The Lleveci gathered, craning long necks, crowding the crowded space.

A water world hung below the *Kokkon*, a smallish planet

wrapped in white cotton, with a scrap of blue showing here and there through a rent in the clouds.

"If any of the fairy tales are true, that's Rayor," MacDonald said.

"Nothing from the surface, Mac," Oscar Achebe reported.

"I expect nothing, Oscar Achebe," Ayyah explained. "I understand Rayorians do not build astronomical instruments on this cloudy world, and they have no need for radio spectrum communications. They will be aware of our presence as a cluster of life-forms in their sky—they are biologically sensitive to such things—but I do not believe they have suitable techniques for long-distance information exchange."

"Whoop-dee-doo," Oscar Achebe answered.

"I do not understand this," Ayyah said.

Oscar Achebe shook his head and spoke to MacDonald. "I think we have synchronous orbit above the largest landmass."

MacDonald peered at the sensor board. "Pretty damned small. Okay, Ayyah, we're here. If you're right, and we have no surface support, the number of things we can do here is fairly limited."

"It is satisfactory, MacDonald."

"Hey, wow, I'm overwhelmed with expressions of gratitude."

Ayyah regarded him gravely, trying to read in his face what she could not understand in his words. Often he said things that seemed to make no sense. She was uncertain whether she misinterpreted the language or the human.

Neither case bore on the immediate future. "I will go to the surface," she said.

MacDonald shook his head. "How do you propose to get down there? There's no amenities for tourists, you know."

It seemed a frivolous question. She offered the obvious answer. "I will take the shuttle."

"You know how to pilot a shuttle?"

"You will tell me how it is done."

MacDonald groaned and covered his eyes with one unhappy hand, an expression of distress. She had done nothing to distress him.

"You're out of your ever-loving little pussycat mind," he said.

"Explain 'pussycat.' "

He did not explain. "It takes a little learning, you know. You try to fly the thing cold, I'll be out a passenger and a shuttle."

"This disturbs you, MacDonald?"

"Damned right. I'd be hard pressed to replace the shuttle."

"I will make the attempt."

"The hell you will. I bet there isn't even a landing pad." He groaned softly. "I knew this was going to happen. Why am I doing this?" Before Ayyah could answer, he said, "I'll fly. You have any idea where you want to go?"

In answer Ayyah went back to the crowded little cupboard and found the map of Rayor among the resources acquired from Ynacy Station.

Unfolding it over the navigation console, she pointed to the largest of a chain of islands straggling northward from near the equator. "The north shore of this place, where a deep bay is found. There we will communicate with Rayorians."

"You sound like you're sure."

"It has been done. Before the Kaz, my people from time to time consulted Rayorians. They are very wise."

"Sure."

"You choose often to doubt me, MacDonald. I do not know why this is."

MacDonald folded the map and handed it back. He busied himself with trying to set automatic systems to maintain their orbit. "Ayyah, you say some purely wild things," he said without looking at her.

"You believe that I lie to you?" She could see no value in his deliberately trying to insult her, so she must infer that he genuinely doubted her veracity.

"Well, not exactly," he answered. "It's just, well, look at this map. It came out of Ynacy's archive files. It's so old, how can you trust it?"

"I think geology does not change much in a few centuries."

MacDonald shook his head, defeated. What had the contest been? "I guess not," he said.

"We will go to the surface now?"

"Might as well get it over with. But, Ayyah, suppose the Rayorians don't know any better than anyone else how to beat the Kaz? Suppose the only reason the Kaz haven't taken Rayor is that it's too wet to tunnel in? What then?"

"Then we will proceed into the Perseus arm and search for the answer there."

MacDonald sighed. "Talk about a needle in a haystack."

Ayyah was taken aback. "I have nothing to say about it. What manner of discourse would occur regarding such a thing?"

"Never mind. It's just an expression. Now, you see, here you go with the wild talk again. So let me tell you one thing straight out. That's where I get off the bus, lady. If you go to Perseus, you go without me. I've got other things to do with the rest of my life."

The matter of a bus was puzzling, but she understood the nature of the statement from the tone as much as the content. She found the notion he was presenting to be most peculiar. "What would this be?" she asked, frankly curious.

"Eh?"

"You have a thing planned for the rest of your life more important than defeating the Kaz?"

MacDonald only stared at her for a long time. She understood they were not communicating well, but did not know how to rectify matters.

MacDonald turned to Oscar Achebe and missed, by a hair's breadth, cracking his head yet again on the low ceiling. "Have we got it right yet? Is it stabilized?"

"I think so, but I'm not sure I'd want to bet my life on it. Maybe I should stay here, just in case."

"You don't mind?"

"Hey, I can get a steam bath anytime I want. I'll just set the environmental controls back on automatic."

MacDonald watched Rayor's endless gray sea lap gently against a rocky shore. Oscar's reference to a steam bath wasn't too much of an exaggeration. The air was filled with water, something between a thick mist and a light rain that merged imperceptibly with the low-hanging clouds.

Ayyah stood at the water's edge where a deep finger of the bay poked into the land as if to scratch away this small impediment to the water's free movement over the world. Around her, the sharp spires and deep crags and tumbles of keen-edged black stone looked as if they had just then emerged from subterranean fires. MacDonald half expected them to be steaming in the wet air. He had found barely enough semiflat ground to land the shuttle. He had been seriously worried for a while that they were going to flop gracelessly into the water.

He leaned against the side of the shuttle with one foot hooked up on the skid and watched the Orian gazing out to sea ten meters ahead of him. It had been that close. He should have stayed inside where it was dry, but after the difficult landing, he felt the need of solid ground beneath his feet, even if there was precious little of it.

A thin green slime shading to yellow on the high spots covered the rubble. He decided it was a variety of algae, for all there were moments when he half believed it was in motion. It must be algae, because he didn't want to think of having charred and crushed any sensible beings putting the shuttle down. He didn't want to be standing on anything that hurt. He didn't want that slimy stuff to have any sense of purpose, or to feel resentment.

He wondered how long Ayyah was going to stay there. She had been there a long time, and so far nothing of interest had occurred. Her fur was not the sort that was much protection against the wet. She looked bedraggled and cold. She was shivering; MacDonald could see the tremors amplified by the long tail turned ratlike when the sodden fur collapsed.

He straightened and started down to the shore to tell her it was time to give up, before she caught pneumonia. She held him back with an imperious wave of her hand.

All right, lady, he thought. Suffer. See if I care.

The waves lapped and the fog rolled, and beneath his feet, the green slime shimmered, but it was only a shift in the dull light. He was determined to believe that was all it was.

"They come," Ayyah said.

At the ocean end of the bay, a scattering of dark forms appeared, mottled humps barely distinguishable among the waves, impossible to count as they showed momentarily above the surface and then slipped out of sight again, appearing and disappearing randomly in a loose group like illusions of sea and sky.

The Rayorians' approach was soundless. They moved through the water as if they were part of it. MacDonald had not realized they were so big.

The school submerged. The surface of the water lay undisturbed.

It looked as if the game was over. The Rayorians had declined the meeting.

MacDonald started once more to the shore to fetch Ayyah out of the wet. He wondered why he cared.

The huge dark shadow lay in the inlet, hugging the bottom,

its boundaries made indistinct by the waves. It lay there, gathering its resolve, then shot forward until its belly grated audibly on the shingle. The front end heaved out of the water in a great cascade of ocean, a wrinkled rubbery cylinder supported on a pair of stubby flippers. MacDonald found himself staring down a triangular maw that looked big enough to swallow the shuttle whole.

The ensuing dialogue was utterly silent. MacDonald's shock and dismay were swamped by the Rayorian's initial response to their presence, a gigantic question mark, as big and overwhelming as the creature itself, occupying that other dimension of space MacDonald normally thought of as his mind.

. . . greetings . . . you are welcome . . . what brings you . . .

His mind. His own private property. He tried to back away from the intrusion and found himself with his back against the shuttle. The trespass was both infuriating and frightening.

He heard—was aware of; he found no suitable vocabulary for this invasion of consciousness—only the Rayorian's part of the communication. If Ayyah was able to reply, he couldn't detect her replies. If the Rayorian was aware of him, it gave no sign. He was not included in the conversation.

Who talks to the taxi driver, anyway? he thought with resentment strong enough to surprise him. One of those invisible people other people forget have any sense or feelings. All through this all-begotten adventure, he had been treated like a taxi driver, getting none of the respect the master of a starship was due. The two mad females used him like part of the equipment, a convenience. He was getting bloody sick of it.

His thoughts were pushed roughly aside. The Rayorian occupation left little room for resentment.

. . . news of the death of Orion has come to us . . .

Consciousness was flooded with a terrible sadness. For the first time MacDonald was aware of the cause of the pain that haunted Ayyah, that drove her though she never spoke of it.

A scene became vivid in his mind, of a place he had never been, the Orian spaceport, of the mad, determined scramble to evacuate as many of the population as possible as the planet's defenses crumbled, the pitiful few packed like cattle into whatever spacegoing vessels were available, clutching the treasures of their race, the computer libraries and the germ banks, not knowing as they fled if they could preserve those precious remnants or not, while all around them their world was exploding.

People with no tolerance for crowding were crowded together until the horror of the conditions on the ships was almost equal to the horror of the slaughter on every hand. Millions died in the effort to get a few thousand away. The terror and the smoke and the noise and the smell of death were as real to MacDonald as if he were standing in its midst.

The Kaz pursued the refugees into space. The laboring, overburdened ships were no match for Kazi fighters. Bright deadly flowers bloomed in the dark as ship after fleeing ship was destroyed.

On the surface, the Kazi program of extermination began, to end years later when not one single Orian remained on the planet.

Horror and pain and loss. Anguish too deep to express. Half a billion died not knowing if their final effort had made any difference in the end.

. . . mourn with you the loss of a world, a people . . . fear with you the growing strength of Kaz . . . first recorded regret for unsuitable physiology for joining the fight . . . what help possible given freely, willingly . . .

The assault of the Rayorian minds was staggering. Ayyah sensed nine functioning through the one, sympathetic in their fearsome way, and overwhelming. She struggled to retain a sense of herself, but it was not possible. She was like a candle burning in a forest fire. Dazed and frightened, her mind struggled like some small thing drowning. The Rayorians' benign goodwill notwithstanding, the loss of control was terrifying.

. . . greetings . . . welcome . . . yield to the link . . . resistance will distress you . . . merge . . . come gently . . . no harm will come of this . . . fear not . . . fear not . . . welcome . . . the time is long . . . the news of the destruction of Orion has come to us . . .

The Rayorians' picture of the death of Orion burned like acid on the spirit. It was all too accurate, calling up all the horror and the anguish buried deep within, agony that had to be buried, to remain buried, if the bearer was to function at all. To have it ripped up to the surface was intolerable. Ayyah swayed on the edge of unconsciousness. The picture faded, engulfed in apology.

Time passed while she recovered, the Rayorian presence reduced to a soothing empty beat, a carrier wave, a neutral presence. In that interlude, she realized that MacDonald had been accidentally included in the circuit. She could feel his frantic, wounded psyche flopping like a beached fish in its effort to escape. The Rayorians seemed unconscious of his being there, or careless of it.

Release the human, she suggested. *His distress serves no purpose.*

. . . done . . .

Others? she asked. *Have you known Oriani from other groups?*

. . . you are the first since the Kaz . . . what brings you . . .

Suddenly she was back in the cold, damp birthing cave on KD2434, hurt and spent, heartsick, her lovely babies lying dead around her.

. . . mourn with you . . . how can we help . . .

Of its own accord an image of her father welled up, alive in her mind as he was in his latter days, weary and graying, losing the battle he had given his life to, fighting on nonetheless, handing the mission on to his only child.

They sat together in the garden of Talan's Orion home on a warm summer day. A reproduction of a Kazi star chart lay between them on a small table and Talan was pointing out an error, provocative because the Kaz made few errors. On this chart, the world called Rayor did not appear.

Satisfaction colored the Rayorian response, and some sense of mild amusement.

It was too much for Ayyah to be yanked from one emotional state to another with scarcely a pause between. Any such sensation was distressing. Many of them, hard on one another, all within a few minutes, had her reeling. The mind, so abused, cringes, closes in on itself, becomes engrossed with its own workings.

The image faded to neutral gray, to the empty, waiting beat. Again, patiently, the Rayorians waited for her to collect herself. How long, she couldn't say. When she felt able, they continued.

. . . an interesting observation by a keen observer . . . Talan was a good mind, remembered well . . .

How is this done? she asked. *Can it be done elsewhere?*

The vision developed into a convoluted puzzle turning in on itself in many dimensions, her own perplexity and concern made manifest.

. . . regrets . . . the answer will not be useful to you . . .

Into Ayyah's mind came the Rayorian view of space, a great

emptiness with objects embedded in it, a world, a star, a distant moon, and Kaz. The Kaz were tied together with glittering threads of infinite thinness. The threads permeated space every-where, except around the world they bent away, leaving Rayor untouched among the workings of a million manic Midas spi-ders.

Ayyah tried to imagine herself with other Oriani learning to do that. The Rayorian response was sadness and negation.

. . . regret you are not able . . .

The perception she received was of an overwhelming burden, of enormous effort.

. . . will not endure . . . for a moment we are invisible . . . energy demands great . . . the Kazi mind is odd, difficult, half its own, half the property of the brood . . .

Ayyah had no image for her sense of loss.

. . . do not grieve what has not come to pass . . . much may be done by courage and agile hands . . . follow the threads to their end . . . seek out the mother . . . the one weakness we see . . . others may be . . . we learn, we study, we work to under-stand the enemy . . . this we know, for now . . . the Kaz are tied to the mother so strongly, the death of the mother is the death of many . . . in time we will know more . . . time changes all things . . .

The Rayorian was growing tired. The effort of the contact and of maintaining itself out of its element were rapidly draining it of energy. Ayyah could feel it growing weaker. The scale of the vision changed. She was given an image of a substantial fraction of the Kazi empire in the Orion arm. All was filled with the Kazi threads, an impossible tangle, without ends. Without ends, but with a direction. There was a degree of order in the tangle, conceivably an order only a Rayorian could fully grasp. The sense of it hung at the edge of Ayyah's mind like something almost understood.

The vision vanished. As it faded, Ayyah was aware of re-ceiving data directly into memory, bypassing consciousness. Alarmed, she tried to pull away. The Rayorian minds began to withdraw, leaving Ayyah her singular self, isolated inside her little shell of flesh, lost in the dark of her solitude, as hurt as if something material were being torn away. She realized the meaning in the human word "alone."

Then she was once again peering out through the holes in her skull at gray waves washing up on black rock and out across the endless heaving sea. The great streaming universe lay all about her, and she was very small.

The Rayorian collapsed back into the water with a crash of spray that soaked her to her ear tips. She backed away, shaking herself. The shadow lingered in the shallows for a moment, gave a sinuous twist, and was gone.

She was deeply disturbed and disoriented. Her head hurt. She was cold to the bone.

Head down, Ayyah climbed slowly up the shallow slope. She passed MacDonald without speaking.

"Hey," he said. "Aren't you going to tell me what happened?"

For a moment she saw him anew, with his curiosity written all over his face, a creature less alien than he had been. For a moment she thought she saw, beneath the hard, world-worn façade, something frightened by the experience of the Rayorian and hurt at being thrown out of it.

"I have been given much to decipher and comprehend, MacDonald," she said.

"Yeah, okay," he answered crossly, and was suddenly hard and remote again. He kicked his boots against the shuttle's skids and swung himself inside. "So, you ready to go, or not?"

Her preoccupation with the Rayorian contact might excuse her, but they were back in the *Kokkon* before she understood that MacDonald's abrupt change of mood had occurred because he thought she chose not to discuss the contact. He didn't realize that she didn't yet know what she had. How could she possibly explain what she herself did not understand?

The *Kokkon* remained in orbit above Rayor while Ayyah worked and MacDonald fretted and wondered just how much he actually owed the Lleveci. They had promised him a starship and had delivered, if one could call the Kazi can a starship. He had promised to take Ayyah where she wanted to go, and he had done that, and his thanks was to be totally ignored. Was he obliged to hang around while she did whatever she was doing?

He seemed to feel that he was.

Lying in orbit was the cheapest and possibly the safest way to wait. *Kokkon* used much less fuel than she would under power, and the Rayorian bending of Kazi sensibilities should protect it from detection. Or so MacDonald hoped.

But by the time he had watched planet dawn straggle across the cloud deck below for the fourth time, he decided he was getting tired of waiting.

The Lleveci were beginning to get restless, too. MacDonald thought it would be wise to find them something to do, before he had trouble with a gang of bored and cranky warriors, but he didn't know what it was going to be. He had tried to interest them in helping to unravel the *Kokkon*'s mysteries. Ellid Rullenahe was intrigued by the problem, and Delladar Oll dogged MacDonald with questions and poked her long neck into everything he was doing for a couple of days, but soon tired of it. Most of the Lleveci seemed to think this was not warrior's work. They just hung around, got in the way, and talked among themselves.

Oscar and Ayyah were busy at the computer. Oscar had finally begun to get a little sense out of the machine and had called a star chart onto the main screen for the Orian. On the smaller screen next to it, Ayyah was refining a reproduction of the Rayorian view of the universe. Delladar Oll was trying to talk to her whenever she could distract the Orian from her work. MacDonald smiled wryly to himself. Maybe tedium would overcome Delladar Oll's contempt toward Ayyah in a way nothing else could. Boredom made stranger bedfellows than politics.

MacDonald had been putting in the time trying to familiarize himself with the ship's controls. He had made one useful discovery, that he could get some of the monitors to respond in Sindharr, which helped, but he still wasn't overwhelmingly confident of his ability to handle the ship.

It was head-cracking work. He thought he might just wander over and see how long it was going to take Oscar and Ayyah to do whatever they were doing.

That was a gross exaggeration of what he actually did. MacDonald could no more wander on the flight deck of the Kazi ship than he could dance in a closet. He could only sidle with his head bent and his elbows pulled into his sides. He could ease himself between environment control and the navigator's station by tucking his tail bone tightly in and sucking in his gut. After a few days of doing those things, he was getting a permanent and painful crick in his neck, and becoming extremely tense and irritable.

So when he asked Ayyah if she was making any sense of the

Rayorian information, it was not so much in the spirit of friendly curiosity as it might have been under other circumstances.

Oscar said, "Excuse me a moment," got up, and made his way carefully across the bridge. MacDonald took his place on the floor beside Ayyah.

"It is not so difficult," Ayyah said, "when you understand the representational conventions."

"The representational conventions."

"Yes. Almost all reasoning peoples have some convention of display. With humans, it is one of distance. If you were to draw a picture, you would assume a common understanding that the objects in the bottom corners of your picture were nearest the observer, and those near the center top were farthest away."

"Yeah, I guess I would."

"With Rayorians, the conventions are those of perceived importance and subjective direction. Our first chore, therefore, is to determine the orientation of our contact relative to some more objective coordinates. This is only a matter of mathematics, but with minimal assistance from the computer, it is time-consuming.

"I am correct in believing it is time that concerns you?"

MacDonald nodded. "Well, yes. Aside from the fact that inactivity is making everyone restless, and aside from the fact that supplies are not unlimited, and aside from the fact that Kazi rations won't kill us but I for one don't like them much, this bug bucket surely must be the most uncomfortable blasted ship since *Gemini*."

"Gemini? An element from early human folklore?"

"Now how would you know that? Yes, but also one of the very first Terran spacecraft."

"Indeed? To answer your question, soon I expect to know the location of the Broodmother. It is very odd, this remembering what you never knew."

"So what's this brood—"

Oscar returned. "Mac, there's something I think you ought to see."

"What?"

"I don't know."

"Where?"

"In the head."

"The head?" That was another horrendous problem. The sanitary facilities fit Kaz. They were remarkably unsuited to humans, Lleveci, and Oriani. In an enclosed environment like a spaceship, matters of sanitation were of utmost importance.

"Do I want to see it?" MacDonald asked, not relishing the possibilities that came to mind.

"Probably not," Oscar said. "But I think you should."

Reluctantly MacDonald heaved himself off the floor and managed to scrape the point of his shoulder on the edge of the terminal keyboard doing it. He sighed in resignation, rubbed his shoulder, kept his neck bent, and followed Oscar down the short corridor. Ayyah followed, perhaps needing a break from her work, perhaps merely curious.

The tiny chamber had an opening—it could scarcely be called a door—across the full width of the forward end, slightly more than waist high. When one was within, a sliding panel closed it. The chamber itself was lined with a smooth, translucent material in which the lighting elements were embedded. There was a shallow trench and a drain in the floor. Flushing had meant getting thoroughly soaked by shower heads mounted at intervals on walls, ceiling, and floor, a distressing arrangement, particularly for Ayyah, until Oscar had gone to work and put the controls outside the chamber.

Plumbing was obviously not the thing the Kaz were best at. There was a tendency for fittings to drip a little. But MacDonald had not noticed the yellowish-green stain around the wet places before.

He reached in warily and scratched a little of the stain off the wall with his thumbnail. Slowly the scraping pulled itself into a minute green sphere balanced on the end of his nail. Small as it was, its color varied as if two immiscible liquids were streaming sluggishly by one another just below the surface. Repelled, MacDonald flicked it away from him.

He thought about it for a minute. "Well, it's kind of disgusting, but it doesn't look that dangerous," he said.

"But it does bring two questions to mind," Oscar said. "First, where did it come from? And second, what's it living on? It's alive and growing, so it's eating something. Are the recyclers losing efficiency?"

"Oscar, my friend, I do not like what you are saying."

Merciless, Oscar continued. "Our bunch probably produces different waste products from the Kaz. Maybe the system can't handle them. If that's the case, we're in serious trouble. We're a long way from friendly assistance."

MacDonald bit his lip. "You're right." He frowned furiously, thinking.

"Can we check it out?" he asked. I knew something just about this dumb was going to happen, he thought. He had told Ayyah from the start it was stupid to go buzzing off into hostile territory in a ship you knew practically nothing about when you couldn't even read the instructions.

"I can look at the system, but I'm no kind of biochemist. If there's a mechanical problem, maybe, just maybe, I can figure it out. Otherwise, not."

"Any idea what we've got for backups?"

Oscar shook his head. "I don't know if there are any. Could be Kaz have never run into this problem."

"Shit," MacDonald said.

"That is the subject of the moment."

MacDonald glowered. "You pick the strangest times to be funny."

"I could cry, but that would just add to our troubles."

"Yeah. Here's my bucket of guilt for you. I think I probably brought that stuff up from the surface. It looks about like the junk that's growing all over the rocks down there."

Ayyah had been following the conversation, eyes flicking from one speaker to the other. "Your assumptions are unreasonable. I, also, might have been the vector. Perhaps decontamination of the shuttle was incomplete."

"Or," Oscar added, "maybe it's always been here, for all we know. Whatever, it's done us a favor. We might not have had any warning we could recognize without it."

"Yeah, okay," MacDonald answered. "I appreciate what you guys are trying to say. Oscar, you go do your looking. I'll get this so-called ship started for the nearest friendly place, just in case. Ayyah, you come with me. I need your help."

"Are we going to tell the Lleveci?" Oscar asked.

MacDonald thought about it, then shook his head. "They'll find out soon enough. Let's put off the general panic as long as possible. Maybe we're worried about nothing."

"Yeah," Oscar said dubiously. "Maybe."

As they headed back to the bridge, Ayyah stopped MacDonald in the low corridor. "Where is this 'nearest friendly place'?" she asked.

"I don't know. That's one of the things we're going to have to find out." He urged her out onto the bridge proper where the ceiling was a little higher. "Can you make the computer cough up a map of this sector of space?"

There was a miniscule hesitation before she replied. "The Kazi version, in which Rayor does not appear."

"That will do."

"I do not like this, MacDonald."

"Me, neither."

The Lleveci milled restlessly around, wondering, no doubt, what was going on. Ayyah fiddled with the computer for a few moments, then went to talk to Delladar Oll.

The display came up on the main screen, and MacDonald located a not-too-inconvenient free port out of Kazi space called Kincaid's World, made an educated guess about the course to it from where Rayor would be if it were there, and punched the numbers into the navigation console. It took him awhile. He was having trouble adapting to the Kazi system of numbers.

He set the helm on automatic and called Ayyah. "Come and watch this for a few minutes while I tend to the engines. If it starts to drift, sing out. Don't touch anything."

"Where do you plan to go?" she asked.

MacDonald pointed out Kincaid's World on the chart.

Her ears tipped back slightly. "This is the wrong direction, MacDonald."

MacDonald was busy at the power board and didn't answer.

"You have made a commitment to the Lleveci and to me. I would hold you to it."

The engines fired and gave *Kokkon* a little nudge. The Lleveci looked up and chattered among themselves. Delladar Oll came over. MacDonald wished for the umpteenth time for an intercom so he could warn Oscar of coming acceleration. The Kaz must have had some way of communicating with various parts of the ship, but so far MacDonald had not found it.

Ayyah was watching the board in front of her with intense concentration, but she wasn't through with him yet. He decided she had the potential to become a first-class nag. "Your reputation describes you as a man of your word. Your promise means nothing whatsoever to you?"

"Damn it, Ayyah," MacDonald growled, stung. "We can't."

A bristly Delladar Oll strode across the deck and took up an aggressive stance in front of Ayyah with her arms crossed over her chest, as if to physically defend the Orian from MacDonald's failure to live up to his agreements. "Have agreement, Mac-Donald," she said with menace. "Take Orian where she wants."

Ayyah backed away, trying to get a little space, until she was hard against the navigator's console. MacDonald reined in a fit of temper. He hesitated, then went on, abandoning his hope of keeping general alarm at bay for a time. "We may be in deep trouble with the life support. We've got to get somewhere with air and water and facilities for repair."

"Know this sure?" the Lleveci asked.

"No. But I don't plan to take the chance. There are pleasanter ways to die."

"Air, water, lots on Rayor."

"Fat lot of good it does. There's no way to get it from there to here, and if there was, it won't fix the recyclers. If we hang around, we could find ourselves having to choose between suffocation and looking below for a place to stand above the high-tide line, if there is such a place on Rayor. It doesn't strike me as the way I want to spend the rest of my life."

On the forward view screen, Rayor's fuzzy white image drifted off the lower righthand corner.

"Reserves?" Delladar Oll asked.

"Let's hope. As soon as we clear the planetary system and can set this flying hive on automatic, everybody's going to be pressed into service looking for them. But it'll be a few days at most."

"A few days are all we need," Ayyah said.

"Wrong. Those few days—and we don't know yet if we've even got them—are our safety margin. We're a minimum of nine days out of Kincaid's World, and our first jump is going to drop us right into the middle of Kazi town."

"You could choose a safer route."

"But longer."

"The problem is that serious?"

"It could be. I don't know yet."

"We are abandoning our efforts because of a problem that possibly does not exist?"

"Yeah."

"I do not understand this."

"Come on, Ayyah. You saw the green glop in the can. Think about drinking polluted water for nine days. You'll get the idea." Cautiously he set the power controls on automatic. "Hold it steady for a few minutes. I'm going to get Oscar."

* * *

MacDonald had only left the bridge when Delladar Oll turned to face Ayyah.

"Orian, know where going?"

"I believe so," Ayyah answered. The engines gained power steadily. They didn't need her attention.

"Is far?"

"Several days."

"Air, water there?"

"If I have interpreted the Rayorian message correctly, a major population of Kaz live there. Kaz require conditions similar to our needs. I do not doubt facilities for servicing starships are also there. Getting access is another matter."

"Know how make course there?"

"Yes."

"So. We go there."

"MacDonald is determined to proceed to Kincaid's World."

The warrior pulled a heavy handgun from the folds of her tunic. She smiled her open-mouthed smile. "Change mind."

"No." Ayyah was appalled. "I cannot agree to any such thing."

"Good talk. Not so good think. Spend lots time, money, have much danger, get here. MacDonald say leave here. Orian say okay. No fight. Think maybe come back, start over? Not happen. Decide, Orian. What you have, clean hands or dead Kaz?"

It was a long speech for the warrior. And, Ayyah thought, perhaps the Lleveci was right. Perhaps she was not thinking well. She knew she was stressed. Living and working with aliens in close quarters strained her tolerance. The communication with the Rayorian had disturbed her deeply, and she was only beginning to feel recovered.

The Lleveci was determined. Opposing her, Ayyah might find herself the target of the ever-ready weapon, or at the very least, losing Lleveci support. Delladar Oll was easily irritated and tended to act without thinking far into the future.

Truly, Ayyah's objective was becoming more remote with every throb of the engines. On an alien world, the last shreds of the Orian race were dying. But if she agreed to this, what survived? A shape, a form, without meaning?

What meaning could be found among the dead?

"Without the humans, we cannot operate the ship." Ayyah

felt relieved to find this one rock-solid reality from which there was no retreating.

"No problem. Fix course. I fix humans. Orian do nothing. Say nothing. Orian hands clean."

"Why do you want to do this? What you are considering is very dangerous."

"Mother wishes."

"Your mother shows a fine disregard for the lives of her children."

"Kaz kill many. All time more. Small chance better no chance."

"This I understand well." Ayyah could hear footsteps in the corridor. "The humans are returning."

"Be ready," Delladar Oll instructed. Ayyah turned to the navigation panel with a sense of having acquiesced to a deeply immoral act. In her imagination, the martyred philosophers of ancient Orion who led their people from brutal savagery into reasoned civilization turned away disapproving eyes.

Oscar was already on his way back. MacDonald met him in the low, narrow corridor near the engine room. "We've got to invent some kind of intercom," Oscar complained as they hunched their way along to the bridge. To MacDonald's questioning look he said, "I don't know. The life-support system looks all right. The recyclers look like they're working. I didn't *see* anything wrong. On the other hand, I've never seen anything quite like it before. Do I know what I'm seeing?"

All was quiet forward. Unusually quiet.

Maybe it's finally gotten through to these people what kind of trouble they're in, MacDonald thought. "Okay," he said to Oscar. "Take the helm from Ayyah. We'll take her to Kincaid's and see if we can find someone who understands Kazi machinery to look it over. Or better yet, sell her for scrap and use the proceeds to make a downpayment on some decent rig."

Oscar studied the board in front of him for a moment, glanced up at the chart, then leaned over to read the settings on the navigation console.

"Kincaid's World, you said?" he asked.

"Yeah. It's the nearest neutral territory." MacDonald took the power board off automatic for the business of building speed for the hyperspace jump. The Orian and the Lleveci had moved off a way, into a corner where they had a little room. They seemed to be arguing, which was more in keeping with their incompatible characters.

"Mac, the settings are all wrong."

"Eh, what? You think suddenly I can't plot a course?"

"I'm not kidding. Just a minute." Oscar went over to the computer terminal and worked there for a moment. On the overhead chart a dashed red line appeared.

"That's our projected course," Oscar said.

MacDonald came over to see the boards for himself on the off chance that Oscar might be hallucinating.

Oscar, as always, was eminently sane. The settings had been altered. The red line ended deep, deep in Kazi territory.

"How in the name of the nine worlds—Ayyah!"

Ayyah turned from her argument with her yellow eyes innocently wide, her ears pricked forward. Delladar Oll moved toward the rest of her people, as if to get out of the way of MacDonald's obvious displeasure.

"Just what did you think you were going to accomplish here?"

"This is where we must go, MacDonald."

"Yes? Tell me, when did you learn to navigate?"

"Approximately eighty-two Terran years ago, when I was required to join my people in their efforts to defend their world. We failed, MacDonald, but I have not forgotten all that I learned in that evil time. I am not so clever at it as you are. I think I could not have found Rayor from the old charts. But my skill is adequate for this."

"You just neglected to tell me all that?"

"You neglected to ask."

MacDonald was vibrating with fury. Oscar put a hand on his arm in a sympathetic effort to help him control his anger, but Oscar himself looked less than happy.

When MacDonald could trust himself to speak, he spoke very quietly and very precisely, and if any of his passengers had known him better, they would have realized it signaled a dangerous state of mind.

"Ayyah, I think I made it sufficiently plain for everyone that all our lives may well depend on getting to a safe port as soon as possible. When we get to Kincaid's World, we may discuss possible future destinations. I assure you it will not involve any insanities like dropping in on the Kaz in the most securely held part of the sector. Until then, there will be no argument. Is that clear?"

"I understand you," Ayyah said. "You must understand, our lives are not significant in this matter."

"Wrong," MacDonald said as he turned to reset the navigation controls. "My life is important to me, and I'm responsible for yours for the time being. Once we set down on Kincaid's, you're welcome to pursue suicide in whatever manner pleases you."

Oscar's shout of warning came a moment too late. MacDonald turned in time to see Delladar Oll with her arm raised just before the butt of the blaster collided with his skull right behind his ear. Then he knew a couple of seconds of blinding pain before the darkness closed in.

Klact

The Empire class light cruiser *Klact* made good time from Ynacy Station to Llevec, and its commander ordered the shuttle to the surface as soon as the vessel achieved stable orbit. The commander was excited about the information retrieved from the reluctant librarian on Ynacy and would have been pleased to be allowed to act immediately on the new data. It chafed at the delay.

However, the delay was by no means unreasonable. *Klact* left Llevec following nothing more substantial than a rumor. If something should happen to the *Klact*, the data would be lost. The leaders had a need and a right to know what had been uncovered. One might wish for a more efficient method of communication.

The commander brought along a technician from its vessel to the governor's office, and while the technician labored to get Kazi computer equipment to read the alien records, the commander described its visit to Ynacy. The human female maintaining the library on Ynacy had been hostile and disrespectful toward the empire, but she kept immaculate records. It glanced toward the image forming in the large navigator's display tank that it had installed on the governor's desk. The murky swirls of color were beginning to take on form.

While they waited, the commander explained to its leaders the provenance of the charts they were about to see.

These are the charts the Orian pirate examined during her stay on Ynacy Station. They are strangely old, more than fifteen twelves of standard years out of date, originally prepared by a pre-empire alliance of spacefaring worlds in this region known as the Interstellar Community. The copies at Ynacy are certified.

In other signs, some authority of the time guaranteed them accurate.

One might have hoped for something more significant than a clawful of computer records containing old maps, the governor said.

We have confirmed the existence of the Orian, the commander pointed out.

Little enough return for the effort made, the governor signed. *It is difficult to understand why pirates or anyone else other than a historian should exhibit an interest in old charts.*

In the tank, the image cleared.

The broodmaster made sluggish signs. It looked about to collapse. It was not well versed in the navigational arts, it said. One chart looked much like another. Could the commander explain the importance of age as it pertained to star charts?

The galaxy does change, though slowly, the commander said. It tapped a claw near the upper edge of the tank. *Here is shown the blue-white giant star 316A. But 316A became a supernova almost nine twelves of years ago. Several nearby systems were evacuated. To navigate this region, depending for information on this chart, would put one in danger of encountering the remnant of the supernova, with survival extremely doubtful, and of expecting civilization on worlds now lifeless. The question is, why should the pirates take so much interest in charts that would be dangerous to use?*

The governor shrugged and suggested that aliens were often incomprehensible in their ways.

The broodmaster disagreed, weakly. *We may not always understand the motives,* it signed, *but all actions are motivated, alien as well as Kazi.*

The commander instructed the technician with the abbreviated signs the military often use with one another. The image in the tank faded, to be replaced with another, larger-scale chart of a small region.

It drew the broodmaster's attention to the more sparsely populated image, then asked the technician to overlay a modern map of the same region.

After a period of confusion while the technician adjusted the scale and orientation, gradually the twinned points drew together and merged. There were minor differences to be sure. Bodies rotated about their common centers. Dust clouds billowed or collapsed. The galaxy turned and dragged its members unevenly along. But fifteen twelves of years was a ridiculously short time as the stellar dance was measured. Though it did not consider itself well informed about astronomical matters, the broodmaster did not expect any very large differences. Particularly, it did not believe a star had winked out of existence without a trace in that small span of time.

The governor was not impressed. *So much for the guarantees of alien authorities,* it said. It did not see how inaccurate old maps could be of much value in the search for a stolen starship.

What is this place which is not on our charts? the broodmaster asked.

The commander signed its puzzlement. *I know of no such place. I once assumed it to be a cartographic error. Yet what other reason to seek out old charts except to find a place not on new charts? I now think the bandits have gone in search of this star. Where better to hide than a place the empire believes does not exist?*

Does it exist? the governor asked.

I believe it does not. Our cartographers are reliable, the commander said. *I have been in this region. However, if the pirates believe it does, there is no reason we could not intercept them in empty space.*

Our cartographers are infallible? the broodmaster asked. *You know every star in the sector?*

Rather than answer questions for which there were no answers, the commander turned to the governor with an interrogatory gesture, requesting permission to pursue the pirates into the region.

The governor's scent recommended caution. *To order vessels to be maneuvered based on so thin a hypothesis would not be wise,* the governor said. *Even so, could you catch them? You must be some days behind.*

Leaning back on its legs, the commander admitted, *At least a twelveday behind a vessel of similar speed. However,* Kokkon *is not so fast, and the pirates do not have much experience with it. We do not pursue an armed force, only a few, isolated rebels in an unarmed broodship. The* Klact *is here and ready; the time would not be unduly long, the danger minimal.*

The broodmaster thought perhaps the commander underestimated the few, isolated rebels. Two twelves of them had, after all, made off with a Kazi starship and eluded pursuit thus far.

The governor rocked slightly side to side, showing its indecision. *This sector is endlessly in need of ships*, it complained. *If a warship had been nearby earlier, we would not have lost the* Kokkon *in the first place. The* Klact *would be useful here. If a ship dispatched to examine empty space finds nothing, we would look at least naive, at worst, criminally wasteful of empire resources.*

The broodmaster saw things differently. Its scent was intense. *We must send the* Klact *to this place at once, with all possible speed*, it told the governor, showing more energy than it had in a long time. *This is the place the* Kokkon *will be found.*

The governor was relieved. A direct order would absolve it of responsibility. The broodmaster was watching it intently for a sign of its agreement. What it saw was the governor's signs of compliance. *I defer to you as broodmaster. If resources are wasted, you are responsible.*

Let it be so, the broodmaster replied. It fell back on its legs, its little store of energy exhausted.

The commander expressed its appreciation to the broodmaster and wasted no time getting the *Klact* into space.

Six days later, the *Klact* dropped into space normal within sensor range of the point in question.

At that moment, both the navigator and the sensor operator registered surprise and began to sign something, then indicated a mistake.

As the star field came on the main viewing screen, the commander itself was disconcerted by a subliminal sense of a yellow star dominating the view, when in fact there was nothing on the screen nearer than four light-years. The feeling was so strong that it checked the mass sensor over the sensor operator's back, as if the screen might be in error. All was in order.

Proceed with great caution, it ordered the bridge crew, though caution seemed unnecessary. The *Klact* eased its way toward the precise point marked on the old map. The sensors swept the way ahead, searching for the missing ship.

The course curved away from the intended direction.

The commander instructed the pilot to pay attention to what it was doing.

The pilot replied with an apologetic posture. It had been paying attention. It was at a loss to explain the way the ship was behaving. The helm was responding as if the *Klact* were approaching a large mass.

The mass sensor still said nothing.

The commander had a degree of confidence in its crew. Small, uncharted black holes and collapsars were not unknown. Instruments sometimes went awry without warning. The mass sensor should be reliable, but a possibility of failure existed.

The commander also had its own persistent feeling that something was amiss. With some misgivings, it yielded to its intuition.

Engines on standby, it signaled. *Navigator, observe the ship's drift. Determine the possibility of any nearby mass.*

Obediently the navigator bent to its calculations.

Suddenly the star was there, huge, blinding, overwhelming the forward view screen, looming directly in their path. Suddenly a dozen sensors on *Klact*'s bridge were blinking in alarm. The mass sensor was heading off scale. The ship's skin temperature was much too high and climbing. Motion sensors were completely confounded by the writhing, seething, flaring surface below. Radiation and particle sensors were flooded. The *Klact* was falling into the sun.

Shocked though it was, the commander did not stop to ponder the mystery.

Emergency restart, all engines. Full reverse thrust.

The ship shuddered under conflicting forces. The commander watched the sensors intently to see if the *Klact* was going to be able to pull away from the star. Its claws dug into the deck as if it would lift the ship by its will.

The *Klact* was a good, trim, fighting ship, powered by a pair of the best engines the Kaz were capable of building. The ship groaned and slowed and stopped, and then began to climb away with engines straining for every centimeter.

Much later, when the commander had time to assess more objectively its performance in that crisis, it understood it had not hit upon the best solution to the problem. Later in its life, when its career bent toward teaching others the nuances of journeying through space, it would discourse at length about the use of hyperbolic trajectories in emergencies.

At the time, it was only relieved and baffled and shaken.

When it felt it was reliably able to do so, the commander put the *Klact* into a parking orbit, a comfortably distant parking orbit with a fifty-million-kilometer perihelion. It gathered its crew around and asked for an explanation of what they had just seen.

All agreed on the major characteristic of the phenomenon, that a star appeared where no star had been moments before.

The computer record, on the other hand, showed the commander calmly driving its ship directly into the sun, with the quiet, unperturbed complicity of its crew.

No one could offer any reasonable explanation.

Once commander and crew recovered their equilibria somewhat, the technicians made such astrophysical measurements as *Klact*'s instruments allowed.

In due time, the head technician reported to the commander. *The star is a perfectly ordinary middle-age yellow dwarf,* it said. *Six planetary bodies, nine moons, and some smaller debris have been located. Undoubtedly, more elements exist in the system, but a fully equipped astrophysical survey party will be needed to make an exhaustive catalog.*

Assuming the system didn't vanish again the moment they turned their backs, the commander thought. However, it did remember to look for the *Kokkon*, even though its original objective seemed of little import compared to the remarkable fact of having a star pop out of empty space almost between one's legs.

There was nothing supernatural in the Kazi tradition. Kaz admitted only two realities: explained phenomena and unexplained phenomena. The assumption was that unexplained phenomena would, in time, become explained. Nonetheless, commander and crew shared an uneasiness about remaining in a region where stars materialized without warning. More than one crew member looked up suddenly from its work to check that the star was still there. All were anxious to do what had to be done and be away.

One biogenic planet only, the head technician reported. The commander was relieved that the painstaking search of planetary surfaces should be limited to one. If the *Kokkon* had visited this phantom system, most likely it would have gone where other life existed.

The planet is almost wholly covered by ocean, the technician continued, *and all its advanced life-forms are aquatic. No industrial development, no evidence of technological civilization has been seen, and no sign of the missing ship.*

Nonetheless, the water world seemed the only possibility. The commander put the *Klact* into orbit around it and set the technicians to work scanning the available bits of land, its reasoning being none of the pirates was of a species who would be comfortable under water.

Work of that sort took time, even when only a few, small dry sites needed to be considered. The commander's anxiety was noticeable, particularly when the bulk of the planet hid the sun from view.

The almost continuous cloud deck hampered the technicians. In time, they hit upon the solution of placing an instrument package below the clouds on a steerable balloon. The investigation then proceeded more quickly. The instruments returned only one item worthy of investigation, a scorched spot and two parallel marks in the yellow-green slime that uniformly covered the land above sealevel.

The commander accompanied the technicians to the surface.

While the technicians applied more precise instruments, the commander measured the distance between the parallel lines with its outstretched forelimbs. The distance matched the distance between the skids of a Lleveci shuttle.

Kokkon had been there.

The *Klact* returned immediately to Llevec with the news. The governor was both amazed and relieved by the *Klact*'s discovery. Its decision to dispatch a warship to an apparently empty location was vindicated in a most spectacular way. Convinced that the old broodmaster had deeper insights into the psychology of rebels than anyone, including itself, had previously appreciated, it issued a general alert to Kazi ships in the region around the newfound star to be on the watch for the *Kokkon*. It asked the district supervisor to construct a sensor net along established routes through the region. The value of the *Kokkon*, after all, was less significant than the fact that the pirates had gotten away with it, and the 44th Battalion deserved some vengeance. The empire's subjects should not imagine anyone could do such things and survive.

The *Klact* did not join the hunt. Its environmental and recycling systems were undergoing repair. The fouling wasn't extensive, but it needed cleaning out before it became serious, for the alien organism growing there had insinuated itself into every tube and filter. In time, the system would fail completely.

Meanwhile, the commander was summoned to bring a copy of its records to the Academy of Anthropology on one of the core worlds, to discuss its discovery and, particularly, the events preceding it. The world of water, the academicians noted, fit nothing so well as the description of the illusive world known as Rayor, mentioned in the early history of the empire in this region, but not since. The Rayorians, the commander might be interested to know, were noted in the legends for their mind games, for their skill at creating illusions, often lethal illusions.

Although the long journey took it far from its proper work, the commander was heartened by the possibility of an explanation.

In the seas of Rayor, the great bodies gathered in the ocean deeps, exhausted and mourning, seeking what comfort they could find in one another. They had done their best to make the crew of the Kazi vessel believe that Rayor's star did not exist, and they had failed. If the Kaz had been a fraction less quick to react, if the ship's engines had been minutely less powerful, they would have succeeded. They could no longer maintain their deception.

The Kazi exploration had been brief, but thorough. The Rayorians had heard the instruments bleating to one another, had seen the probes' energy fields slicing down like burning blades, sweeping over the land, delving into the water, had been touched, had seen their comrades touched. They had felt the Kaz above, brooding, malevolent presences pulling in the threads of information.

What the Kaz might want with Rayor, the Rayorians could not imagine. They only knew the enemy had come. They foresaw their world destroyed.

Deep Kazi Space

The thin whine penetrated the darkness. It was important, that whine, if he could just remember why. It was desperately important, but the pain in his head made his stomach sick.

Something else was important, too, about the foul taste in the air, but it was too hard to think. It would be better to lie back down and stop fighting until his head felt better.

"Mac, damn you, wake up."

That was Oscar, sounding urgent. The weak, ragged groan was his own. MacDonald pulled his eyelids open. The greenish light stabbed at him. Slowly the deck plates came into focus, vibrating slightly under him. That was wrong. Deck plates shouldn't vibrate.

There was an argument going on somewhere.

He wished the whine would stop.

He got almost sitting up. An arm around his shoulders helped him finish the job, then handed him a glass of water.

"Out of the reserve tanks," Oscar said. "It should be okay."

Oscar's strong hand under his arm almost lifted him to his feet. The deck swung around him. MacDonald frowned in concentration, trying to orient himself, and staggered toward the engine control panel.

Engines. Overloaded engines, whining with too much strain. That was what the noise was about. He had to stop it. Now.

Ayyah was in the way.

He grunted at her and pushed her aside.

She didn't move.

He frowned at her, trying to understand. She looked back at him with wide yellow eyes and an expressionless face.

He looked around for Oscar and grazed his scalp on an over-

198

head brace. The pain made his knees buckle and his eyes water. Oscar appeared from somewhere and made concerned noises.

"What?" MacDonald croaked out. "What?"

"These idiots are trying to make the center of the sector in one jump. Please tell them it can't be done. Maybe they'll believe you. I've tried to tell them this Kazi can is going to come apart at the seams. They don't believe me."

"No." He was going to shake his head, and stopped himself just in time. "Abort. We've got to abort. The engines."

"Well, there's a problem."

MacDonald looked back at Ayyah. She had not moved. "We go as the Rayorian directed, MacDonald," she said.

He looked for the Lleveci. They were standing around like a hunching crowd of sharp-eyed buzzards watching a bullfight and waiting to take on the loser. "Don't you understand?" he asked them.

Delladar Oll shrugged. She still had the gun in her hand. MacDonald took that to be evidence that he had not been unconscious very long. Then again, no doubt the weapon had been keeping Oscar at bay.

"You've all decided?"

She gave him the waggley Lleveci nod.

"No," he said. "You can't do it this way."

She pulled her neck down into a double curve and shook her mane out as if she were trying to mimic a short-necked creature. It meant she had no intention of debating the issue.

MacDonald took a deep breath and tried to pull himself together. He wanted so much to lie back down on the deck until he felt better.

"You're wrecking the ship," he said.

Delladar Oll said nothing.

"Wherever you think you're going, where you'll be is in little pieces scattered across a sizable fraction of the known galaxy." MacDonald paused, trying to think of a compelling argument. "You hear the noise? You know by now that's not normal. The engines are straining. That can't go on for long."

The Lleveci gave no indication of listening to reason.

MacDonald gave up on explanations. "The hell with it," he muttered hoarsely. "I might as well be shot down as blown up. Oscar, give me a hand here."

When Ayyah realized the humans would move her bodily out of the way if necessary, and that between them they could likely do it unless she was prepared to fight them, she let them by.

The aborting of a hyperspace jump was a delicate operation, best done coolly and calmly. Having a gun held to a head full of scrambled brains was not conducive to good operating procedure. Add to that minimum cooperation from the ship's computers and a control board only half understood, and it made for a rough drop into space normal with more residual speed than one might prefer.

The engines stopped whining, though, and the silence was welcome.

Oscar's warning of a reading on the motion sensor came a fraction of a second too late. "Vessel, dead ahead, closing fast." By the time he got it said, they were down, and stars showed through the forward view port.

"How far?"

"I don't know. Kazi numbers, Kazi units. Close. Too close."

"Let me see."

"I don't think you've got time."

Frantically MacDonald reversed the procedure he had just done. A fraction of a second before they were suddenly elsewhere, the hull rang like a bell hit with a rock.

The field compensators were not designed to accommodate two transitions in two minutes. The direction of down took on some interesting variations before everybody crashed to the deck.

Climbing back up to the pilot's station, MacDonald feared he was going to lose the precarious hold he was maintaining on his stomach contents.

"They're shooting at us," he complained indignantly.

He had not wasted time changing jump coordinates. The ship still thought it was reaching for the center of the sector. The engines started to complain again. A little more carefully, they set the *Kokkon* back into normal space.

For a while neither Oscar nor MacDonald did anything. They sat hunched over on the short little Kazi benches side by side and breathed, in spite of the stale and increasingly humid air. The Lleveci warriors clumped together around Delladar Oll, chattering nervously.

When it felt like it was time to move again, MacDonald asked, "Can we do a damage survey?"

"Could try," Oscar answered.

"Any idea where we are?"

Oscar transferred the navigation chart with its green dot to the pilot's station. "Roughly," he said. "The computer is working out the details. It's taking its bloody time about it."

The ship lay deep in Kazi space. There wasn't a friendly site anywhere around.

MacDonald swung around to confront the others. He had begun to think of them as that, a unit, the willful, self-contradictory, incomprehensible, sometimes criminally stupid others.

The warriors had crowded in close, still chattering, looking for reassurance. MacDonald glowered up at them. "Shut up," he snapped. "Get out of the way. Go sit down somewhere."

To his surprise they did quiet down and disperse somewhat. They understood the tone if not the words. No doubt about it, the Terran was mightily peeved.

"Ayyah."

The Orian responded with ears tilted in his direction.

"You realize I am quite within my rights to drop you two conspirators outside."

"I do not understand you, MacDonald."

"What you're doing here is called mutiny. Your techniques are a little less than refined." He touched the sore spot on his head gently. "Barbaric, I'd say." He got a small satisfaction from seeing Ayyah wince. "After all the lectures you've been giving the Lleveci, I must say I'm disappointed. What did you think you were going to accomplish?"

"You would not take the ship where we must go. You control Oscar Achebe. I could see no alternative."

"I don't 'control' Oscar. He has enough experience and plain common sense to know what a stupid thing you were up to. Exceptionally stupid for a person who comes across as smart most of the time.

"I told you before, there's only one master on this ship. Do you understand me now?"

"I understand your words, MacDonald. I do not know how you plan to enforce your edicts."

"You think about how long you'd last if I decide to resign. Try reading a bit more of our operations manual. It might help. You may notice it says Kazi ships are not designed for prolonged periods in hyperspace. They skip along it like a bouncing rock. That's an old technique, hard on fuel if you don't do it exactly right. It has some advantages, like the best speed and range from rather small engines. One damned thing is certain, it's no business for bloody amateurs. Keep this in mind. There is a little more to running a starship than taking a course in navigation eighty-whatever years ago. Times have changed, my dear.''

"The stars have not.''

"The equipment to get about them has.''

Ayyah said nothing more, apparently deep in thought.

MacDonald caught Delladar Oll in his glare next. She still held her gun, and the warriors were ready to back her up, but she seemed uncertain about how to proceed. Her hawk-eyed scowl met his, but it lacked her usual self-confidence.

"You're just about as stupid as she is," he said. "And furthermore, I owe you a crack on the head.''

Delladar Oll's indignant snarl was interrupted.

"Mac," Oscar called, "the ship's back. Tentative identification as a Kazi light cruiser. I have to warn you, she doesn't like us. Firing projectiles.''

"Get up some speed. We'll try a few evasive maneuvers.''

"We can't outrun her," Oscar said. "She's got sublight speed on us for sure.''

"How did it find us?" MacDonald complained.

"The commander would employ simple statistical analysis," Ayyah answered. "It would assume a course the same or near the observed course as the first probability, a reversed course as the second, and calculate the probabilities for a hyperspace jump of random length. It would then investigate the most likely locations in order. Its first guess would be a somewhat greater distance—''

"Shut up, Ayyah. Oscar, plot us a couple of sideways jumps and—''

Kokkon was taken with a fit of the ague. Things rattled and chattered. Sparks flew here and there.

"That was no damned projectile," MacDonald complained.

"I didn't say only projectiles.''

"Jump.''

"Where?''

"Anywhere.''

Kokkon staggered utterly gracelessly into hyperspace and out again almost at once. Some of the Lleveci warriors were beginning to look intensely unhappy and a bit green around the edges. MacDonald questioned Oscar with a look.

"I noticed the Kaz don't like short jumps, but I have to tell you, this is playing hell with our fuel consumption."

"I figured."

"They don't need Ayyah's fancy math to follow, you know. This close, they can pick up the ion trail before it disperses."

"I know. Get us off this course."

"Can't."

"Eh, what?"

Oscar was working the board with furious concentration while he talked. "The navigation computer isn't accepting input. I think that plasma charge kind of scrambled it. If you need a new setting, we're going to have to put it in by hand. Got a pencil?"

"Haven't got time."

"There's another problem," Oscar said quietly so the others wouldn't overhear. "I didn't really want to bring this up but—"

"Let's have it, Oscar."

"Have you noticed yourself feeling a bit nauseated and breathless?"

MacDonald had. He assumed it was the aftereffects of a whack on the side of the head.

"I've been watching the pCO_2. The amount of carbon dioxide in the air has been going up quite dramatically the last little while. Kincaid's is now about eleven days away. I don't think we can make it. Matter of fact, I'm damned sure we can't."

"Reserve?"

"We're breathing it."

They were going to suffocate, trapped in this stupid bug buggy. There had to be a way out of it. MacDonald's brain flopped around like a beached fish trying to find its way back into the water. Oscar was beginning to fidget before MacDonald finally asked, "How far to Ayyah's place?"

"Two days, eleven hours forty, given jumps of reasonable length."

MacDonald's look was a continuing question.

"Maybe. If everyone holds his breath a lot."

"It will take half a day to calculate an alternative by hand. We don't have much choice, do we?"

"Not much."

"Vent the shuttle's tanks into the system. It'll help a little."

"That cruiser's going to keep following. It's faster than we are. Sooner or later, it's going to catch up."

"True." MacDonald chewed his upper lip for a moment. "I guess it's time to implement your cargo-unloading technique."

"You said it was too dangerous, remember?"

"Everything is relative, my friend. Just now, we don't have too much to lose compared with surrendering to the Kazi military."

"Point well taken. You think the cruiser will stop to pick up the bodies?"

"I don't know. Who knows how Kaz feel about their dead? As far as I know, they reprocess everything. Maybe it's like a religion. Would they be willing to abandon some good raw material in space? I don't know. I hope not."

The sensor net had warned of a ship in hyperspace and calculated a probable course. The commander of the light cruiser had not expected the net to be so remarkably accurate. The vessel appeared in space normal directly ahead, right in the cruiser's path.

The commander was hard pressed to imagine what a broodship was doing so far from the normal nursery runs. Moreover, the vessel's behavior was decidedly odd. The commander expected it to veer off and identify itself. That was normal procedure. Neither of those things happened. Nor did it answer communications. Instead, it picked up speed, preparing to drop back into hyperspace. That was far from prescribed conduct.

The commander ordered its gunner to fire the sublight, unarmed missile as a warning. It would bounce harmlessly off the broodship's hull, but it would certainly wake the crew up.

The gunner signaled contact just as the broodship winked out of normal space.

Very strange indeed. The commander didn't spend much time thinking about it before deciding to give chase. In minutes, the ion trail would be too dispersed to indicate direction accurately.

Something was most peculiar.

A broodship was a valuable asset, all the more so if precious eggs were aboard. It told a crew member to replay the computer record to try to identify the vessel.

The jump was so short, hardly more than a few minutes, the cruiser overshot it and had to backtrack. The vessel, the crew member informed the commander, was the broodship *Kokkon*.

Are you certain? the commander asked, though it had no reason to doubt the crew member.

The crew member's upward tilted head and crossed forelimbs signified that it was indeed certain.

The *Kokkon* was the vessel that had been stolen from Llevec, with the loss of the 44th Battalion of the Army of the Empire. The *Kokkon* was the ship the *Klact* had been seeking when it encountered its phantom star. The more the commander heard about the *Kokkon*, the odder it appeared to be.

The crew member brought another point to the commander's attention. A note from Llevec was appended to the Fleet directive. A broodmaster there requested the hijackers alive if possible.

The commander gave the request a moment's consideration. Broodships, designed to ply only the safest lanes of transport, were sturdy and fast, but carried no weapons. The broodmaster's request would severely limit the commander's options but in no way endanger its own vessel. Though the broodmaster had offered no explanation, it undoubtedly had its reasons.

The empire would probably be best served if the broodmaster could have its way. When the cruiser caught up with the *Kokkon*, the commander ordered two low-yield missiles directed at the vessel's engines.

Whoever the alien pilot was, he was alert and quick. The *Kokkon* swerved and the missiles passed harmlessly along the broodship's port side.

Swinging the cruiser around to follow, the commander decided to try once more before taking the more pragmatic step of annihilating the *Kokkon*. A plasma charge, a compact bundle of ionized particles, if it hit the ship squarely, would disrupt its electrical systems and leave it dead in space, but biological activity would be unharmed, at least not much harmed, at least in the short term.

Once more the alien pilot defeated the commander. The *Kokkon* zigged at the crucial moment. Only the edge of the charge brushed it before it dropped once more into hyperspace.

This is a clever one, the commander thought as the cruiser took up the chase. Once more they overshot and had to backtrack. But a clever one should have taken his prize into neutral territory, not be traveling more deeply into empire space. Some mischief was afoot, surely.

When they found the place, nothing was there but a dispersing trail pointing toward the center of the sector. The commander relaxed a little. This would undoubtedly be a longer jump. The cruiser would catch up with *Kokkon* in hyperspace and have done with it. There was no chance a broodship could outrun them.

Except for position updates, the navigator was idle while the ship followed its sensors, so it indulged its curiosity by plotting a hypothetical course for the broodship from the several places they had encountered it. The results of the plot were surprising, so the navigator brought its work to the commander's attention.

The commander regarded the projected course with some concern. It gave the navigator a set of coordinates and asked it to include those in its calculations.

This is empty space, the navigator protested.

These coordinates show the location of the Klact's *phantom star, where* Kokkon *is known to have been,* the commander explained.

The point fit perfectly on the course line.

The projection pointed directly at the sector nidus.

The nidus was the place where the eggs were laid and cared for until they could be shipped out to the places a new generation was needed. It was the place of the Broodmother, the nearest thing to a holy place there was in a Kazi's universe.

For a moment, the commander imagined rapacious pirates descending upon the helpless Broodmother and her unsuspecting attendants. It shuddered at the thought, and around the bridge the Kaz, ever sensitive to others' movements, trembled in sympathy without knowing the cause.

A moment later, it relaxed. The aliens would never be able to approach the nidus.

But the more it thought about it, the more credible the idea became. The aliens had already bypassed most of the controls and defenses that would normally keep them far from the region. The course projection was definite. They were using a Kazi broodship. Any ship's commander would, as the commander itself had done, hesitate to fire on a broodship. Space is so big and empty. Chances were they would not meet another vessel once they cleared the area of active patrols. The nearer the nidus the *Kokkon* came, the more normal it would seem, one among the many broodships transporting eggs.

The pirates had been clever, but they could not know their destination was anticipated. The cruiser could outrun them handily, alert the nidus world, and await their arrival. They would not succeed in spite of their cleverness.

The commander's ruminations were interrupted by signals from the sensor operator. A swarm of small objects, it said, directly in the cruiser's path.

The commander asked for an identification. The operator expressed its puzzlement. *Partly metallic, partly biological,* it said. *No life signs.*

Possibly the clever pirates, operating unfamiliar equipment, had invented their own disaster and saved the commander the trouble. To be certain, the *Klact* would have to stop and investigate the debris.

Be quick, the commander instructed its crew. If these things were not pieces of the *Kokkon*, it wanted to know as soon as possible. It didn't want to lose track of its quarry.

Nidus

"This is the end of the line, folks," MacDonald said wearily. A fellow ought to face his death with a little more interest, he thought. But his head felt like a lead weight on the end of his neck, and his mind was working as if he had to push every thought through an overlay of tar. There was a drummer in there somewhere, keeping time with his heartbeat. It was an effort just to keep his eyelids from crashing down.

"This is the place," Ayyah said.

"Yeah," MacDonald answered. He didn't know what she meant, and he didn't care either.

"The way I see it," he said, "we can stay here and suffocate, or go below and get reprocessed. Shuttle's leaving in fifteen minutes. All ashore who's going ashore."

"No way we're going to make it down there," Oscar said. "It's a Kazi world. I read no surface vegetation, no surface water."

"I know. I'm sorry, my friend." MacDonald felt a bit light-headed. "But *Kokkon*'s had it. We can't go and we can't stay. It's a matter of choosing a way to die."

In spite of the gray weight that pulled his features down, Oscar tried for a smile. "Such melodrama," he said.

MacDonald started to nod, then thought that once started he would be unable to stop, so instead he turned and crossed the bridge, heading for the gangway that led to the shuttle bay. He wanted a brave, firm stride, as much as was possible bent over beneath the low ceiling, but what he did was more like a shamble.

Behind him, Ayyah said to the Lleveci, "Everyone will be needed on the surface."

For what? MacDonald wondered.

He never had understood the Orian's motives. If this was just a way to provide the Kaz with some fresh raw material, it was a damned complicated way of delivering it. Delladar Oll answered something, but MacDonald couldn't make it out. He had to concentrate on where he was going. Wherever that was.

The packed shuttle broke through the cloud deck over a barren plain. Such hills and valleys as this world might once have had were leveled. If it had ever had life of its own, there was no sign of it now. The uniform, sterile land rolled beneath them.

"Where is everyone?" Oscar asked. "I was expecting a reception committee." He had brightened considerably in the last few minutes. Everyone had. As soon as he had read enough air pressure, MacDonald had opened the scoops and let fresh air ram into the shuttle's holding tanks. Now the pumps had it up to breathable density and had started it circulating.

"This has been a Kazi world for hundreds, possibly thousands, of years," Ayyah said. She had taken over the navigator's position. Under other circumstances, MacDonald would have chased her out of it in short order, long-ago navigation lessons notwithstanding. Now it didn't much matter where they went.

"For almost that long it has been a quiet, orderly place without external disturbance. The Kaz would not expect to have to defend it. Internal disorder is almost unknown. This is the safest, most secure world the Kazi command in the region. There are likely few Kaz trained as soldiers stationed here, and possibly no military craft. We arrived in a Kazi vessel of a type common to this world. It would be taken as a normal event, at least to begin with, though port controllers must be wondering why their inquiries have not been answered. No doubt the shuttle is being tracked."

"Great. Just the place for us," MacDonald said. Behind him, Oscar cleared his throat and the Lleveci warriors murmured among themselves.

Delladar Oll said what they all were thinking. "So, Kaz where we land."

"I expect it to be so. For this reason, I propose we remain airborne until our destination achieves planetary night."

MacDonald was about to ask what difference it could make, but instead asked, "What destination?"

Ayyah regarded him with that wide, frank, through-the-skin

stare of hers. "You believe I am quite mad," she said, head slightly cocked, ears pricked forward. "Only now I understand this."

She worked with the navigation terminal for a moment, setting the shuttle into a wide, slow spiral angled toward the terminator. MacDonald didn't argue. One course was as good as another until the fuel got low.

"This expression is correct—'Achilles' heel'?" she asked him without looking up.

The sensors had picked up another craft. MacDonald watched the readings while he answered. "It's an expression. Whether it's correct or not depends on how you use it." The newcomer looked to be about the size of a small fighter aircraft. It was pacing them. If all Ayyah's information was as accurate as her assumptions about military craft, they could be on the wrong world entirely. If there was a right one.

"We seek out the Achilles' heel of the Kaz," Ayyah said.

Their last circle had taken them out of twilight into shadow and back into the light again. MacDonald overrode the autopilot and sent the shuttle toward the nightside to see if the other would follow. "Ayyah, my dear lunatic, Kaz ain't got no heels."

"Yes?"

Their shadow was still with them. "We've got a tail," MacDonald announced. "If we're going to set down on our own, I think we'd better do it now."

Ayyah's tail waggled. "I do not understand you," she said.

"We're being followed. If any place on this planet appeals to you over any other place, tell me now, before the shooting starts."

Ayyah transferred the chart on the navigator's terminal to the pilot's screen. The place she had picked out was distinguishable only by planetary coordinates. It was marked as a port facility. MacDonald thought they might do better in a wilderness area, except, of course, there was no such thing. He experienced a moment of wry amazement at his own thoughts. Where there's life there's hope, the old saying went. As long as a man was breathing, he would struggle to continue, even when there was no hope at all.

"Listen to me," Ayyah said, in a tone MacDonald might have at another time resented as being a shade too imperious. She turned in the navigator's chair to address everybody. Her ears were pricked, her eyes bright, her expression impassive.

"We seek on this world the breeding female. She will be found in a large chamber deep underground. The place we will land is the place from which the eggs are shipped that make the next generation of Kaz. There will be connecting tunnels.

"You must know the Kaz will defend the breeder by all means at their disposal. They will call as many as needed from any occupation to this most urgent of tasks. Our chances of success will be best if we act quickly.

"You must also know our chances of success are not great. However, we cannot survive our present circumstances. The destruction of the Broodmother will give death some meaning."

"Why here?"

"Here is where the Rayorian said."

"We find. Then?" Delladar Oll asked.

"We must kill her."

"Much trouble, one Kazi."

"One important Kazi, which will affect many. Look to your weapons. You will need them."

"Ah, the sweet sounds of the pacifist." Oscar's sudden anger had made his features stony. He almost knocked MacDonald off the pilot's chair pushing his face into Ayyah's. The Orian leaned back over the board, trying to keep an acceptable distance between them. MacDonald was astonished. Any man was capable of anger, but Oscar didn't often express his.

"I heard it said the Oriani were schemers," Oscar continued. "I never knew how ruthless until now. You understand Lleveci psychology pretty well," he said. "Come to think of it, you've manipulated us all with sublime efficiency. Maybe you were a xenopsychologist in real life?"

Ayyah's head cocked slightly to one side. She seemed fascinated. "I was a teacher," she said, "when there were young to teach. I do not 'manipulate.' You are mistaken."

Oscar shook his head, a sharp, short gesture. "No way, Ayyah. You engineered events to bring about this impasse. You wanted us here, hopeless, to do your work."

"No, Oscar Achebe. I use what I can find. I do not understand your anger. The tools are not of my choosing."

"You're a bloody liar."

Ayyah's ears flattened close to her head, and her tail twitched. Her fangs seemed more prominent than usual. MacDonald thought he should warn Oscar to cool it, but Oscar was saying many of the things MacDonald would have liked to say, and what the hell did it matter anyway?

"You came looking for us, for Mac," Oscar said. "You knew what you were doing, right from the beginning."

"You imagine I knew the Kaz would attack your refuge?"

"I'm almighty sure you knew your sudden appearance on Riga would get the bugs all excited. Something was bound to come of it. It's damned obvious you've made a thorough study of the Kaz. You know a lot about them."

"You believe I predicted the events on Llevec? That I anticipated the failure of the *Kokkon*'s life-support mechanisms? You have a high opinion of my ability to see the future, Oscar Achebe."

"I'll tell you this much about the future, Orian. If a miracle occurs and we get out of this mess alive, watch out for me. I'll kill you. I swear it."

"Perhaps. It would not be so simply done as you might suppose."

"I'm not a simple man."

"I did not believe you were."

It did matter, MacDonald was surprised to discover. Where there was life, there was hope, and for the moment they were alive. "Cool it," he snapped at the combatants. "Fight each other later. I need some help here."

The Lleveci murmured unhappily, deprived of their entertainment. Ayyah's destination had appeared through the forward port as an irregular smear of light in the darkness. The sensor monitor continued to register the aircraft, about two kilometers above and behind.

"We're coming down," MacDonald announced. "The bad guys are still right on us. Ayyah, either man that board or get out of the way."

Ayyah left the navigator's station and pushed her way stiffly through the crowd of Lleveci toward the rear of the shuttle. Oscar slid into her place.

"That was a dumb thing I did," he said.

MacDonald grunted noncommittally. "Give me point one two on the forward verniers," he said.

Oscar manipulated the thrust controls. "Are we going to go through with it?"

"Got a better idea?" MacDonald asked.

" 'Fraid not," Oscar answered miserably.

MacDonald had slowed the shuttle to a subsonic crawl and was holding it at a steady hundred meters' altitude. He was going for a visual landing, dark or no dark, ignoring the frantic Kazi characters running along the bottom of the pilot's screen—the traffic controller no doubt, screaming as best a Kazi could for their attention.

The features of the facility were discernible now, such as they were. No buildings showed aboveground, only half a dozen low mounds, communications antennas consisting of a tall mast and four parabolic dishes of various sizes angled toward the sky, the pad itself, some pieces of machinery, and dark knots of Kaz gathering, like ants at a picnic blackening the ground around a tasty crumb.

"One suggestion, though," Oscar said, "dependent upon your peerless skills as a pilot. If we made a couple of super-low-altitude passes over the field, the exhaust might do a lot to scatter the reception committee."

MacDonald nodded, and the shuttle roared over the pad scarcely twenty meters above the surface. Oscar tensed.

"What?" MacDonald asked.

"I had a horrible feeling the mast was going to snag on the underbelly."

"Trust me."

"Let me guess. You're a doctor, right?"

"Hell, no. Doctors can't fly worth spit."

When they came around to the field again, Kaz were scrambling every which way, as disorderly as any mob of frightened creatures.

After the second pass, he got a little altitude, then, over Ayyah's protest, brought the shuttle down blind, in the dirt, in a spray of dust and small rocks, accompanied by Oscar's white-knuckled grip on the navigation board and squeaks of alarm from the Lleveci, hoping for something solid beneath rather than knowing it was there. One thing about having nothing to lose, he thought. You can take insane chances with aplomb.

The ground was neither as hard nor as even as a pad. They bounced once and came to rest with a definite starboard list about a kilometer from the lights of the field. The debris they kicked up rained down on them. As the racket subsided, MacDonald heard the engine of the aircraft, receding.

"Now what?" he asked nobody in particular.

"This is a thing you say often, MacDonald," Ayyah said from the rear.

"I don't remember that it ever came up before I met you," MacDonald answered.

"We must get below ground before the Kaz reorganize."

"Below ground," Delladar Oll said with a bit of a snort, "more Kaz."

"How long before light here?" Ayyah asked.

MacDonald shrugged. "We're about twenty degrees east of the terminator. Tell me the period of this planet, and I'll take a guess. But don't expect the Kaz to wait for dawn. Whatever you think they haven't got, they'll have vehicles of some sort, and lights."

The warriors were the first out, fanning into a semicircle around the hatch, weapons drawn, eagle eyes scanning the empty night.

MacDonald was the last to step down onto the loose dry soil. He stopped before closing up the shuttle and asked Oscar, who was just ahead of him, "Before we left *Kokkon*, did you happen to notice other vessels in orbit?"

Oscar nodded. "A couple registered on sensors. I confess I didn't stop to figure out what kind."

"What do you think about the odds of our commandeering another ship to get us out of here?"

"So close to zero the difference isn't worth mentioning," Oscar said, belting his weapon at his waist. "Which makes them infinitely better than anything else we've got. I have to tell you, I'm not keen on Ayyah's suicide mission."

"Me, neither. Let's see what we can do."

The shuttle's passengers started off toward the only distinguishable feature on the planet, the lights of the port. They walked in silence, agreed for once upon at least one thing, a direction.

They met the first party of three dozen or so Kaz just outside the perimeter of light, a milling group streaming out toward the grounded shuttle armed only with powerful hand lights. The Kaz appeared to be motivated more by curiosity than by any sense of alarm. When the lights they carried first met the shuttle's passengers and made long shadows streak off across the barren ground, the Kaz stopped, as if startled. The waving forelimbs and the posturing were meant to tell them something, MacDonald was sure, but the warriors were in no mood for conversation.

Blasters raked the Kaz and left a twitching, smoking ruin. Their hand lights lay among them, casting a manic illumination on the slaughter.

Even with Kaz, it was sickening. Ayyah had turned her face away, looking wilted and pained. But she didn't say anything. MacDonald thought she might finally be coming to terms with the reality of what she wanted.

"They didn't expect people?" Oscar asked.

"If Ayyah's right, we're their first aliens in a good many generations, so maybe not," MacDonald said.

"Well, don't start feeling too confident," Oscar said, pointing past the pile of dead Kaz to the field. "Killing that lot will make sure any others we meet will be thoroughly hostile. And I think we're about to meet some others."

The lighted area was almost completely covered with a shimmering carpet of black backs. Small clumps broke off and hustled themselves from one place to another. Individuals raced around the periphery as fast as a dozen legs could carry them. Bunches jostled into lines and squares. Some kind of organization was going on.

"Oh, my God," MacDonald said. His skin prickled. "Let's get the hell out of here."

About that time the ground behind him exploded, the concussion throwing him forward into the Lleveci. His instinct was to throw himself into the dirt with his hands over his head. Which would, of course, be much too late. Debris rained down on them.

"What happened?" Oscar yelled into his ear.

"The cruiser's found us," MacDonald answered.

"Get cover," Delladar Oll commanded. MacDonald could hardly hear her through the echoes of the explosion inside his head.

"Like where?" Oscar asked, his voice upscale from its usual low rumble. The Lleveci were already running for the nearest of the low mounds, which lay between them and the Kaz. MacDonald followed rather than be left, though it seemed the wrong way to go. That huge conglomeration of Kaz had started toward them. He could hear the rustling shuffle of them, in spite of eardrums that felt physically damaged. He could smell them in the dust they raised.

It was hard to move toward them. A second explosion, centered not much more than a couple of meters from the place he had been standing moments before, urged him along with a hot, rocky shove at his back.

There was a small arched opening in the side of the mound. The shuttle crew threw themselves into it without a thought of what they might find in there. It couldn't be worse than what they were leaving behind.

Blaster fire followed them. Dirt sprayed. The warrior behind MacDonald collapsed with a scream. MacDonald started to turn back to the wounded girl, but a Lleveci grabbed his jacket and yanked him stumbling down the slope.

The entry narrowed rapidly into a low tunnel, forcing them into single file. Around a sharp bend, they lost the light from the entrance. They mobbed up in the dark, hunched over, running into each other.

MacDonald pushed the warrior's hand away angrily. "Dammit," he shouted. "That girl was hurt."

The warrior chattered something, and Delladar Oll's voice came out of the darkness. "She was dead."

Something warm and wet was creeping down MacDonald's neck. He reached for it. His hand came away sticky. Still angry, he yelled, "Ayyah!"

"I am here, MacDonald."

She sounded so calm that he felt ready to do mayhem.

"You said they didn't know how to defend themselves."

"I did not," Ayyah answered, "I said I thought they would not be experienced at it."

"Explain that to them. They'll be after us in a moment."

"If you stop shouting, perhaps they will not find us so quickly."

MacDonald's mouth was open, ready with a loud and scatological reply. He closed it without uttering a sound.

Ayyah's voice came out of the darkness. "Undoubtedly the warship that was giving chase has arrived. Follow me."

"How'm I going to do that? I can't even see you."

A light bloomed in the midst of the group, and Assall Oll held up one of the Kazi hand lamps.

"You're a provident fellow," Oscar said wryly. "You know, human mythology has a special place for the torchbearer."

Delladar Oll translated for the warrior, who smiled his open-mouthed smile and nodded his head in appreciation. MacDonald frowned. It was hard to believe that these people had lost one of their own just a few moments before. They had a funny way of mourning their dead.

"You're bleeding," Oscar said.

"It's nothing. What is this place?" MacDonald asked.

Oscar shrugged. "I don't know. It looks like the tunnels in Rullenahesad."

"Yes," Ayyah said. "A Kazi habitat. They are all built to a similar pattern."

"Great. The perfect place to hide from Kaz."

"We do not hide from them. They smell us. They know where we are. Come. We have little time."

"It occurs to me," Oscar said sourly, "that for high-flying, spacegoing pirates, we've spent a damned lot of time underground the last while."

"Call us versatile," MacDonald answered. "Or better yet, call us Wednesday."

Oscar groaned at the pun. In the swinging light of the hand lamp, Delladar Oll was staring at them as if she thought they were demented.

Ayyah led them on a winding route downward. MacDonald wondered if he would ever again come to a place where he could stand upright. The air was warm and moist, nauseatingly thick with the smell of Kaz.

They paused in a wider spot where several tunnels joined theirs.

"Why are we following this crazy Orian?" Oscar asked.

"Because she's leading," MacDonald said, "and we don't know where else to go."

"We're bound to run into some bugs down here."

"We're bound to run into some on the surface, too."

"I think I'd like it better if I could die under the stars, with some space around me. I feel half buried already down here."

"Now who's being melodramatic?"

"It looks to me like our leader is as confused as the rest of us."

Ayyah was prowling—that was the only word for it—from tunnel mouth to tunnel mouth, her nose tipped up, nostrils dilated, mouth slightly open as if tasting the air. She went a little way into one, retreated, then tried another.

In all the tunnels, the lights came on.

Ayyah started off down a tunnel angling to the right and down.

The rest followed. MacDonald imagined he could hear the scritch of Kazi feet at his back.

"Wait," Delladar Oll called. She spoke briefly to the warriors, and two of them directed their blasters at the roof of the tunnel near the entrance. Oscar's cry of dismay was lost in the snarl of blaster fire and the roar of falling earth.

Coughing in the dust, they followed the Orian. Behind him, MacDonald could feel Oscar's shudder.

"You okay?" he asked.

"Christ, no, I'm not okay. I'm going to die down here, Mac, and I'll be damned if I can get comfortable with the idea."

"We're not dead yet," MacDonald answered. Oscar said nothing. He trudged along behind in silence.

Six Kaz met them at the next junction.

Before Ayyah had time to react, Delladar Oll had pushed her aside and was firing past her. The Kaz fired back, though it wasn't until the warrior ahead of him howled and staggered and clasped his side that MacDonald realized the Kaz were armed. The Kazi weapons were silent, and invisible until Delladar Oll's blaster had raised some dust. Then he could see the violet streaks of light.

"Lasers," he said.

"Makes sense, down here. Blasters keep bringing the roof down." Oscar's dull tone suggested he didn't care much anymore. His horror of being trapped in the tunnels overwhelmed any other sense of danger.

After the first shot, the Kazi fire was erratic and shortlived. They had to shoot into the mouth of the tunnel. Delladar Oll might be nervous about space travel, but in hand-to-hand combat, she was iceberg calm and steady.

They stepped over the bodies into the wider space of the junction. Ayyah studiously ignored the dead Kaz and resumed her sniffing inspection of the tunnels. Under Delladar Oll's direction, the Lleveci were yanking overhead cables down. Suddenly it got dark again.

The route to the next junction was short and straight, though still angling down. They could see that the lights were still on at the end right from the beginning, so Assall Oll wisely saved his lamp. The wounded Lleveci wasn't making good time. He didn't seem to be bleeding much, but he responded to the queries of his companions with short, pained grunts.

In the third junction, MacDonald knew that the sound of Kazi feet was not his imagination. He could see Ayyah's ears twitching, scanning like sensor probes, to the sides and back. She chose their route more quickly that time, urging them into the rightmost entrance.

The injured warrior sank down to the floor near the entrance with his back against the wall, blaster in one hand, crystal knife in the other. MacDonald took his arm to help him up. The warrior pushed him away with an elbow.

He tried again, thinking the warrior had misinterpreted his intentions. The Lleveci cursed him roundly in a language he didn't understand.

Delladar Oll got between them and urged MacDonald away.

"He can't stay here," MacDonald said.

Delladar Oll shoved him roughly toward the opening that had swallowed up the rest of the crew. He'd had just about enough of that. He turned around and pushed her back, sending her stumbling into the warrior behind.

"Ha, MacDonald. Want fight?" Her neck extended until her head was brushing the roof of the tunnel and her mouth was open in a smile.

Her good humor collapsed when the sound of a blaster came down the tunnel.

They caught up to the rest where they had stalled at a bend. MacDonald peered between waving Lleveci necks to try to see what was going on.

Ayyah, at the head of the group, was confronting the biggest Kazi MacDonald had ever seen. Standing with its upper body erect and the two pairs of forelimbs off the ground, it nicely filled the tunnel, a living plug that was reaching for the Orian with a great, ridged foreclaw that looked as if it had been forged of gunmetal. Ayyah had a gun in her hand, but she seemed too stunned to fire. A warrior pushed her against the wall and fired past her.

The backwash from the blast was like a belch from hell's furnace. Dirt rattled down from the walls and ceiling. The air stank of burnt Kaz and burnt hair.

The lights went out.

A wave of totally irrational irritation washed over MacDonald. A man could get royally sick and tired, he thought, of fumbling around in the dark. Unseen Lleveci chattered to one another. He was getting a little tired of them, too, always shooting first and thinking later. Though, deep down where his honesty lived, he had to give begrudging admiration to Lleveci reflexes. If the warriors had been less alert, he wouldn't be standing there in the dark resenting them.

Assall Oll's Kazi light came on. The dead Kazi, surrounded by fallen rubble, still made an efficient block at the bend. Ayyah was leaning against the wall, brushing ineffectively at scorched fur. Drooping ears and drooping tail suggested that she wasn't feeling very well.

A pair of Lleveci eased their way past her and began hacking away at the corpse with their knives, pushing still-twitching sections back into the tunnel. MacDonald could feel his stomach heaving. He had to turn away and face the walls to regain his equilibrium.

He was surprised to find Oscar's arm across his shoulders. His friend's hand was comforting. "Why are we here?" he asked.

"I think because you said we have no place else to go."

"Do I still believe that?"

"We can't go back."

"We were going to look for another ship."

"I don't think we'll find one in here."

"Are you all right?"

"The human animal is amazingly adaptable. It can get used to anything."

They followed the others past the pieces of Kazi, over the mound of dirt. When they were far enough down the tunnel to make the operation less hazardous, the Lleveci directed their blasters at the roof, sealing the tunnel behind them.

The downward slope had lessened. A muted rustling sound seemed to be all around them. The smell of Kaz was overlain with a new scent now, an unpleasant sweetness, like fermenting fruit.

At the next bend, they met another of the giants.

Assall Oll's light clicked off. In the darkness ahead, Mac-Donald could hear a murmured conversation between Ayyah and Delladar Oll. It sounded like an argument.

"No," Ayyah's voice said sharply.

"You see; I do not," Delladar Oll answered with exaggerated patience.

They broke off abruptly.

There was some movement and a thump. The light came back. The Kazi was lying on its side with a Lleveci knife stuck between its quivering forelegs. Ayyah was regarding her wet hand with its plastered-down fur as if it had only just grown there and didn't belong to her. The Lleveci made their way around her still form to begin a second act of butchery. Delladar Oll retrieved her blade.

Delladar Oll took the lead, easing by the remains of the body. When it was MacDonald's turn to make the passage, Ayyah was still standing there. He reached out a comforting hand, but she pulled away from him, giving him only a glimpse of the pain in her eyes. He wanted to say something encouraging, but the hurt look was already gone, buried under layers of furious Stoicism. She went on ahead of him without a word.

He felt put down in some subtle way he couldn't define.

The tunnel ended.

The Broodmother

Ayyah's greatest difficulty, among many difficulties she experienced dealing with aliens, was the way people constantly wanted to be touching her—pushing, bumping, guiding, being guided—MacDonald's sympathetic hand meant to comfort but in truth was only annoying. Ayyah stopped in the bell-shaped tunnel mouth and shook herself. He meant no harm.

The room ahead was big and looked bigger after the narrow tunnels, worthy of a moment's consideration even now, even knowing that while elbow room was welcome relief from confinement, the constricting tunnels had worked to the invaders' advantage.

The Kaz had used no building material other than packed soil; the engineering was remarkable. The unsupported arc of the domed roof seemed impossible. Clever Kazi optics made the smooth sloping walls of the circular chamber glow with the soft, greenish light the Kaz most favored.

"Move," Delladar Oll directed, wholly uninterested in architecture. She shouldered her way by without waiting for space to be made. She started down the ramp that led toward the floor. She didn't go far.

The floor of the chamber was lower than the tunnel entrance, with a sharp slope leading down. But the floor itself was not visible. A seething mob of Kaz covered it, until it looked like a great cauldron of boiling tar. They raised a dry, muted rustling roar. They raised ancient dust, smelling of the ages.

Behind her, Ayyah heard MacDonald gasp.

All around the perimeter of the room, other tunnels ramped down, and Kaz poured out of them until she thought they would soon be standing on one another's backs.

"Clear opening," Delladar Oll ordered. "Make room for fight."

The unnerved humans had come up on one side of Ayyah and stuck close together to give each other courage. The Lleveci squeezed between her and the wall on the other side and fanned out across the tunnel entrance.

The turbulence on the floor had a direction, toward the intruders.

"Where the hell are we?" MacDonald demanded.

"This place?" Delladar Oll asked.

"Yes," Ayyah said, directing with a gesture the warrior's attention to the center of the chamber. It was exactly as she remembered it, having never seen it except in her mind's eye, memories planted by the Rayorians.

A raised mound of packed clay stood above the churning mass below. On its flat top, ignoring the ferment around them, a ring of busy Kaz attended a thick, dark, quivering cylinder of flesh. A visible spasm traveled the length of the cylinder, and from beneath it one of the Kazi attendants carefully retrieved a small, roundish object that gleamed dully white.

"We're not going down there," MacDonald said quite firmly. Ayyah didn't argue with him, or even answer. Her travels were over; the humans were now largely superfluous. If they did not go down, the Kaz would come up. In all sense, it was of little importance. Yet she was deeply disturbed to see MacDonald clench his fists, revolted, frightened, trapped now after reluctantly serving her purpose against his better judgment, indeed, against his will. He and Oscar Achebe had been badly used, and in a better life, Ayyah would have been haunted by the immorality of such treatment of unwilling allies.

This was not the time for primitive sentimentality. Her objective was in sight. Only several hundred Kaz stood between them now.

She was tired, muscle weary, and heartsick, and the possibility of getting through the seething horde below looked vanishingly small.

The Lleveci wielded blasters like scythes, mowing down Kaz by tens, but the living climbed over the bodies of the dead without hesitating. The Kaz were unarmed, depending on the weight of numbers. It seemed sufficient.

"We will die here," Delladar Oll said.

"Yes," Ayyah answered truthfully. That truth grieved her,

and for a moment she gave in to despair. No one could pass the Kazi horde. It could not be done. Retreat was not possible. She had sacrificed all these others for a goal that was, in this final desperate moment, unattainable.

She felt stunned. Out in the starry void, she had been able to make herself believe it could be done. It had been hopeless from the outset. She had just never let herself admit it.

The air grew blue with smoke. The stench was overwhelming.

The smell of death is never sweet, Talan had once said.

This is depraved and vicious, brutal. This is not the way of our kind, the ancestral ghosts moaned.

A light touch on her shoulder startled her. "Come," Delladar Oll shouted over the snarling weapons.

A tight wedge of warriors cut its way through the massed Kaz. Delladar Oll propelled Ayyah into the open end of the V. She scooped up the weapon of a fallen comrade and thrust it into Ayyah's hand. The gun was hot with destruction. Ayyah clung to it, detesting it.

She stumbled over bodies, not all Kazi, confused by the press around her, dazed by the noise, overwhelmed by the horror. Through the smoke, she glimpsed Oscar Achebe and six or so Lleveci backed into a circle, firing into the Kaz. The wedge inched forward. For a moment she and he stood eye to eye. Oscar Achebe held a gun leveled and steady. No sympathy showed in his features. The blast of the weapon singed her fur. She heard a body fall behind her. The warriors advanced, sweeping her along. The Kaz flowed in behind. The center of the chamber was impossibly far away.

Black claws reached for the warrior nearest her. She fired the blaster at them, surprised and horrified to see the Kazi collapse. The warrior nodded his thanks and turned back to the battle.

Appalled, Ayyah felt unable to move.

A hand on her elbow urged her forward. She pulled away from the intrusion and looked into MacDonald's gray eyes. The fear was gone from them now, replaced by iron resignation.

"Oscar Achebe did not kill me," she said, still perplexed that this was so.

"Yeah?" MacDonald snorted. "Stay close," he said. At that moment, he appeared very big and very capable.

The warriors' formation was collapsing. One after another fell beneath the weight of the Kaz. The chorus of weapons lost voice after voice. MacDonald's blaster quit, drained. He threw it at an oncoming Kazi. The weapon bounced harmlessly off the black carapace. Ayyah fired past him as he backed away, kicking over a container of sorts. They had a one-breath-long respite as the nearest Kaz abandoned the battle and turned to the recovery of the precious eggs.

"You're getting the hang of this," MacDonald said breathlessly, with the grim humor only a human could appreciate.

They were backed hard against the platform now. The angle was too sharp to shoot effectively at the enemy above. Kaz beat down at them. Ayyah saw one gathering itself. It was preparing to drop onto MacDonald's head. Before she could respond, Delladar Oll was between them. The Kazi launched itself onto the warrior's crystal blade. Dying, the creature clamped its foreclaws around her neck. They fell together, lost in the melee.

"Can you get up there?" MacDonald asked.

Ayyah turned to regard the earthen wall. It was only a few centimeters above her head. She handed MacDonald her weapon and crouched to spring, seeking a gap among the defenders.

Just as she caught the upper rim, the weight of a Kazi crashed into her, smashing the breath from her, loosening her hold. It clung to her back with all its claws. Hot pain surged from a dozen places. Her diaphragm strained. Her own claws dug and scratched for purchase.

She saw MacDonald turn to toss her the gun and fall headlong. The weapon bounced uselessly away.

She was on her hands and knees before the gross, distended body of the Broodmother while the fury on her back gouged into the flesh, seeking a vulnerable spot. Another Kazi was coming at her over the gross mound of flesh. She slashed at it blindly, arm and hand moving by instinct. She felt her claws strike and tear and withdraw as from a distance.

The Broodmother squirmed futilely. Ayyah dug her nails into the quivering hide to pull herself and her malign burden forward. Her legs trembled. Just to move took all her energy. Her strength was leaking away with her blood, and consciousness had diminished to include only the center of her visual field and that spot where the swollen shape joined a head made trivial in comparison.

Her universe became only that point. All around it, a roaring blackness beat in time with her pulse. Deep in the heart of the darkness she could see limp, wet babies lying silent and unmoving. She saw Lawr, turning his head away in pain. She saw her father, dying, fighting death.

I cannot, her thoughts screamed out to these importunate specters.

You must, they insisted.

Dragging the weight of the Kazi with muscles gone watery, armed only with the weapons she was born with, attention fastened upon her tiny goal, she heaved herself onto the rubbery body that only trembled in return, and sank her fangs into the neck.

The slow, thick ooze filled her mouth with horror and offered one small spark of satisfaction before the darkness folded her inside.

Escape

MacDonald saw Ayyah leap for the top of the mound like some avenging tiger just before something clamped around his ankle and yanked his feet out from under him. He fell hard, banging his head.

He was towed along by the ankle as if he were already dead, the spoils of the hunt. He thrashed in the Kazi's grip, throwing his weight one way, then the other, trying to free himself. He expected chitinous claws at his throat.

The dirt floor of the chamber was worn hard and smooth by a thousand generations of Kazi feet. MacDonald clawed at it with bleeding nails, trying to get a purchase to fight the slow drag out of the chamber. He kicked furiously with his free leg and met only empty air.

His motion stopped, though it was none of his doing.

The Kazi pulling him along hesitated, changed direction, back toward the center of the chamber, stopped again, and changed direction again, and again, bouncing MacDonald over the body of its kinsman, whose claws were still locked around Delladar Oll's neck. MacDonald's frantic hands found a hold on the dead Kazi. He arched his body and spent his remaining strength in one last desperate pull against the claws wrapped round his ankle.

For a moment he was stretched out like a string. Then the Kazi dropped him and he fell onto the linked bodies with a crash. He lay as still as he could and watched, hoping the Kaz would think him dead. It was a damned feeble hope, but it was the only one he had.

The Kaz took no further notice of him. Those still living seemed to have lost interest in the situation. They wandered about randomly, in sharp contrast to their usual brisk, business-like purposefulness. Two of them met face to face. They stopped, touched one another, forelimb to forelimb, and then wandered off again in different directions as if the encounter were totally meaningless.

After a while, MacDonald risked rolling off his grisly resting place. Nothing happened.

He sat up, keeping a wary eye on the aimless forms moving around him, and examined the ankle gingerly. It was bleeding quite freely where the Kazi's hard claws had cut through the skin, and it was bruised and swollen and hotly tender, but nothing seemed broken. On hands and knees he crawled to Delladar Oll and fumbled the elaborate knot on her sash undone. Shock was beginning to set in. His fingers were thick and awkward.

Winding the fabric tightly around the damaged ankle took all the energy he had. He just sat there for a while, looking up at Delladar Oll's dead face. The hawkish eyes were still staring, but the fire was gone. Her hand was still clamped around the haft of the knife buried to the hilt in the body of the Kazi who had killed her.

You deserve a warrior's funeral, old girl, MacDonald thought. I'm damned sorry I can't give it to you. I promise you this much: If I get out of here, they'll know on Llevec they had a hero to be proud of.

Gently he released the Lleveci's grip on the knife. Then he had to brace his good foot on the Kazi's body and get both hands on the handle to pull the blade free.

Around him, the Kaz had stopped moving altogether. Were they waiting for something? Only Kazi gods knew what.

Some sense of urgency began to return, pushing through his stunned incomprehension. He had no way of knowing how long the Kaz would remain immobile, no reason to suppose it was a permanent state of affairs, and no way of knowing how widespread it was. At any moment a thousand Kaz might come pouring out of the tunnels to avenge their dead parent.

He got cautiously to his feet. The ankle would support his weight, though not comfortably. Hobbling and hopping, climbing Kazi bodies like a ladder, he made his way up to the platform where Ayyah lay sprawled across the gross body of the Broodmother.

Even dead, the Broodmother incited a shudder of disgust. She looked naked, skinned. The tiny head and cluster of legs at one end were out of all proportion to the bloated abdomen. Where

Ayyah's teeth had all but severed the head from the neck, a stinking, thick yellowish fluid still oozed. MacDonald swallowed hard. This was surely the ichor proclaimed in song and story, the genuine, goose-bump-raising article.

Ayyah's claws were dug into the Broodmother's body, teeth clamped shut through the gruesome flesh. MacDonald touched his fingers to Ayyah's neck beneath the torn ear, searching beyond reason for some sign of life. There was none. He rested his hand for a moment on her shoulder, just about the only place on her body where her fur was not matted down with her own blood. It was the first he had ever really touched her beyond a momentary and begrudging contact. The hair was soft and thick.

There was no compensation he could offer the Orian. She would have no truck with heroes or funerals. She would have been indignant at the suggestion. His vision blurred. Only now, too late, did he realize how fond he had become of this difficult and wholly admirable person.

He wiped at his eyes impatiently. This is insane, he told himself. We had nothing in common. We fought all the time. She used me unmercifully. Get out of here, MacDonald, while you still have the chance.

He slid back down onto the main floor, finding scarcely a place to stand amid the Kaz, and worked his way cautiously toward the perimeter, cringing every time he touched a black body. He came across a mound of dead, and the scene hit him like a blow to the stomach. In the heat of the battle he had been aware of his friend falling. But the loss had not sunk in.

"Oscar. Damn," he said aloud, the sound of his own voice foreign in the silent chamber. "What'd you have to go and do that for, just when I need you most? Somebody's got to tell me—I don't know what the hell's going on here." He leaned against the side of the ramp for a while and kept his dead friend company. "I don't know what prayers to say," he told the dead man. "I never asked you what you believed in."

Shock closed in and unmanned him. Grief racked him. For a period of time he floated disoriented and unaware.

A great draining effort was required to take himself in hand. "Look, MacDonald," he told himself, "you can't stay here. You have to get moving."

It seemed wrong to leave Oscar there, to whatever scavengers prowled this world. He could see nothing else he could do.

He picked an entrance at random, the one nearest him, worried, though not as much as he thought he should be, about how he was going to find his way out of the maze and up to the surface. It turned out to be ridiculously easy. He just followed the trail of stalled Kaz, edging nervously, pressed against the smooth tunnel wall, past groups who had been heading toward the chamber when the strange paralysis overtook them.

He came to the surface in bright sunlight, with a stiff breeze blowing across the landing field. It was empty now, deserted, a flat, barren, rectilinear plain with little skitters of dirt meandering across it. Barely visible in the dusty distance, his shuttle waited.

It dawned on him that he wasn't going to be able to handle his ex-Kazi starship all by himself, and even if he could, it wouldn't support him. He could manage the shuttle, but without hyperspace, he would be a hundred years getting anywhere. Besides, it had a very limited range.

He leaned against the tunnel entrance to rest his ankle and tried to think what he was going to do. His head felt thick and slow, as if the Kazi lethargy were beginning to overtake him, too.

A drone, he decided eventually. That was what he needed. An automated freighter. One with a controlled environment, so he wouldn't either suffocate or freeze. Escape that way would be possible, though slow and likely uncomfortable. Possibilities were all he had. He didn't want to hang around and wait for the Kaz to wake up.

The place to find out if such a ship was to be had was the traffic control station, where parking orbits would be charted. Assuming, of course, that the computers hadn't come to a dead stop along with the Kaz.

The next part of the problem would be finding the station. Like everything else the Kaz built, it would be underground.

Communications. The antennae were aboveground, and it seemed reasonable they would be near the station. He looked around and spotted the mast and its attendant great metal flowers near a mound at one edge of the field. He pushed himself erect and hobbled off in that direction.

A small arched opening in the mound let him into a tunnel that sloped sharply down without branches. Bluish light from the terminal displays illuminated the wide, low-ceilinged underground room. It was crowded with machinery and stalled Kaz. Some piece of equipment was flashing a red signal like a strobe, asking for attention and giving the place with its petrified attendants a surrealistic air.

The Kazi at the main control board squatted on its bench unmoving. MacDonald gave it a shove, and it fell off. It struggled slowly to its feet and stayed where it was. MacDonald took its place at the bench. He discovered he still had the knife in his hand. He laid it down beside him. Hunched over the board, trying to fit himself to the Kazi-size instrument, he had a moment of despair when he thought he wouldn't be able to understand the images. Fortunately, ground-based Kaz used the same conventions of display he had become almost familiar with aboard the *Kokkon*. He faltered again when he discovered there was nothing above like the thing he wanted. Then he thought perhaps he would give up. He was all out of fight. It wasn't worth the struggle.

He stared listlessly at the terminal.

In time, he perceived one minuscule possibility. A large freighter lay almost directly overhead, her cargo doors hanging open, in the process of being loaded when the Kaz stopped. MacDonald recognized the type, an unsophisticated Caparan design, not much more than a bare hull and an engine. No environment control, but big enough to take the shuttle if MacDonald was very, very careful about his approach. He could use her engines and the shuttle's life-support systems. Normally, he wouldn't have tried it on a bet without guidance systems on the ship, without a proper shuttle bay. But what did he have to lose?

The freighter was starting to drift. He would have to hurry. Committing the orbital parameters to memory, he started away, stopped, limped back and picked up Delladar Oll's knife, then made the best time he was able up to the surface and out to his shuttle.

There comes a point beyond which exhaustion no longer registers in the conscious mind. MacDonald worked in a numb haze, hardly aware of what he was doing. He went first to the *Kokkon* and packed food, and water from the reserve tank, to the shuttle, gasping in the foul, stinking air of the ship and resting in the better atmosphere of the shuttle. He wrestled with the bulky pressure suit as if with a mythical monster, finally subdued it, and stowed it.

He treated himself to a stimulant and a painkiller from the first-aid kit, either of which could have made him liable to arrest and prosecution in other sectors of space. He would need his wits about him and a bit more energy than he currently had for the tense moments of entering the freighter. Swallowing the pills, he remembered Ynacy Station and Peter Allen's nervous ambivalence about supplying them, the bureaucrat in him unhappy about breaking the rules, the businessman anxious for the exorbitant profit. That memory seemed distant now, something that had happened a very long time before. It had been funny at the time. It wasn't funny anymore.

For a short time everything was preternaturally clear and slow while he freed the shuttle from the *Kokkon* and dropped back to match speed and orientation with the freighter.

In spite of the pharmaceutical assistance, he came up on the drone too fast and was within a hair's breadth of ramming through the freighter's forward bulkhead before he got the shuttle stopped inside the hold.

With shaking hands, he got into his pressure suit, a difficult and painful business around the swollen ankle.

Outside of the shuttle's field compensators, he was in free fall and could move around without too much difficulty, though he took a few hard knocks before his foggy brain remembered what every dock rat knew about the relationship between acceleration and mass in the absence of friction.

He found the drone's control systems housed right next to the engine compartment. His training aboard the *Kokkon* stood him in good stead as he puzzled out the manual override. Setting the series of hyperspace jumps for an arbitrary point outside of Kazi space, he got the distress beacon going and almost fired the engines before he remembered to secure the shuttle to the freighter's frame so it wouldn't slam around like a cannonball inside a paper bag as soon as the ship started to accelerate. The weightless environment was the only thing that made it possible.

The stimulant wore off by the time he had packed himself safely inside the shuttle and the freighter's acceleration as she headed out was shoving him deep into the pilot's seat. He hardly noticed himself sliding away into the void. Just before he lost consciousness completely, he addressed his father's ghost.

"Are you happy now, Pop?"

Gnatha

The Gnathan tug, flying idle after dropping off an ore barge, picked up the beacon the moment the freighter dropped out of hyperspace. It dropped almost on top of the startled Gnathans, and they were understandably annoyed by such disregard for safety margins until they realized it was robot controlled and calling for help. Anticipating a handsome return on salvage, they gave chase.

Catching it wasn't easy. Confident in the false clarity of mind induced by the stimulant, MacDonald had completely forgotten that its computer would try to take the freighter to its programmed destination the instant the override instruction sequence was complete. So, no sooner was the jump sequence over than the ship began to accelerate for the return, the Gnathan tug in pursuit.

Though not built primarily for speed, the tug was all engines. The Gnathans did finally catch the freighter and manage to lock their vessel to the service port. They got inside and disabled the controller minutes before the jump was due.

It was like fishing for a whale and snagging an old boot. The freighter was empty except for a shuttlecraft containing one severely battered Terran who was clinging for dear life to a Lleveci knife as if it were his best friend.

The Gnathans might have been forgiven for abandoning the whole thing as more trouble than it was worth. However, they decided the hull would fetch a fair bit in scrap alone, considering its size, and the shuttlecraft wasn't exactly junk, and they weren't doing anything productive anyway, so they towed the whole rig home.

He was lying on the floor. The place looked and smelled like a stable. The wide slabs of rough, silvery material that formed the walls of MacDonald's ceilingless enclosure had narrow gaps between them. The light came from panels high overhead. The floor was covered with a thick layer of dry yellow sand.

The place seemed familiar, as if he had been there a long time, and strange, as if he had never consciously seen it before. He didn't know where he was. Shifting around, peering through the gaps on three walls, he saw empty enclosures similar to his own. Beyond the fourth, he chose to call it the front, was a corridor, with more gray slab walls beyond.

A panel in the front wall opened and a creature came in, addressing him in rapid Sindharr.

He looked like a bundle of snakes, woven and knotted together in midbeast to form a body. The sound emanated from the middle of the knot, though there was no obvious opening there.

"So, you wake. I am what you would call your doctor. You are feeling how?"

"A minute, please." MacDonald frowned, trying to make sense of it. "You talk so fast. I can't follow you. Where is this?"

"The world humans call Gnatha. This medicine you do yourself is not so good. Also some days, no food, no water. Also serious infection in joint of basal limb. You very nearly kill yourself."

"How long have I been here?"

Some of the doctor's appendages terminated in a pair of digits like fleshy tongs, biological pliers. He manipulated these rapidly for a moment as if doing some fast binary finger math. "I think fifty nights."

"Fifty?"

"I have not had a human patient previously. I begin to worry."

"I am all right, I think. I feel all right. A little weak. Actually, a lot weak."

"So, this is expected. You go home now. Others come soon to make arrangements."

"What arrangements?"

"Arrangements for your to return to Earth."

"I have to go to Llevec."

A wave of motion made the circuit of the many limbs. It might be called a shrug. "Speak with those who come."

The doctor turned to go.

"Wait a minute. I want to know something. If I've been here fifty nights, how come I didn't remember any of them?"

"Understand human, dangerous patients are kept sedated."

"Dange—"

The doctor was gone.

MacDonald had concluded that regardless of color, race, creed, or number of legs, whether bilaterally or radially symmetrical, all bureaucrats exhibited certain similarities. One of those similarities was that having once successfully pigeonholed an individual and determined the prescribed procedure, bureaucrats exhibited a degree of inertia out of all proportion to their mass. The Gnathan immigration official looked so much like the doctor that MacDonald couldn't tell them apart. But the official had a typical bureaucrat's attitude. He had made arrangements for MacDonald's passage to Earth. He didn't want to hear about Llevec.

Sindharr was an excellent language for description and instruction. It was not so good for argument, especially since he was not particularly fluent. MacDonald could only insist again and again that he had to go to Llevec.

"The Gnathan government has no authority to send foreign nationals to Llevec," the official explained.

"So, do not send," MacDonald said. "Let me go where I will. You are not responsible, yes?"

At last the official shrugged his circular Gnathan shrug and agreed this was possible. "Of course, you must deal with the Lleveci Port Authority when you arrive as best you are able. We will not assist. We will not be held liable."

"Agreed. Now, about my stuff."

"I query the meaning of the word 'stuff.' "

"My belongings. The shuttle and its contents, for example, and the Lleveci knife. I want that knife."

"So, yes. The knife is an excellent piece, I am told. It will bring much from a discriminating collector."

"It is not for sale."

"Do not be so hasty, human. There is a matter of payment for rescue and medical services."

"Now just a damned minute," MacDonald roared in English. The official scuttled backward toward the door panel. It was amazing how fast the slightly thickened snakes at the bottom could move him.

"Please, human," he said somewhat less officiously, "control yourself."

MacDonald took a deep breath.

"Understand I am very grateful for rescue and medical services," he said in Sindharr. "Understand, also, I am not stupid. Gnathans are well known—" MacDonald almost said "for rationalized theft," but decided that it was not in his best interest to antagonize his hosts any more than necessary. "—for making strong bargains. The shuttle and its contents are valuable salvage. I would make this deal: that the shuttle be sold. From the proceeds, I want passage to Llevec and five hundred credits in cash. Gnatha can distribute the rest according to local custom. I keep the Lleveci knife. That is not negotiable."

The official argued a bit more. MacDonald suspected it was a matter of form. Argument was expected of him. But MacDonald's offer was more than generous, better than the official should have expected to be able to make. With any luck the official would be anxious to get MacDonald gone before he had a chance to change his mind.

On the other hand, MacDonald's willingness to be diddled was not entirely folly. If the official simply decided that Gnatha was fully entitled to expropriate the whole kit and caboodle, there was not a lot he would be able to do about it.

Ollsad

The Lleveci Port Authority proved to be less troublesome than the Gnathan official anticipated. The new Lleveci government was still picking up the pieces and reinventing the rules of its existence. Lleveci port entry procedures had become lax since the collapse of the Kazi regime. Nobody knew exactly what he was supposed to be doing, or exactly what the new policy was. When an irritated MacDonald, at the limits of his patience with bureaucratic dithering, offered a few credits on the one hand, or to use the warrior's blade he was carrying to slice sandwich meat from the reception officer's skinny neck on the other, he was let through on the understanding that he would leave again the moment his business was done.

He used a few more of his credits for information and to get passage on the public transportation system as far into the hills as it went.

The village called Waellsad at the end of the line showed little Kazi influence; the brightly painted buildings with their conical roofs were typically Lleveci. The inhabitants, mainly clipped-maned lowlanders with a sprinkling of long-haired types, stared with frank curiosity, but politely refrained from asking stupid questions.

It was just as well. Not knowing the language made Mac-Donald's task difficult enough without questions. After he had tried several passersby, one helpful soul directed him with drawings in the roadside dust to a larger than average building that appeared to function somewhat like an inn. A gray-maned individual of indeterminate sex and a minimum of lisping Sindharr met him at the door and sent him with much pointing and waving of arms to a stable at the edge of town.

MacDonald trudged down the neat dirt road in the designated

direction with a sense of heads turning and whispers following in his wake.

Leaning against a stout corral enclosing half a dozen of the scaly beasts the Lleveci rode, the stable owner frowned in her effort to understand and be understood. When it didn't work, she wrapped long fingers around MacDonald's arm and dragged him fifty meters down the dusty street to a house with sulfur-yellow walls and azure roof.

Inside, four mountain people seated around a small table were sharing a prodigiously large roast of dark and smelly meat. "Tiktall Oll," the stable owner called from the door. One of the warriors looked up as if a bit surprised at her impudence. He came over to them, looked at MacDonald with the most neutral look MacDonald had ever seen, and spoke to the stable-keeper. The two Lleveci chattered away for a while, then Tiktall Oll turned back to MacDonald. "What is it you want?" he said in English, without the slightest warmth.

"I'm looking for a guide to take me to Ollsad."

"This is three days. The weather is getting bad."

"It's two days. How bad can the weather get?"

Tiktall Oll's neck crooked in surprise, the equivalent of a human's raised eyebrows.

"Very bad, Terran," he said.

"I can pay," MacDonald said.

"Yes?"

"Yes."

"How much?"

The warrior haggled like any merchant over the fee and finally agreed to take MacDonald into the mountains. MacDonald was glad to have found a guide but a little disappointed that a warrior's services were so easily bought. He had had the notion that Lleveci mountain warriors were proud, aristocratic folk.

The mounts slogged at a gentle pace up the rocky trail at MacDonald's insistence, for while the Lleveci warrior sat his animal as if he had been born to it, MacDonald felt no more secure than he had the first time he rode one.

The sun shone brightly, but the air held an underlying chill that spoke of snow. Birdsong was sparse. When MacDonald mentioned this to his guide, the warrior said only that most birds spent the cold season in the lowlands.

Beyond that, they said little to each other. The warrior was a taciturn fellow, and MacDonald didn't feel unduly sociable. At dusk they made a rough camp in the shelter of a rocky bowl and shared cold provisions from the Lleveci's carryall.

Toward noon of the second day, as they rode along a stony ridge high above a river valley, MacDonald realized the curve of the river and the dark forested slope rising out of the valley were familiar. He pulled his mount to a stop. Tiktall Oll reined up alongside, curious about what had attracted his employer's attention. Far below, on the bank of the Illah, a pile of metal lay rusting in the sunlight.

"That's my ship," MacDonald said.

"You're lucky," the guide said.

MacDonald gave him a sharp look.

"You're alive."

"Yes, I guess I am." MacDonald regarded the wreck for a moment, while he picked at the leaves of a nearby bush handsome in autumn purple. He didn't know what he expected, but he was surprised that he felt nothing beyond a vague regret. Turning his mount back onto the trail, he discovered a violet stain on his fingers.

"Springberry," Tiktall Oll explained. "On high mountain slopes where the deepest color forms, weavers gather the leaves to dye the autumn wool. I think it will not come easily from your skin."

It was the first information the guide had volunteered since they set out the previous morning. "What do the weavers do?" MacDonald asked.

"Wait. Time takes care of it. But in autumn they are called the clan of the purple hand."

"I see. Do they take recruits?"

Tiktall Oll did not answer so foolish a question. "We have another four hours or so. There will not be another satisfactory campsite. Do you want to spend the night here, or do you want to go on? It may be dark before we reach the village."

"Let's carry on. I want to get done with this as soon as possible."

"You never told me what business you have at Ollsad."

"No, I never did."

The guide's face betrayed his curiosity, but Lleveci manners forbade him from probing further. MacDonald relented. "I made a promise to a dead warrior. I have a story to tell them in the village," he said. "You want to hear it?"

"I would like that," Tiktall Oll said.

As they rode on, MacDonald spoke softly of Delladar Oll and the death of the Broodmother. In time, the emotion-laden words took on the cadence of the mounts' plodding uphill pace.

The guide was a good listener, silent when the story was going well, gently prompting when MacDonald stalled on a rough spot. By the time the tale was done, they had crossed the height of land and were descending into the mountain meadow where Ollsad lay in the shadows of towering, snowcapped peaks.

MacDonald was surprised. Hearing Delladar Oll speak of her hometown, he had envisioned a bigger place, and one perhaps not so quaint.

The village was picturesque, bordering on archaic, with its solid houses with their pointed roofs snuggled together beside a quick stream whose eddies flashed a bit of silver as they caught the last of the light. Lamps glowed warmly in the windows, a friendly sort of anachronism. People went about their business, bundled up against the cold, and if their dark shapes in the gathering night seemed a bit strange, it didn't detract much from the scene.

The silent, snowy mountain stretched above them. It was peaceful, Christmas-card peaceful, this warriors' village.

As their mounts sloshed across the stream, splashing icy water on his leg, MacDonald had a strong sense of an ending, as if something large and significant had been completed by this crossing.

Then he was busy with the villagers' greetings, spoken in the chattery language of the Lleveci, which the guide interpreted in part as a welcome, and offers of shelter and food.

They were shown to the guest house, and given time to clean up, time to eat, and time to rest. Later, a messenger knocked at the door, held up a big lantern, and announced that the chief elder was ready to receive them. Time seemed present in abundance in those timeless mountains, and the mountain folk were generous with it.

MacDonald wrapped the crystal knife in Delladar Oll's sash—cleaned and pressed after its duty as bandage—and asked Tiktall Oll to come along to interpret for him. The man agreed, and they went out into the night, following the messenger and his circle of light.

The night was overcast, dark. A small wind had come up,

driving flicks of icy rain. The chief elder's house was in the center of the village and in the center of the house a fire burned. They were seated on benches near the fire. In a few moments the chief elder joined them from somewhere within to form a pleasant, comfortably egalitarian group. Tiktall Oll addressed the elder as Mother—a title, he hastened to explain, not a claim of relationship—and prefaced his translations with "Mother says," but the old, white-maned, impressive individual seemed no more female than male, sexless as far as MacDonald could tell, for all the forceful character that radiated from her.

"Mother says she has not seen a Terran for some time."

"Tell her I'm honored by the hospitality of her people and by her willingness to see me."

"Mother says we could dispense with the formalities if that would not displease you."

"Tell her I have something that belonged to a noble warrior from this village that I would like to return."

"Mother says she would be pleased to receive it in the name of Ollsad, and will see that it finds its rightful place."

MacDonald unwrapped the knife and laid first the embroidered sash and then the blade in the chief's lap, hoping that was an acceptable way of going about it. The old person seemed disturbed by the thing rather than the manner of presentation. She bowed her head and closed her eyes briefly.

"Mother says this can only mean that Delladar Oll is dead."

"Tell her it is so."

"Mother asks, can you tell the manner of Delladar Oll's death?"

So, for a second time, MacDonald told the story of the Kazi Broodmother, more slowly this time to give Tiktall Oll a chance to translate, remembering therefore more of the details, the remembering bringing forth anew the panic and the pain and the faces of the dead. When it was done, the place was quiet for a time. The fire sighed and muttered softly to itself.

MacDonald was talked out. He was content then just to sit. The twice-told tale had been a cathartic for him, releasing tensions he had been scarcely aware of, and he felt more at peace than he had in a long time.

The wind had risen, sounding cold and distant through the thick walls of the chief's house. Within, the only light was the gently wavering fire that enclosed them in its warmth. Muted clinks and rattles of domestic activity preceded the appearance of the erstwhile messenger now turned serving person, bearing heavy, steaming mugs on a metal tray.

"Mother says she hopes this meets with your approval."

MacDonald tasted the offering cautiously. The flavor was heavy and rich, sweet and definitely alcoholic. He smiled his appreciation. The drink seemed perfect for the ambience. He stretched his legs out toward the fire and allowed himself to relax.

"Delladar Oll once told me her people had no taste for alcohol," he said to the guide.

"A warrior in the field is expected to abstain," Tiktall Oll answered, and then translated the exchange for the chief.

"Mother says she feels you have been a good friend to Delladar Oll. She asks, do the Oriani know of this tale?"

"Tell her I don't think so. I think they have a right to know, but I don't know where they are, or how to find them to tell them."

"Mother says this will be done."

"Tell her thank you."

"Mother asks, do you have plans for your future?"

MacDonald's head sagged. He had put off thinking about that since he first had regained consciousness in the Gnathan hospital. He pushed the thought away whenever it surfaced, for his future looked sadly blank and pointless. Everyone and everything that mattered to him was gone.

He shook his head. "No," he said. "I don't have any plans. I'll go home, I guess. Maybe I'll find something to do there, I don't know what. There must be something a tired old ex-pirate can earn a living at."

The chief speared him with a piercing look. After a moment she looked away, into the embers of the fire, and took a long draft from the mug she held. She spoke at length to the dying fire.

"Mother says it must seem strange to you that so much here is done in the old ways, done the way it has always been done. There is a comfort in that, in providing for your life with your own hands, and in the connections it makes with what is past and with what is to come. A way of doing can hold much meaning. Mother asks, do you understand this?"

"I think so," MacDonald said. "I think I understand."

"Mother says among our people, the winter is taken as a time of preparation and planning for the new life that begins with the spring.

"Mother says you are in a winter of your life. You are welcome to spend it among us. Spring will come in time. It always does."

"Mother says we will learn from one another, if you are willing."

"Tell her I am deeply, deeply honored."

Later, on their way back to the guest house, MacDonald asked the guide, "Will you be staying the winter, too?"

"You mean the rock-headed lowlander didn't tell you my name? You must have heard it." Tiktall Oll smiled the openmouthed Lleveci smile. "Of course, you would not understand the link of name and village. To answer, yes. I will be here until the mating season. This is my home."

MacDonald glared at him but couldn't make much of his expression in the wind-wracked, moonless night. "You just neglected to mention that before?" he asked.

"Why would I mention it?"

"Is it some kind of secret?"

"No, no secret. I am a warrior. I do not normally work the tourist trade, nor would I often agree to take an unknown Terran into the mountains for any price. I have had some experience with Terrans, enough to know they are often loud and disruptive, and often insistent about changing centuries-old traditions in the name of modern efficiency.

"But the whispers on the streets of Waellsad spoke of a Terran in the village carrying a Lleveci warrior's knife, and this was, at least, disturbing. The whispers conveyed a description of the tribal markings on the handle, so I knew where the blade belonged.

"Now consider my position, MacDonald. You must admit it is not the most common thing on this world to find a Terran journeying alone to a high mountain village. I did not know you, or what your intentions were. You were carrying my kinsman's blade, which could only have been taken from her body. I saw no reason to alert you if you proved to be a danger to my people."

"If you had decided I was dangerous, what then?"

"Who could say? It is possible you would still be wandering the high passes with winter coming on. You might now be lying on the banks of the Illah beside the wreckage of your ship. Perhaps my sister's blade would have avenged her.''

MacDonald paused at the door to the guest house. The wind had hard needles of snow in it now, and they stung where they hit.

"Am I safe now?'' he asked.

"You are safe, MacDonald.''

Epilogue—Earth

"Now see here, young man, you get right back into that bed. What's the use of me telling bedtime stories if you won't even try to go to sleep?"

"Yeah, but, Grandma, what happened then? After, I mean, when Great-great-grandpa came home and everything?"

"Then the new mayor of Centauri City made a big long speech and bored everybody to tears, and the people put up a monument because your Great-great-grandfather MacDonald was a hero. But he never did like it. He always said he wished he had the fortitude to pull it down some dark night."

"What's that mean, 'fortitude'?"

"Being brave and strong, something like that."

"Great-great-grandpa MacDonald was so brave. I know. I bet he was strong, too. I just betcha."

"Maybe he just didn't want to hurt anyone's feelings, especially after they went to all that trouble."

"Yeah. Yeah, that could be it."

"Anyway, the monument is still there. If you ever get to Centauri, you'll be able to see it."

"Did all the Kazes die then, Grandma?"

"No, Malcolm, certainly not. Only the ones who were the children of that Broodmother. Great-great-grandfather MacDonald showed the way, but the fight goes on. Brave people are still dying. I don't know if it will ever end."

"That makes you really sad, huh, Grandma?"

"I guess so."

"How come you know so many sad stories?"

"I've lived too long, I guess."

"How old are you, anyway?"

"Never you mind. It's time you went to sleep now."

"I'm thirsty."

"You're nothing of the sort. You're just playing games with your old grandma. I'm going to put the light out now."

"But there's lots and lots of Broodmothers, right, Grandma?"

"I guess so."

"There'll still be some when I grow up, right?"

"I imagine so."

"When I grow up I'm going to get this hu-mongous starship with these hu-mongous guns and I'm going to blast those Broodmothers dead. Then you won't have to be sad."

"Humongous? What kind of word is that?"

"You know. Great big. Bigger, even."

"I see."

"Wouldn't that be good, though, Gram? If I could do that?"

"It certainly would. It would be a very good thing. But if you don't get some sleep, you won't grow up very big, you know."

"Is that true?"

"That's what they told me when I was a kid."

"Ha. That's pretty funny."

"What is?"

"You being a kid."

"You think I was always an old lady, do you?"

"I don't know. I guess."

"Well, I wasn't."

"Oh."

"That's it? Oh?"

"Did they have the Tri-D when you were a kid, Gram?"

"How long do you think it took to reinvent the wheel? Or do you think I'm pushing my second century? Yes, we had Tri-D when I was a kid, though not so much and not so fancy as now. Now it's almost as good as before the Kaz, if you can believe the people who say they know."

"Does being old make you sad, Gram?"

"Not when I remember the alternative."

"I love you, anyway."

"I love you, too. So give the old lady a kiss and shut your eyes. There's a whole new day coming tomorrow."

"Yeah, but, Grandma, did he live happily ever after, like in the story stories? I mean not like the real stories about Great-great-grandpa MacDonald and stuff like that. I mean story stories, like Cinderella and the Three Bears and Puss in Boots and like that. Great-great-grandpa MacDonald, I mean."

"Hmm. Well, now, I honestly don't know. Your great-grandmother never told me. I think he must have. All good heroes do, don't they? Eventually, when he came back to Centauri, I think Great-great-grandmother Shirley must have made him happy. They had a nice big house where the museum is now, and they raised a lot of children. Before that, he spent some time with the Oriani. That must have been peaceful, if nothing else. Now, you've delayed enough. Go to sleep, or else I'll have to call your mother."

"Yeah, okay."

"Good night."

"Hey, Gram, I forgot to tell you. I saw a Orian. Me and Mom. In the market, eh? It looked like Puss, except bigger."

"Malcolm, we don't call people 'it.' "

"Well, I couldn't tell if it was a boy or a girl. It wasn't wearing clothes or nothing. Just fur, like Puss."

"It sounds to me like significant aspects of your education are being seriously neglected. I think I should have a few words with your mother."

"What'cha going to tell her, Gram?"

"Never you mind. Good night, now. Lights out."

"It sure is dark in here."

"That should make it easy for you to fall asleep."

"Gram?"

"Now what?"

"Will the Kazes ever come back here? You think they will? Sometime will they?"

"What, with bold warriors like you out there in your humongous starships with your humongous guns waiting for them? They wouldn't dare."

"Yeah. We'd get 'em, right, Gram?"

"Right."

"Good night, Gram."

About the Author

LESLIE GADALLAH was born in a small town in northern Alberta on October 8, 1939. She graduated from the University of Alberta in 1960 with a B.Sc. in chemistry and spent the next fifteen years or so plying her trade and raising a family before abandoning the practice of science for the opportunity to write about it.

Ms. Gadallah has written popular science extensively for newspapers and radio, and served as a technical editor for the Alberta Research Council for a number of years.

Ms. Gadallah lives with her family on a small farm just outside of Edmonton, Alberta, which they share with four cats, a budgie, a goat, and an uncertain number of rabbits. There they pursue the firm but distant goal of becoming independent of the supermarket.